Opening Blinded Eyes

A Modern Day Parable

Peggy Sue Miller

A Special Thanks:

To the many people who have helped me create this book. In particular, my husband, Lynn, thank you my dear, for your never-wavering support and being the first to edit and edit and edit and edit... You are my constant.

To my children and grandchildren: even though they all know my shortcomings, they watched me write with encouragement.

I'm deeply grateful to you, Greg and Mary Kuk for your editorial insight.

Mac Campbell for your relentless drive for perfection while proofreading.

Thanks to Lemuel Miller for your patience and technical assistance.

I'm indebted to Melissa McGhee for your unwavering support and boundless enthusiasm, as you did a myriad of tasks behind the scenes, along with making sure things ran in chronological order.

Thanks to my dear friends Polly Bainbridge and Liorah Norris, for aiding me in shaping this novel from inception to completion and holding it to a Godly standard. You both have my most heartfelt gratitude.

Thanks to you all for cheering me on over the years.

I'm so fortunate to have such good friends and family, and I'm humbled to see this story take its first steps out into the world, knowing that I couldn't have done it without 'God first' and then every one of you.

Thank you all again!

A brief summary of: Book 1

In HIS Eyes

Chuck was in love with Kate McClure, a Christian woman, but she did not return his love. So when Chuck saw a man flirting with his Kate, he, along with his friend Leroy, followed the man into the country where Chuck pulled out a concealed gun and shot the man in cold blood.

Meanwhile, two couples camping heard the shots and the men went out to investigate. In the shadows of the early morning light, Cody inadvertently laid his hand on the dead man's shoe and then screamed, revealing their presence, leaving them no choice but to turn and run for their lives.

Cody seized his wife Shelly's hand, and along with their friends, ran as fast as they could. None of them seemed able to shake the feeling that at any moment a flying bullet, which could end their life forever, might hit one of them. They pushed themselves hard to get away from the two men who chased them deep into the Smoky Mountains.

Cody, who had seen the dead man's eyes staring blankly back at him, was haunted by those dead eyes. Eyes that seemed to point out to him the deadness he held in his own heart. Those eyes lead him to deal with the dead man in himself; 'the old man', his flesh.

Days passed, then weeks, and Shelly (Shel),

knowing the most about hunting and gathering, felt the full weight of that responsibility fall on her shoulders. Through her trials, she also began to examine herself and found she had been rebellious toward Cody's God-given responsibility to protect and provide for her. She found that she wanted her husband's guidance, his protection, and that she still loved him and needed his strength to get through this ordeal. It made her willing to put down her own flesh and step up to the challenge of becoming the wife God had called her to be.

During the chase, Chuck became more obsessed to find and eliminate the persons who had witnessed his heinous crime. His accomplice, Leroy was feeling just the opposite. As they got ever closer to catching up with the two couples, Leroy knew he might have to kill at least one of the witnesses to appease Chuck's need to include him in his crime. So Leroy made an attempt at suicide, only to have the Lord stand in his way and spoke to him through a vision that he, at the time, could not understand.

As the inevitable day of catching up with the witnesses dawned, Chuck who had grown tired of the dead ends they had encountered, shot the tracking dog, Duke. Duke's owner then turned on Chuck and shot him, and then fled the scene, leaving Leroy alone and broken to cry over his seemingly dead friend.

Watching the whole thing from the trail, the two couples who had been chased throughout the story, stepped from the bushes and ministered to Leroy. Using Chuck's truck, they took Leroy, Chuck, and Duke into town for medical attention. During that trip into town, Leroy came to know the Lord through their witness.

The tracking dog, Duke, was taken to the veterinarian, and after being treated, was adopted by Cody and Shel who took him back to their home in Ohio.

Last, but most certainly not least, Kate McClure met the man who investigated the case, Police Detective Samuel Trusty.

And so begins the story.

Opening Blinded Eyes

A Modern Day Parable

Peggy Sue Miller

1

Daydream

"...When I found the one I love.
I held him and would not let him go,"
Song of Solomon 3:4 NKJV

Small town of Ponder, Appalachian Mountains

"How can you love someone you only met one time three months ago?" Mandy's disheveled corkscrew hair looked like so many springs being set free over her slender shoulders, gently encircling her round mocha colored face. Her nearly black eyes sparkled with flecks of gold as they peeked out over pinkened cheeks, reflecting the way she looked at life - with enthusiasm. Her full chocolate lips pursed as she waited for the answer to the question she had just asked her friend, Kate McClure.

"I didn't say that I loved him, I said that I can't stop thinking about him. Every time the bell over the diner door rings, my heart leaps into my throat until I see it's just Old Lem coming in for his daily serving of ice cream, or someone else coming in for their breakfast or lunch."

"Well Kate, that sounds like love to me. Why don't you just try to think about something else?"

"Like what? I'm open to any suggestions! I've tried everything and when I finally think it's working, I realize that even the thought of it working is related to my thinking about him. Of course, it doesn't help that Granny at least once a week says something like, 'When he comes back ta town and ya'll get married'..." Kate mimicked her Granny's voice for dramatic effect.

Mandy just smiled at the thought of Granny toying with Kate. "I guess you might as well face it Kate, you're smitten."

"Oh thanks for your help!" she said, reaching out and pushing her friend playfully, causing Mandy to stumble sideways, almost running into a shop window. The two women continued down the street side-by-side as Kate sighed. "Seriously Mandy, what am I supposed to do? I know that I'm never going to see him again. I mean, why would he want to come back here to this sleepy little town after living the exciting life of a big time police detective in Bennington?" Kate dropped her head as her tears wet her cheeks.

Mandy put a hand out to stop Kate and then took her in her arms. "I'm sorry Kate, you got it bad and I shouldn't be teasing you. You know," Mandy stopped suddenly, caught Kate's shoulders and looking into her tear filled eyes, "I've been thinking it's time for us to go on an outing, let's go shopping! I've been needing some new things and it'll do you good to get out of town for a while. Come on, what do you say? It will be fun!"

Kate smiled and nodded in agreement, but the thought tumbled through the back of her mind that she might just see Sam while in Bennington. And her heart jumped once more to choke her up with another tear that this time brought a skeptical smile to her face.

"Ok, good, let's get out of this snow then! It's freezing the bejeebers out of my toes!" Mandy took her arm and practically ran with her friend to the car.

Sam moved mechanically throughout the day while doing all the things he needed to do. Like a mindless robot, he didn't realize that he had completed a task until he came back to do it again. The image of the woman named Kate McClure stood before him every day and he replayed his encounter with her over and over again in his mind...

When he first met Kate's Granny, she put her hands out to him, palms up and said, "Shall we dance?" He took her hands nervously as she jested with him. "Now you mind yourself officer. Iffin' ya try anything, I'll gum ya to death!"

He had to laugh as he remembered her flashing her gums at him in mock chewing.

"Now tell me officer, why do you think you came in here today?"

He had taken a second to process the question and then said, "Well, I'm looking for a Kate McClure. She lives here, right?"

"Oh, she sure do! Alright young man, what's your name?"

"I'm Detective Samuel Trusty, ma'am."

"Are ya a Christian Sam?"

"Yes I am, I go to church regularly." He had smiled, feeling as if he was playing some kind of game with the jolly old lady.

"Are ya single?" she had asked him with a grin.

"Am I single? May I ask you where these questions are going?" He added as he raised an eyebrow with a slight smile.

"Relax Sam, I'm not interested in a young'un like you at my age." She looked at him, tilting her head to

3

one side, then raised her eyebrows and nodded as if
to say, 'well Sonny, I asked ya a question'.

"Alright, let me help you out a little," he had told
her. He smiled before saying, "I'm forty-one years old
and I've never been married. I am looking for a nice
Christian woman but I haven't found her yet, no
offense."

"Good! Now you're goin' ta want ta know
somethin' about my Kate," she stated.

His smile faded as he stopped dancing and
stepped back. "I'm sorry ma'am but I'm only here to
give her some bad news, that's all."

"Now Kate," the old lady had continued, paying
no heed to his state of mind, "she grew up in church
but she wandered away for a while, lookin' for love,
ya know. Of course she can't find it thataway, but she
do try. Now, I been prayin' for her since she were
born. Her mama done died and her papa left her
with her Gran-daddy and me. Her Gran-dad died
nigh onto eight years ago now, and I'm not gonna be
livin' much longer bein' just a mite over twenty-nine
myself. Now the good Lord done told me he'd be
bringin' someone ta love my Kate before I go, and in
ya come."

She was quiet for a little bit but then added, "Now
you'll be needin' time to be prayin' on this a mite, I
expect. I'll leave ya here 'till Kate gets back. She done
stepped out for a minute but she'll be back real soon."
Sam could still feel the panic that urged him to run
for the hills.

He had suddenly remembered the prayer that he
had prayed repeatedly before that day. "Lord, please
make it clear, to my sometimes slow perception, that
I would only have eyes for the woman You have for
me." Then as he stood in front of the old jukebox
listening, it began to play a song that, prior to that
day, he had never heard before. As he sat at his desk
in his office, he hummed the tune to himself.

Remembering Kate entering the room, while the song played on, ♪ 'I Only Have Eyes For You'. ♪

Just then Kate had come in, "Hello. My Granny said you wanted to talk to..."

When Sam heard her voice played back in his head, he turned in his chair as if he might see her behind him again. He drew in a deep breath as he remembered her standing there and how he took her in with one quick glance. Her cheeks had pinked as she brushed a dark curl aside, which had been hanging over one eye. Her green eyes sparkled as she looked back at him. He had felt like he couldn't breathe as he said, "Kate McClure?"

"Yes! That's me," her chin lifted slightly higher in recognition of her name as her breathing sped up with nervousness.

"I'm Police Detective Samuel Trusty ma'am," he had smiled then, and he smiled again, as he remembered stepping forward to take her hand. He felt the electricity again as he recalled their fingertips touching, then the clasping of their hands. He then imagined pulling her into his arms and...

"Okay Sam, I'm back from lunch. You can go now," Martin said as he sat down at his desk across from Sam. His phone rang. "Hello," – "Ah, yes ma'am, this is the state police but this is the detective unit. Let me connect you to the right department." After Martin selected the right connection, he sat back looking at Sam. "Sam, did you hear me? Earth to Sam!" He waved his hand in the air.

Sam looked up with a blank expression on his face, shaking himself free of his daydream as if Martin might know what he had been thinking.

"Well?"

"Well what?" he smirked in disgust. "I'm working here!" as he quickly busied himself with sorting the papers on his desk.

"Where is it you go ta in that head of yours? I said you could go ta lunch now. Come clean buddy, what is it, that small town again?"

"Yeah, that small town," Sam lied, not wanting to expose his true thoughts to ridicule.

"Hey, I'm fine with you movin' out ta the sticks, it'll probably mean a big promotion for me, but I'll miss you man." Martin looked again at his friend's vacant face. "Well, I guess I should say I'm missin' you already."

"What?"

"Ahhh, nothin'. Go back to your daydream. I swear Sam, if I didn't know you and your puritan ways better, I'd say there was a woman involved in that new job prospect of yours!"

Sam looked up with a smile and a little chuckle like it was an absurd suggestion.

"Well, what's this?" Martin said as he picked up a piece of paper from his desk to examine it closer. "How'd this get on my desk?" He looked at it for a moment then added, "Well Sam, it looks like daydreams do come true." He handed the form to Sam as he continued with, "while you're lookin' at that, see if there's any mention of a promotion for me?"

2

Respect for the Dead

To everything there is a season,...
A time to be born, and a time to die;...
A time to weep, And a time to laugh;
Ecclesiastes 3: 1a, 2a, & 4a. NKJV

People had misunderstood the relationship between Kate and Maclean Farrell, the man that had been murdered last fall by Chuck Atteberry and Leroy McCoy. The chief of police of Ponder had told Sam that Mac had been Kate's boyfriend.

Her spending time with Mac had, in fact, just been her witnessing to him, trying to draw him out of his depression, but many misinterpreted that as being a romantic attraction.

Yes, she was with him the night he died but so had the pastor of her church and several others who were praying for him. That night, Mac gave his life to the Lord and when he left Pastor Smith's house early in the morning he was happier than he had ever been his whole life. Kate knew God had given Mac another chance, as it had quite literally been the last thing he would ever do this side of heaven.

Kate was truly upset when Mac was found dead. Not because there was some kind of romance going on between them, as everyone seemed to assume, but because she had hoped to see Mac have a long life walking happily with the Lord. She loved seeing the transformation God did in people when they finally gave their lives to Him. Besides, she had grown up with Mac and that in itself was enough to make her heart burn with loss at his murder.

Sam didn't know all of this, he liked Kate and she seemingly liked him. But because of Mac's death, he wasn't sure how long he should wait before pursuing a relationship with her. He felt like he should stay at arms length until after the trial for Mac's murder was over. So he busied himself everyday in a thousand different ways, with a thousand different things. It should have been enough to get his mind off of Kate, but still he could not stop thinking about her.

Days and weeks passed into months as Sam finally decided he had waited long enough to merit respect for the dead. He didn't know Mac after all, didn't owe him anything, and there wasn't anything more he could do for Mac. So he would go to Kate's hometown under the pretense of getting things squared away for when he was transferred over to be their new police chief.

Sam drove into Ponder and parked his car in front of the police station, looking around as he got out and went in. "Good morning." He stepped up to the desk of the secretary, "I'm Police Detective Samuel Trusty. Can I speak to Chief Burt?"

"Oh, you're our new chief of police!" she said with delight as she half stood and leaned forward over her desk to take his hand. "Go on in detective. It's the first door to your left." She pointed to the hall.

"Thank you, Ma'am."

"Pauline."

Sam nodded with southern respect, "Thank you, Pauline." He turned and walked towards Chief Burt's office. Knocking on the door he heard from the other side, "Come in." Stepping inside he moved to take the older man's hand. "How are you today, Sir?"

"Fine, just fine," Chief Burt said with a smile as he stood and took Sam's hand. "How are you doin' detective? What brings ya to our neck of the woods?"

"Oh, I just thought I'd save you a stamp and come out and sign those papers you have for me."

"Oh yeah, I was about ta have my secretary take those over ta the post office." He lifted a manila envelope off his desk and handed it to Sam. "No postage due!"

Sam smiled. He opened the envelope, signed the papers and then handed them back to Chief Burt. "There you go."

"Is that all ya came ta town ta do?"

"Oh, I thought I'd grab a bite to eat with you while I was here."

"My treat Sam. I was about ta go over ta 'Sally's Big Burger'. They make a mean burger there and I can acquaint you with the town as we eat."

Sam was derailed by his own indecisiveness. "Ok, that sounds good." He decided to make the best of it and still maybe drop by the diner later for some ice cream.

The two men jumped into the patrol car and started down the street towards the burger joint. When they arrived, they stepped inside, sat down, and were approached by the waitress who was a teenage girl. "Good morning Chief Burt. What can I get for you gentlemen?"

"Good morning Rachel, how are you today?" He didn't wait for her answer but just went on, "This here is Samuel Trusty, the Police Detective that is soon to be my replacement."

Rachel laughed as she laid their silverware in front of them. "Is that your real name, 'Trusty'? Or is the chief pulling my leg?"

"As far as I know, my parents, my grandparents, and my great grandparents went by Trusty. So if it's made up, it was made up a long time ago." Sam smiled having heard that question before.

"Welcome Detective Trusty. It's nice to meet you. Now what can I get you today?"

Chief of Police Burt asked, "Can we have two of Sally's Famous Burgers with the works and a basket of fries with each? And I'd like a large cola. Do you want something ta drink Sam?"

"I'll just have water."

"Are ya sure ya don't want a soda Sam?"

"I'm sure, thank you."

Rachel scribbled on her pad and then said, "Alright, I'll be right back with your orders."

As soon as Rachel left, the police chief began with, "now Rachel comes from a nice family. Ya won't have any problems with them. There are a few in town that will give ya trouble most every day. There is one feller in particular who will call and complain about the neighbor's dog digging up his flowerbeds and defecating on his lawn, you name it - that poor dog has done it. It's a small dog so it's never as bad of a problem as he makes it out ta be. Sometimes it turns out to be a gopher digging holes, or something other."

"And then there's Miya Fay, now how I figure it, she just needs someone ta visit with. All her folks are gone including her son who died close ta ten years ago now in a motorcycle accident. She calls at least once every week claiming her son has wandered off or has been kidnapped. I expect she'll start calling ya Ralph too. That was her son's name and it doesn't seem to matter to her if you're blonde or an old gray-haired man like myself." He ran a hand over his butched off silver gray hair. "Don't be thrown by it Sam. It's just her way of dealing with her son's death and keeping him alive. Respecting her dead as it were. It's harmless, she's harmless Sam."

"Some folks around here make sure ta take care of her. They visit with her, take her shopping, have her come to tea, or even take her to church. I don't know what church does for anyone, but I guess it gets her out of the house. Others in town avoid Miya or laugh at her. Now that's a heartless person who would kick a woman who has lost everyone in her life, but there's nothin' anybody can do about it."

Just then, Rachel came back with the biggest burgers Sam had ever seen. "Here ya go gentlemen, enjoy your lunch." She slid their burger baskets onto the table with a smile and then walked away, trailed by the two men's thanks.

Chief Burt continued to talk about what he believed or rather didn't believe, "I don't hold to Christianity none, but I've observed it does tend ta make people better citizens for the most part." He continued to talk about the town's people. Sam found it hard to follow the police chief's comments as the names had no faces. Anyhow, Sam had decided long ago to make up his own mind about people rather than believe what someone else had to say. He had found in his thirty-seven years that even the best of people could and did carry around tainted, unjustified opinions of others they didn't understand.

Sam tried to live by this motto as best he could, but didn't always succeed. After all, he was human and in so being, self-seeking himself.

As the police chief's words quietly rumbled through Sam's head, his mind drifted with thoughts of Kate and how he wished she would come walking through the door. Sam was disappointed he hadn't spoken up and suggested that he and Chief Burt eat at McClure's Diner. He knew the chances of Kate walking into 'Sally's Big Burger' were slim but still he watched the door intently. *'Maybe I wasn't supposed to see her yet; maybe it is still too soon after her boyfriend's death. This obviously didn't work out the way I had hoped it would. I think I need to just go home and wait on the Lord to lead me in His timing.'* But he didn't know if he could wait that long.

"Sam, did ya hear me?" the police chief asked.

"What?"

"I said I have ta get back to work and I guess ya have ta get back ta work too. Am I right?"

"Ah, yeah, I have to get back." Both men stood as the police chief pulled out his wallet and dropped a bill on the table before leaving. The two men slid into the patrol car and drove back to the police station. Arriving, Sam stepped out of the passenger seat and walked around to shake Chief Burt's hand. After saying their good-byes, the police chief stepped into the building as Sam waved at the secretary through the window. Walking over to his own car, Sam opened the door before looking down the street towards McClure's Diner. He paused for only a moment before climbing in and driving toward home, thinking to himself, *'What a waste of time.'*

Several weeks later, the detective's phone rang. "Hello, Sam? This is Police Chief Burt. Hey, I'm calling ta let ya know that we're going ta have our own little Country Fair here this weekend. I know ya don't know anyone here in town yet, except me, so I thought this would be a good time ta get ta know some folks here 'bouts. Ya think ya might be interested in coming?"

"I'd have to shift some of my hours around, but I think I could swing it."

"Good, it's going ta be fun, with lot of things ta see and do."

Kate worked in the kitchen of the diner making breakfast for those who would be coming in this morning. Cutting out biscuits, she set them aside to be baked as needed and then went to grate the potatoes she had baked last night. When she heard the bell over the door ring, she wiped her hands and went out with her order slips to see who it was. Setting in his regular spot was Chief Burt.

"Good morning chief, what can I get you today?"

"Oh, ya better get me biscuits and gravy this morning. I went and told the new chief of police he was going ta have ta try them when he comes ta town, and then I couldn't get my mind off eatin' them myself. So here I am."

Kate's heart was beating fast as she took as calm a breath as she could manage and asked, "Oh, is he going to be joining you this morning too?"

"Nah, not this morning but he might come Saturday for the fair if he can work things out. I'll have a cup of coffee with some cream too Kate, if ya please."

Kate nervously flipped the notepad open and wrote down what he wanted.

"You're going ta like this new police chief. He's as nice a young man as you would ever want ta meet. I do believe ya met him Kate, he's the young man who came in ta tell ya that Mac was dead. I don't expect ya remember too much about him..." Kate all of a sudden turned and walked away, leaving the police chief mid-sentence. "...You being distraught about Mac and all," his voice trailed off behind her.

3

Biscuits & Gravy

"Hold on to instruction, do not let it go;
guard it well, for it is your life."
Proverbs 4:13 NIV

At about five o'clock Saturday morning, Sam decided it was no use trying to ignore the butterflies that seemed to be having a 'fair' of their own in his stomach. He crawled out of bed and walked to the window, looking out at the neighborhood still lit by streetlights. There were no signs of life anywhere except for a cat walking toward some bushes, where it crouched, waiting for an unsuspecting mouse to run past.

Sam sighed deeply as he closed the curtains and turned to his closet where he stared blankly at his clothes. Pulling a pair of jeans from a drawer, he laid them out on his bed along with a light blue t-shirt. "No, I don't want to dress too casual. I have to look respectable, first impressions and all." He put the jeans and t-shirt away and pulled a freshly pressed uniform from his closet, holding it up to inspect.

Kate walked through the diner with a tray of six plates of biscuits and gravy balancing on one hand and a large pot of hot coffee in the other. As she neared Sam and Chief Burt's booth, she tripped over her own feet and stumbled forward. The tray teetered and swayed back and forth on her hand as she tried to keep it from falling. She was concentrating on the tray when the spout to the coffee pot dropped too low and coffee came pouring out in a stream. She spun around while still trying to balance the tray. The pot fell and bounced across the floor with a tinny 'clink, clink, clink.' The remaining coffee spewed out of the spout in a stream as the coffee pot spun and came to a stop.

Catching a glimpse of Sam's disapproving face, she was humiliated and mortified as she stepped in the puddle of coffee and slipped. As she fell, all six plates of biscuits and gravy flew into the air as if in slow motion. Just before she hit the floor and was pummeled by biscuits and gravy, she jolted awake and sat up with a start.

Kate sighed with relief at the realization that it was all just a dream. Downstairs she could hear Granny getting ready for the big day. 'Clink, clink, clink,' she heard as Granny hit her spoon on the edge of a metal mixing bowl. Kate's hands flew up over her face as she turned to look at the clock while stumbling out of bed to go take a shower.

Wondering why Granny had let her sleep in so late, Kate quickly took her shower and then rushed around while picking out her favorite top. She put on her makeup with extra care and tied her hair back so it tumbled gently over one shoulder. Kate smoothed her hands over her top once more while looking in the mirror and decided she liked what she saw; she then turned and ran downstairs to the kitchen.

"Ya okay Kate? I never known ya ta sleep in on a big day before."

"Yeah, I'm fine. I just didn't sleep well. Why didn't you wake me? You shouldn't be making the pies for the auction all by yourself."

"Oh, stuff and nonsense! I've been doing this for longer than ya have been alive missy."

"But you're getting older Granny and you need to slow down."

"Oh, go on with ya. When ya see me slowin' down, you'll know I'm at death's door!"

Kate came over and gave her grandmother a big hug. "Granny, please don't talk like that."

The old woman hummed low and long as she gave in to the embrace, holding the granddaughter she had raised from childhood. "I love ya girl." She pulled back and looked as Kate, touching her dark wavy hair. "Now ya stop frettin' about me and let's get done here before the doors open. Quite a few folks have said they'd be comin' in for breakfast before they start their own preparations for the big day."

"Yeah, Chief Burt said he'd be coming in with the new chief of police this morning," Kate spoke, trying to sound casual.

"Sam? Sam is comin' here this morning? No wonder you didn't sleep well!"

"Now Granny, don't you go making trouble for me."

"Trouble? Now Kate, being cantankerous at my age is to be expected!"

Kate rolled her eyes and turned away with a smile as she shook her head slowly with fond affection for her dear old Granny.

The bell above the door tinkled as Chief of Police Burt and Police Detective Samuel Trusty walked into the semi-busy diner.

"Let's sit here by the door and that way I can introduce ya ta as many folks as come in," Chief Burt said as he slid into one of the booths just inside the door. "Ah, here comes Lemuel Clayton. Folks around here call him Old Lem. He's a good man ta go ta if ya need someone ta think something through. Smart old fart he is, but don't expect ta get much said yourself." The tiny bell rang as the old man stepped in and the police chief stood to greet him. "Lem, have ya met our chief of police ta be yet?"

"No I haven't," Lem said as he extended his hand to the tall young man that struggled to free himself from the bench seat. "Well howdy young fella, I'm Lemuel Clayton. 'Lem' ta those that know me and 'Old Lem' ta those that know me best." The old man shook Sam's hand veraciously.

Sam nodded as he said, "Samuel Trusty."

"Good name, good name, sounds a mite like my own." The old man smiled before going on. "So ya ready ta get ta work are ya or did ya come for the Country Fair? It's going ta be a passel of fun! Ya have ta see the greased piglet contest, my personal favorite, with all the young fellers tryin' ta catch 'um a piglet. There was a day when I was one of the chief players in that contest, but even the best of us have ta retire at some point. I caught the piglet three years in a row, in my younger days. Then one year, the sow broke into the pen ta protect her young'un and knocked a couple of the boys around good before they could jump the fence like the rest of us did, one of 'um with a broken arm. After that, they left the mother of the piglet at home. The little porkers weren't goin' back home anyways so it just made sense ta do it that-a-way, ya know. So Sam, ya think ya might try catchin' yourself a piglet?"

Sam shook his head no; being glad he had decided to wear his pressed uniform, instead of jeans and a t-shirt.

"Oh, I guess ya can't go mussin' up that uniform of yours. I recon' you're a mite too old anyways. Well, I better be movin' on. I'm powerful hungry and I have a lot ta get done yet today. It was real nice getting' ta know ya Sam. I hope we can talk again real soon." With that the old man bustled off to set at the bar where he sat every day.

Kate peeked out from the kitchen as the people started to come into the diner for breakfast. When she saw Sam and the police chief, her heart stopped. She took a deep breath and started to walk toward them. Just then, Old Lem came in and after shaking Sam's hand started to talk with him.

"Oh, that's just great," she grumbled to herself as she disappeared back into the kitchen and pressed herself against the wall, hoping to calm her pounding heart. *"There are other people to serve Kate,"* she said to herself as she stepped back out and made her way to the booth at the end where a couple sat waiting. She took their orders and walked back to the kitchen to wait for Sam and the chief to set down before she went out again to get their orders. But first she would get Old Lem's order, so she didn't seem too anxious.

When Lem finally took his seat at the bar, Kate approached him, "Good morning Lem. And what can I get for you today?"

"Good mornin' Kate. Ooo-wee, you're sure lookin' purdy today! Now, I thought I'd have ham and eggs this morning. I'm getting' ready for that greased piglet contest. I ain't had a lot of young fellers sign up this year yet. I get fewer and fewer every year ya know. I guess young fellers are afraid of a little exertion these days. But I think being able ta catch yourself a wee piglet is something ta be proud of. It ain't an easy thing ta do and it's a mess of fun for the doer and the watcher alike. It brings us together as a community, if ya know what I mean?"

Kate did know what he meant. She had seen the simplest of things where neighbors played and worked side-by-side laughing and crying together, drawing them closer as a community and giving them a sense of belonging. Kate was only thirty-five but she too had seen the decline in community comradery because of lack of participation in things such as this. She had seen people move away from community interaction by using their TV, phone, or some other electronic device for a false sense of socializing. "I do understand," she said, "but now let me get your ham and eggs started, ok?"

Sam saw Kate at the counter with Old Lem and his heart skipped a beat as he tried to keep his attention on the breakfast menu he held out in front of him. "So you said the biscuits and gravy are good?" he asked the police chief casually.

"No, I said they're the best you'll find anywhere!"

Sam watched Kate from the corner of his eye as she disappeared back into the kitchen. A couple came through the door with four kids. One of the boys was considerably older then the other three.

"Oh Sam, this is Gil and Mary Tillman. Gil works at the local hardware store across from your soon to be office. Gil, Mary, this is Police Detective Samuel Trusty. He'll be our new chief of police here in town."

"Welcome." Gil put his hand out to Sam.

"It's so nice to meet you Samuel, but I need to get my brood settled in." Mary nodded and then stepped away, walking backwards as she said; "I hope to talk to you later."

Sam nodded with a smile.

"I'm afraid I can't talk very long either Sam. Oh, can I call you Sam?" Gil asked.

"Yeah, you sure can. In fact, you're the first one to even ask, but I don't mind. I actually prefer Sam."

"Good, Sam it is then." Just then a dispute broke out between two of the youngest of Gil's children over who got to sit by the window. "Sorry Sam but the natives are restless." He shook Sam's hand again, nodded at him, and went to sit with his family.

After Gil left, Sam heard a voice behind him that made him suddenly turn.

"What can I get you gentlemen today?"

"Biscuits and gravy," Sam blurted out and then collected himself and repeated it quieter, "Biscuits and gravy please, Kate." Her gentle smile melted his heart. "How have you been Kate?"

"Fine, I've been fine Sam, and you?" A slight giggle escaped her lips and she was embarrassed. She was much too old to be giggling like a schoolgirl so she did her best to quiet the nervous reaction, which sounded like a bird twittering in her view. Kate smiled shyly, "Biscuits and gravy it is then." And she walked away, oblivious to the fact that she hadn't even taken the police chief's order.

Kate buzzed around the diner with a gentle smile on her face, delivering the orders she had taken earlier. Finally, she brought the police chief and Sam's biscuits and gravy.

"It's a good thing I love Granny's biscuits or I might be put out," Chief Burt said with a grin.

"What, why?" Kate said as her eyes flashed open with the realization that she had never asked him what he wanted today. Her hands flew to her face as she blushed with embarrassment. "Oh no, I'm so sorry! I can get you something else if you like," Kate said as she started to retrieve his plate. He grabbed it back, patting her hand until she released it. "It's fine really Kate, please don't worry about it. I love these." He picked up his fork and shoved a monstrous bite into his mouth. "Mmmmm!" He said as he bounced his eyebrows up and down.

Kate turned to look at Sam as his clear blue eyes twinkled with amusement, and she couldn't help but laugh as well.

"Ya know what?" Chief Burt asked as he stood and picked up his plate. "There is something I have to talk ta Old Lem about. Why don't you sit down here Kate and get to know our new chief of police better while ya wait for more customers ta come in."

"I can't, I..." but Chief Burt was already gone. "I can't," she said timidly to Sam, "I have to help Granny in the kitchen as there's a lot we have to get done before the Fair starts." When Sam smiled up at her, she giggled nervously and blushed again.

"Well, could you use some help? As soon as I'm done here, I won't have anything to do until later and I'm a hard worker." He tried to sell himself with a smile that never seemed to leave his face. With his fork he picked up a biscuit covered with gravy and took a big bite. He then stood up and grinned down at her as he chewed.

"No, no," Kate struggled with what to say next, before blurting out, "I wouldn't get anything done with you watching me." Kate gasped and covered her mouth.

Sam's smile stretched wider, exposing his perfect white teeth and a dimple on one cheek.

Kate's heart fluttered as she looked up at him.

"Well then," Sam asked, "may I have the privilege of escorting you to the Fair?"

"Yes, I think we'll be, I mean *I'll* be finished and ready to go at about 11:00. Would that be ok?"

"Yes, that sounds perfect. I'll see you then." He nodded and sat back down to eat his breakfast as he happily watched her walk away.

4

Finger in the Pie

...It is good for a man not to touch a woman.
Nevertheless, because of sexual immorality,
let each man have his own wife,
and let each woman have her own husband.
1 Corinthians 7: 1-2 NKJV

Sam sat on the bench outside the diner waiting for Kate to emerge. When he heard the door open, he stood to greet her but found instead Granny stepping out to say, "Hey Sam, would ya mind carryin' some pies for me?"

"No, I wouldn't mind." Sam had met Granny once before and he had liked her, but the idea of her joining him and Kate shattered his dreams of promenading her down the street on his arm, with the birds singing in the background as they made their way merrily to the Country Fair.

"The pies are there on the counter Sam." Granny vanished inside as quickly as she had appeared.

Sam stepped inside and moved to the counter where he stood admiring the pies that sat before him. The smell of the freshly baked pies made his mouth water; blueberry, apple, peach, wild berry, pecan, and a strawberry/rhubarb. All but the pecan had a hand-pinched crust that had been toasted to a golden perfection, shimmering with a glaze of crystalized sugar. The juices from all had bubbled up from beneath each crisscrossed crust, adding its color to each pie. The pans were still warm to the touch. As Sam stood there alone, he touched his finger to the blueberry syrup that had bubbled out on that pie's edge. Looking to make sure he was still alone, he started to stick his finger in his mouth just as Kate walked in. Quickly, he tucked his hand behind him still feeling it on his finger as he struggled to act normal.

"What's the matter?" Kate asked with concern.

"Oh, nothing," he said.

But as he looked at her oddly, she became self-conscious and began wiping at her face. "Do I have flour on my face or something?"

"No, you don't have flour on your face." But still the fear of being found out distorted his expression.

"What is it then?" She began to brush at her clothes. Sam began to laugh being unable to conceal his guilt any longer. Bringing his hand out from behind him, he showed her his sticky blue finger. Then he put it into his mouth to taste the gooey sweet goodness. His eyes got big and rolled back in his head as he wrapped a smile around, "Mmmmmm, that's good!" As he hammed it up, they both began to laugh.

"You better not let Granny see you doing that!" Kate covered her mouth as she continued to snicker at the secret the two of them now shared.

As they walked down the sidewalk with a pie in each of their hands, Kate asked, "So Sam, are you planning on bidding on that blueberry pie you just had your hand in?"

"My hand in? I just touched the syrup oozing out the side, that's all! You saw it on the very tip of my finger. Did it look to you like I did a 'little Jack Horner' in that pie?" Sam half laughed at Kate's taunt.

"I know what I saw but how much had you licked off before I walked into the room?"

Sam smiled down at her, "You're a little spitfire aren't you?"

"I hope so. I'm not going to let you off the hook for your indiscretion that fast."

"Indiscretion! Is that what you're going to call it?" Sam looked towards the carnival, happy to be walking side-by-side with Kate. He had passed all the rides and fanfare as he came into town, but it didn't seem to move him like it did now with Kate next to him. Now it was a destination with dream-like capabilities, surreal and even romantic. He took a deep breath of the clear country air and looked at Kate carrying her pies and he sighed before asking, "Do you think Granny can handle the last two pies all by herself?"

"Yeah, she was going to drive over."

"Drive? Why didn't she take all of these if she was going to drive?"

She skewed her brow, "That's a good question. I don't know why." Silence fell between them as the birds sang in the trees, bringing back Sam's dream of having Kate take his arm as they strolled down the street together, towards their destination.

Sam chuckled, "She probably knew I wanted to sweep you up in my arms and carry you to the fair. She was keeping my hands busy with other things." He glanced down at Kate to watch her response.

"Sam!" Kate scolded with mock disgust, but she couldn't keep a smile from giving her true feelings away.

"Well, that wasn't exactly what I was thinking but... close." He nodded with an ornery grin pulling down the corners of his mouth.

Kate's expression got solemn all of a sudden and she stopped walking.

"What's the matter?" Sam stopped and took a step back towards her.

"It's just... it's just that, I don't want to move that fast Sam, I mean..." her face got red and she took a labored breath before continuing. "Sam, I'm not the kind of girl that gives herself to a man just because he call himself her boyfriend. I mean..." a tear made an appearance at the corner of her eye and trembled to be released.

"Kate, shhhh, it's okay, I was just funning with you about scooping you up in my arms. I don't want a fast woman... uhhh... he stopped himself as an uncomfortable silence surrounded them. They turned at the same moment and began to walk again towards their destination.

"Sam?" Kate said timidly, "I don't even want to kiss the man I, ahhh... love until our wedding day." She looked up at him with fear in her eyes feeling like that was going to be the end of their short romance.

But Sam said nothing for a moment, and then he spoke from his heart. "You know Kate, I've never really thought about the way things should be in a Christian dating situation. But now that I have, I have to say that the relationships I envy the most are the ones where the couple are friends with mutual respect for each other. So, if that's what you want, then that's what we'll do." He stopped walking and looked at her, "Kate McClure I would like to be your boy... ahh 'friend' and I'd like to get to know you better, to make sure we can resolve any conflicts between us, before we make any life-long commitments to each other. Does that sound agreeable to you?"

Kate smiled slightly as the tear that had stood in her eye slid down her cheek. "That sounds perfect to me." They turned again to walk.

Finally, Sam asked, "So does that mean we're dating now?"

"Well, I prefer to call it 'courting'. The word 'dating' doesn't mean anything anymore except to have license to have..." She blushed and didn't finish.

It wasn't a long walk to the fair, but long enough that the two of them had set boundaries for their relationship and made a commitment to become friends before anything else. Sam smiled as he thought; *'Maybe Granny knew what she was doing when she put a pie in each of my hands.'*

5
Country Fair

*I know that nothing is better for them than to rejoice,
and to do good in their lives,
and also that every man should eat and drink and
enjoy the good of all his labor-it is the gift of God.
Ecclesiastes 3: 12-13 NKJV*

Sam had shaken so many hands and been introduced to so many town folk that he was certain he wouldn't remember more than five or six of them by name. Gil Tillman stood beside him as they watched the boys that were to participate in the greased pig contest. Gil's son Markus, crawled over the fence as Old Lem made his introduction over the P.A. system and again as each of the other boys stepped over the fence.

"This is his first year doing this," Gil said as he pointed at Markus. "He's been talking about it all week since Old Lem told him all the tricks of how to get ahold of, as he put it, a *'little porker'*." Gil laughed at the old man's wordage to describe the piglet. "That boy next to him is Micah Barnett, Markus's best friend. He's a good boy who comes from a good family. Have you met the Barnett's yet?"

Sam shrugged his shoulders, said, "To be honest I don't know, but I don't think so."

"Well, Ken's standing right over there." Gil pointed across the way to a tall stocky man. As if the man knew he was being talked about, he nodded in their direction and started to move through the crowd to where Sam and Gil stood. Gil continued with, "Ken's boys go to school here but other than that the Barnett's don't make it into Ponder much. It's more convenient for them to go into Bennington on the other side of the mountain."

Ken put his hand out in front of him as he approached Sam. "Welcome to our Country Fair. I'm Ken Barnett. How are the town folks here treating ya?"

"Oh, they've been great. I'm Samuel Trusty by the way."

"Oh yeah, I already knew your name. You're the talk of the town today, you and Kate McClure that is.

Sam looked at Gil, who gave him a look that said 'see I told you'.

Ken continued, "What's going on there with the two of you?"

"Well..." Sam was taken aback by Ken's bluntness.

"Don't pay him no mind Sam." Gil patted him on the shoulder. "We've all been wondering when Kate was going to meet the right man and you walk into town and sweep her off her feet."

Ken added, "You must be an exceptional man. That's all I'm getting at," he slapped Sam on the other shoulder. "Granny would have strung you up by now if not. Now Kate, I haven't seen her since she was a young thing. Is she here today? Point her out for me, if ya would. I don't think I'd recognize her if she was standing right in front of me." He turned as he looked around. He pivoted back to look at Sam adding, "We don't get into Ponder but once a year during the fair."

"She's not here right now, she went to help her Granny get her pies set out for the auction."

"Ok, it looks like we're ready to begin!" Old Lem announced loudly over the sound of a squealing piglet he held tucked under one arm. "Are ya ready boys? Here we go!" He dropped the piglet into the pen and the game was on.

The boys all dashed forward to try and catch the pig. They ran frantically this way, then that. They dodged and shoved each other while the piglet ran in every direction to try and get away.

"Grab its leg Markus!" Gil yelled with the building excitement.

"Yay!" The crowd, made up of primarily men, roared as Micah landed on top of the pig and it shot away with the rest of the boys on its tail. Laughter filled the crowd as the contagious energy continued to build. Micah stood and glanced over at his father with a big smile as he dove again, this time grabbing the piglet's back leg and holding it for a second before the greased leg slipped through his fingers. Another roar went up and just as the piglet was about to shoot away again, Markus grabbed its back leg and swept the piglet up into his arms in one swift movement, clamping it to his side as it wiggled and squealed in protest.

The crowd screamed with delight and roared even louder as the other boys slapped Markus on the back in congratulation and respect. Scratching the piglet's coarse hair and rough hide, some of the boys congratulated him as well. Still laughing, the crowd began to move on to other attractions.

"Good job son!" Gil yelled out loud, "That was fantastic!"

The boys climbed over the fence and joined their fathers as Micah exclaimed, "Dad, did you see it when the pig darted under Phil's legs and knocked him over? That was crazy!" Ken put his arm around his son and walked off with him as the boy chattered on.

Sam stood, taking it all in, until it got quieter, then he turned to Gil who had his arm over his own son's shoulder. "So, what are you going to do with your little porker?"

"He'll have to go back to his mother on the farm. We don't have a place to keep a pig in town," Markus replied before dashing off after Micah and his dad.

"So, why did he bother to catch it if he wasn't going to keep it?"

"For this Sam." Gil passed his hand over the crowd to point out men around them congratulating the boys that had taken part in the contest. "Today these pre-teen and teenage boys gained the respect of their families, friends, and neighbors. They have become more than just boys that wear their father's names. They became individuals today Sam, someone to be remembered and respected."

Sam scanned the happy faces around him.

"You didn't see a lot of women out here did you Sam?"

"A few."

"Well, that's because, for the most part, women don't understand men and their need for respect. It's like breathing to us. You can't just delete it from our nature, but so often that's what women try to do. Now women, they need love the same way we men need respect. If you and Kate can grasp that concept Sam, you'll have an amazing marriage. Take my word for it!" Gil smiled as a woman approached him. "Sam, this is my Mary."

"We met briefly at the diner this morning." Mary smiled, "I wanted to ask you something Samuel..."

"You can call me Sam, ma'am."

"Okay, Sam. Do you have a place to live in town yet? Because old Mr. Fisher has gone to live with his son in Florida and his son is wanting to rent his house out until his father passes away. Old Mr. Fisher is 97 and thinks he'll be coming back here once he gets well, but that's not likely to happen. Anyway, his son was telling me that whoever moved in would have first dibs on the house when he sells. It's a real nice house Sam and you would have some amazing neighbors!"

With a big smile, she turned to look at Gil who finished with, "that'd be us if you were wondering." He pulled his wife to his side and gave her a squeeze.

Mary handed Sam the address on a slip of paper and said, "Come by after the pie auction if you can, and we'll have some pie."

"Sure, why not?"

"I assume that Kate will be with you?"

"I think that would be safe to assume." His face broke out in a grin.

"We can go over and look at the house after we have our pie because I have the key." She smiled again, "that is, if you'd be interested." She glanced over Sam's shoulder as Kate approached him from behind.

"Interested in what?" Kate smiled.

"If he would be interested in renting old Mr. Fisher's house with the option to buy," Mary said.

"Oh that'd be nice!" Kate added.

Gil continued, "Old Mr. Fisher had a stroke a couple of years ago and wasn't the same after that. But he wouldn't hear of anyone helping him out. It'll sure be nice, for once, to have someone in the house that isn't going to be yelling at my kids for playing in our back yard. You're not the 'grumpy old-man type' are you Sam?"

Sam laughed out loud, "No, in fact I like kids a lot."

"That's nice to know!" Mary said as she turned to look at Kate. Kate blushed.

While sitting around Gil and Mary's dining room table, Sam asked, "So what pie did you win anyways?"

Mary popped around the corner with two man-sized pieces of pie. "Blueberry! Granny McClure's blueberry pie!" She sat them in front of the men and added, "You probably had a hand in this pie, eh Kate?"

Kate kicked Sam under the table, "No, but Sam did!"

"Really Sam? I wouldn't have figured you for the baking type." Mary went back into the kitchen to get the ladies pie as Sam pushed Kate's foot back playfully.

"No, I tasted a blueberry pie today and was telling Kate how good it was, that's all." His eyes flared as he threw Kate a playful warning glare.

Kate snickered as Gil sat observing the whole exchange before saying, "Mary, I think they have an inside joke going on here. It'd probably be good not to enquire about it."

Kate stuck her index finger deep in her piece of pie and plunged it into her mouth while looking at Sam. "Mmmmmm, this is really good!" Mocking Sam's antics from earlier.

"It really is," Sam said, stifling a snicker, and after turning away from Kate he deliberately looked at Mary. "Thank you for sharing your pie with us. This is truly wonderful!"

Mary looked at Kate then back at Sam with a puzzled look, "I thought you were going to bid on the strawberry/rhubarb pie?" Sam nodded as he took a big bite. "I guess I should have warned you Sam. Old Lem buys that one every year. He doesn't care how much it costs him and no one stands a chance against his will to have it." Her face drew into a question as she asked, "Didn't Kate tell you that?"

Sam turned to look at Kate, who gave him a knowing nod with a twist of a smile.

6

Out In The Sticks

Trust in the Lord with all your heart,
And lean not on your own understanding;
In all your ways acknowledge Him,
And He shall direct your paths.
Proverbs 3: 5-6 NKJV

Sam pulled into town with all his worldly possessions packed in a small U-Haul trailer tagging along behind his pickup. Kate could see him through the front window of McClure's Diner where she had been standing. All morning she had been waiting for him every moment she could spare. When she saw him coming, she quickly threw herself against the small wall that separated two of the picture windows between the booth-lined parlor. She pressed her hands to her mouth and giggled like a child playing hide-and-seek, when the seeker passed by without a clue of her whereabouts. She pulled herself away from the wall and ventured a peek out the window again to catch the taillights of the trailer glowing red at the only stoplight in town. She stood and watched as it moved on down the road.

"Is he here yet?" Granny asked as she walked into the room.

"What? Who?" Kate said as she turned and began to wash the table next to the window with fervor.

"Sam, is he here yet?"

"He should be here sometime today," Kate said in an overly casual way as if she couldn't care less.

"Now ya either been watchin' at that winder or that table is a sight dirtier then it's ever been. You've been washin' it for over an hour now. Your hand must be downright pruned from holdin' that wash cloth."

Kate looked at her hand and sure enough her fingers were wrinkled just like Granny had said. "Yes, he just pulled into town. There is just no hiding anything from you is there?"

"So why do ya keep tryin'?"

Sam pulled up in front of the Fisher house he was now renting, followed closely by Martin in his Jeep. As the two men jumped out of their vehicles, Martin said, "I can't figure out for the life of me why you would want to move out into the sticks like this. I'd go plumb nuts out here."

Sam opened the back of the trailer, moved a box out of the way, and sat down in the back. Looking around, he sighed and said, "Yeah, but I can breathe out here Martin." His breath stood as a vapor before him in the crisp morning air.

"I can breathe just fine in the city," Martin said as he plopped his butt down beside his friend. "There isn't even a McDonald's in this town. How backwards can you get? Whatever possessed you to move here? Other than Kate of course." He paused before turning back to Sam and said, "She'd probably like living in Bennington! I mean who wouldn't like living in the city as opposed to out here in the sticks?" He looked back down the street.

"No Mart, you don't get it. The peace and quiet is what I love. I love my small office, the small hospital, the small town folks, and McClure's quaint retro style diner. I love it all, and I loved it before I even met Kate. This sleepy little town suits me, that's all. Besides, I won't have to look at your ugly mug anymore. I've had my fill of that." He gave him a shove and Martin's shoulder bumped into the wall of the trailer on the other side.

"Oww!" He rubbed his shoulder. "I think you broke it man! Now you'll have to unload all this stuff by yourself."

Sam shook his head with a smirk, "Oh, be quiet and let's get this done." He and Martin stood up inside the trailer and began to unload the last of the furniture.

"Well Sam, I've never seen anythin' like it. You must know everyone in town and they've all come ta see ya within two hours time." Martin scratched his head, "Oh, I'm not complaining mind you. These cookies are amazin' and that fried chicken was the best I ever ate. Do ya think they'll bring ya food like this every day? Because I could come back with Sheila and the kids, ya know. I'm sure I could talk her into setting up your kitchen for ya."

"Too late for that. Mary Tillman from next door put it together for me while we were packing boxes into the bedroom. She even offered to run to the store for me to get bread, milk, eggs, and a package of bacon. She said I had to have bacon and eggs the first morning in a new house, 'because it's what makes a house a home'. She's probably right too."

Then Sam added, "I couldn't argue with her. I don't think it would of done me any good anyway. She was halfway to her car before I gave her the nod."

"Is that why these kids are runnin' around here?"

"Oh they're fine. Don't you remember running around a mostly empty room listening to the echo?" Sam leaned over and scooped up a little boy of about five.

Martin stepped up and roughed up the boy's hair asking, "And what's this little guys name?"

"I'm Tad. We live next door, right Sam?"

"Yes, that's right. Tad, this is my friend Martin. Can you say hi?"

Tad kept his eyes on Sam and said, "My mom went to the store but she'll be right back. Can I get down now? I have to run."

Sam believed he did need to run. He had felt like a live wire in his arms and now as Tad's feet hit the floor he spun out like his tires had been spinning the whole time he was in the air. Sam laughed to see two boys and a girl under the age of seven as they flew around the room in circles making 'vroom, vroom' sounds like the motors that kept them running.

It took Mary no more than twenty minutes to be back with a paper bag full of groceries. "Now, I got you a U-bake pizza too since I was buying a couple for my own brood's supper. Anyhow, you most likely won't have time to cook tonight."

"Let me pay you."

"Oh no you don't. We're happy to have you Sam. We just want to make sure you get your feet set on the ground because things can get crazy busy around here."

Martin choked on the cookie he was eating and Sam turned and slapped him on the back a little too hard as Martin winced in pain.

"I think you've had enough of those cookies Mart. You've eaten near the whole plate." Sam took it from him and replaced the plastic wrapper.

"Well, I have to get going. Welcome to Ponder Chief of Police Trusty," Mary smiled and shook his hand and then put her hand out to Martin. "It's been nice meeting you, Martin."

"Ma'am," Martin nodded.

"Gil will be over later Sam to see if you need help with anything. See you." She clapped her hands and said, "let's go kids." And without hesitation, the kids zoomed out of the front door and down the sidewalk to their house next door.

Martin stood and watched as they all left before mocking what Mary had said, "You need ta get your feet set on the ground before things get too crazy busy around here."

Sam just punched him in the arm and then turned to shut the door as the two of them stepped outside.

Martin followed him down the sidewalk while saying, "You know, somehow I envy you. Sheila and I have been living in our house for ten years and we don't even know our next door neighbors, except by sight."

Sam smiled, "Well, that's one of the upsides to living in the sticks. I'll meet you at McClure's down the street there." He pointed and added, "I have to run by the office real quick to see Chief Burt off on his retirement. I'll be there as soon as I can."

For months now, Sam had spent time with Kate every day, and talked to her every evening on the phone to say goodnight. But it wasn't enough for him anymore and he found himself antsy, distracted, and even at times irritable. It had been months after all, so he felt it was finally time to ask her to marry him.

Pulling his grandmother's wedding band out of a small box, he placed it on his pinky where it stopped at his knuckle. Settling it in his mind, he decided he would propose to her on Sunday.

After church, the two of them sat on the bench in front of the Diner taking in the perfumed spring air. A cool breeze blew and the tree-lined street was filled with the sound of birds singing happily. Sam sighed and said, "I think I could live here forever."

Kate asked hopefully, "Really?"

"Yeah, in fact," Sam dropped to one knee in front of her and asked her simply, "Will you marry me Kate McClure?"

Kate couldn't imagine a more beautiful setting, or more simple but perfect proposal if she had tried. Because with those words, Sam had made her life complete and she fell into his arms with a resounding, "Yes!"

7
Free Indeed

"...Whoever commits sin is a slave of sin.
And a slave does not abide in the house forever,
but a son abides forever.
Therefore if the Son makes you free,
you shall be free indeed."
John 8: 34b -36 NKJV

Several months had passed and the day of the trial for Chuck Atteberry and Leroy McCoy finally came. After being lead into the courtroom in the County Court House, they were seated before the judge.

A psychologist testified Leroy had acted 'under duress' after Chuck had shocked him by pulling out a concealed weapon and shooting MacLean Ferrell, killing him in cold blood. Leroy had been afraid for his own life and had not only turned himself in to the authorities, but had also helped those he and Chuck had been chasing to get away. Chuck's intent was to kill them as he believed they had seen the murder in question.

When finally Leroy's verdict of 'not guilty' was pronounced, a sigh of relief caused his shoulders to drop and his head to tilt back. His eyes closed for a moment and taking a deep breath he smiled slightly and whispered, "Thank You Lord."

Leroy was the only eyewitness to the murder. When he was called to testify, he cooperated with the authorities turning State's evidence against Chuck. The evidence that was presented was then deliberated upon and Chuck Atteberry was pronounced guilty of murder in the first degree. Therefore he was sentenced to death by lethal injection.

The color drained from Chuck's face as he was pulled to his feet and ushered out of the courtroom. He was temporarily placed back into county lockup until the following Monday when he would be transported to the State Prison.

Deputy Sheriff Paul Damascus came strolling in on Monday and looked over the papers that were to accompany the prisoner being moved this morning. Looking at his coworker he said, "Well, I'm off. I guess you're on your own here until I get back sometime around noon."

"Yeah well, enjoy your time with your friend."

"Yeah right!" The deputy just smiled and shook his head. He knew full well Chuck Atteberry had no friends and he would most certainly be the last person Chuck would ever call a friend.

It was true Paul had a compassion for the man that others couldn't understand. He had tried from time to time to explain it was the love of Christ that caused him to care what happened to Chuck. Most of them would just stare at him as if he were speaking a foreign language.

Deputy Damascus was a devout Christian who had gone to school with Chuck from kindergarten until Chuck had dropped out of school at the age of sixteen. He so wanted to see Chuck happy. He wanted him to know God loved him and to see him fail to respond to God's love was heart-breaking to Paul.

He really didn't want to transport the prisoner today as Chuck's coarse speech and cutting remarks always tore at his resolve. But he was determined to continue to pray for him, in hope that some day his eyes would be opened and he would see God.

'Ok,' Paul thought to himself as he looked up at the clock again, 'you better get going.' he said to himself, before whispering a little prayer and retrieving the keys to open the cell door.

As Chuck sat waiting on his bunk for his ride to the State Prison, he was nervous and sick with fear at the thought of being imprisoned with men who no doubt would make him a victim once again. The thought of that was more than he could handle. *'Was his former stepfather still there? Would he beat him like he used to? Would others follow his lead?'*

Chuck knew he would have to put on some kind of front to make other men in prison afraid of him or just want to stay away from him. But what could he do? He was a small man and was sure some would take pleasure in treating him badly. So he tried to brace himself to become a victim once more, but it just made him feel even sicker and more afraid.

He sat forward and ran his fingers through his short, wavy, auburn hair. "It's not fair!" He said in frustration. "This is the kind of trick only You would play on me God." Chuck blamed the woes of the world on God even though he claimed not to believe in any sort of a Heavenly Father. He had several 'fathers' in his childhood and not one of them, as he saw it, was capable of love on any level. It made him angry there were those who believed in a 'Father God' who was capable of loving. He saw those people as being basically stupid or crazy.

The clanging of keys and the sound of footsteps alerted him it was time to go. He stood and stepped up close to the door with his hands grasping the bars as he looked to see which guard would be transporting him to his new home. Seeing Deputy Paul Damascus coming, he said, "Oh great," he moaned to himself, dropping his hands and glaring at the man who approached his cell. Damascus was the one guard that couldn't ever talk to Chuck without sharing his slant on 'God'. Chuck had grown up with Paul and because Paul was a 'Christian', Chuck had always done everything he could to discredit and test his so-called 'faith'.

When Paul reached the door, he said with a smile, "Now Chuck, you know I can't open this door until you're sitting on your bunk." He fumbled with the hand strap that was commonly used in place of handcuffs these days.

Chuck growled with displeasure at the man as he turned, walked the few steps back to his bunk, and sat next to the book that lay on his bed.

Deputy Sheriff Damascus opened the cell and stepped inside. "Okay Chuck, you know the routine."

Chuck stood and turned, putting his hands behind his back. He waited impatiently, fidgeting, until the hand straps were securely in place. Making sure to clench his fists, Chuck curled his wrist out hard. He had heard that would give his wrist up to a half-inch of play. It might even be enough room for him to gradually work his way out of the offending straps.

Paul at times allowed the prisoners a little 'wiggle room' as far as the rules went. So he said nothing to Chuck about his hands needing to be relaxed as he pulled the straps taut. He knew Chuck would soon be in the back of the transport van with no way of escape.

Anyhow, he was fairly certain Chuck was just angry as usual.

As the deputy finished, he noticed a book on Chuck's bed, titled *Edible Wild Plants*- so he asked, "What's that about Chuck?"

"Oh, I was studying to be an herbalist. I've always liked herbs," Chuck lied in a pleasant tone. He hadn't been interested in herbs at all, but instead he had pored over the book again and again to find out what was edible that grew in the wild. Although he found the discolored drawings to be vague at best, he had distracted himself with it. He checked that same book out of the library repeatedly in the past several months as he waited for his case to be heard.

It was the only book he could find that helped him figure out how the people, whom he had chased last fall, had survived and escaped to convict him of the crime of murder. He was desperate to get as far away as possible. If by some chance he had an opportunity to escape, he wanted to be prepared.

"What did you do to that poor book's binding?" the deputy questioned him.

"I tripped over it." Chuck told the truth for once, knowing he wouldn't believe him anyway.

"Yeah, right," Paul chuckled.

What Chuck wasn't telling him was he had awoken with a start a little more than a week ago as he remembered Old Lem standing in front of the combined Post Office/General Store. Where Old Lem, as a much younger man, was teaching a group of teenage boys how to jump a broom handle. He taught them to jump it backwards when they had conquered the forward jump.

'The trick ta jumping backwards is in the timin',' he had told them. *'Very few can actually do this,*' Chuck could remember him saying as Lem had jumped it easily.

43

Chuck had decided to practice at home Instead of potentially embarrassing himself in front of everyone. He didn't want to make a fool out of himself like the other boys who were tripping, falling, and laughing about it. Chuck couldn't see the humor in looking like a fool. He was thin and wiry just like Old Lem, and he knew he would be able to do just as well. And sure enough, he found it was easy to jump the broom forward, but it had taken him some time to conquer the backward motion. He remembered feeling proud of himself, but as a teenager he couldn't see a reason why he would ever need such a talent so he pushed the achievement aside.

But a week ago he awoke with a start, realizing it might come in handy now. If he ever got the chance to jump over his tied hands, he could put his hands out in front instead of behind him. He wasn't sure that it would really work but what else did he have to do? So he started to practice, determined to jump backward over that unfortunate book.

Chuck walked slowly down the corridor with the deputy sheriff only a step behind him, while another guard looked on. The deputy opened the doors and ushered him into the back of the van, chaining his hands to the wall behind him. Chuck sat back trying to get comfortable. There wouldn't be any jumping over his straps as long as he was chained to this wall. The deputy climbed into the driver's seat and they were off to the State Prison.

Chuck started to think about his former friend Leroy becoming a Christian and anger filled him. That offense, in Chuck's eyes, was much worse than sending him to prison. Leroy had tried to visit him several times in jail, but Chuck had refused to see him. Now, he wished he had Leroy with him to stand between him and those that might want to hurt him.

As he sat in the back of the transfer van, Chuck's brain was working overtime trying to figure out how to get away. *'It's less than a two hour drive,'* he thought to himself. He knew his chances of Paul stopping and opening the back door were slim to none, but he had a better chance of escape now then he ever would. Still, try as he might, he could not figure a way to escape. Even if he did get his hands free, he felt he was doomed.

Paul yelled back through the caged window to Chuck, "You know Chuck, I'll still be praying for you. I know you won't believe this, but even though you'll be in prison it's possible for you to still be free."

"Free?" Chuck cursed with disgust. "How can someone be free who's stuck in prison? What kind of an idiot do you take me for?"

"Well Chuck, John 8:36 says: Therefore if the Son makes you free, you shall be free indeed."

"Who's this Son?"

"Jesus."

"That's enough!" Chuck yelled and then cursed under his breath while spitting out the word 'idiot' at the back of the deputy sheriff's head.

Paul didn't want to push it any further so he stayed quiet for some time as he thought of something else to talk about. "Well Chuck, we'll be passing by the junction that leads to Ponder soon. Susan and I don't get home as much as we'd like to these days, but we still think of it as home. Oh hey! Have you heard Kate's getting married?"

"What! When?" Chuck's head snapped up.

"Well, I think it's maybe next weekend? I'm not actually sure. We got an invitation but I'm not good with dates. Susan writes those kind of things on the calendar," he rambled on just happy to find something Chuck was interested in talking about.

"To who?" Chuck found himself almost yelling.

The deputy looked back at him, puzzled as he continued, "to former Police Detective Samuel Trusty. He's been courting Kate since early this last winter.

She wanted to be married in the Spring and so here we are. You knew Sam gave up his job in Bennington and moved here to take old Police Chief Burt's job, right? Quite the demotion he gave himself, if you ask me," Paul added. "But he loves his job and there's something to say about that. Don't you think?"

But Chuck wasn't listening anymore. Instead, he was going berserk inside. Kate was his gal! Or so he had determined at a young age. Chuck had shot and killed the last man who tried to move in on Kate. He set his jaw, determined to do the same to this man too.

He had to get out, but how? He began to curse and yell in a rage. He threw himself from side-to-side, pulling on the ties with all his might, not caring if he broke his wrists or took the skin off of them in the process of freeing himself.

"Chuck! What in the world are you doing back there?" Damascus screamed in disbelief. His eyes were diverted from the road as he looked through the rear-view mirror and into the caged back of the van.

Soon, Chuck had himself bleeding as his skin peeled back off his wrist and thumb.

"Chuck, stop! What are you doing?" Damascus screamed louder. He pulled the van over to the side of the road and jumped out in an effort to make it into the back before Chuck had successfully freed himself. He didn't know what he was going to do but he had to try to subdue him somehow. As he put the key in the backdoor and turned it, he thought to himself, "He can't get out so what am I doing?" But as luck would have it, the blood on the hand tie worked to help him slip loose. Chuck's hands pulled free at the same moment Paul started to push the door back closed again. The door flew wide open with force, smashing into Paul's face, knocking him backwards onto the pavement, cracking his head and rendering him unconscious.

46

Chuck jumped out of the back of the van. He looked at the man he had considered his enemy as a small red puddle formed to one side of the deputy's head. The man lay flat on his back with his eyes closed, his arms extended outward bent at the elbow, and his hands palms up as if he were surrendering. The keys had flown out of his hand and slid until they lay hidden under the bushes along the side of the road.

Chuck took in a deep breath when he realized he was free. He turned this way and that, looking to see if anyone had witnessed what just happened, but he was out in the country. There were no witnesses and because of the early morning hour, there was no traffic coming from either direction.

He was too relieved to feel any remorse as he took the deputy sheriff's gun from its holster and looked around briefly for the keys. He paused just long enough to say, "Now 'I AM' free indeed." He laughed as he turned and ran off through the woods.

8

Here Comes the Bride

I will greatly rejoice in the Lord,
my soul shall be joyful in my God;
For He has clothed me with the garments
of salvation,
He has covered me with the robe of righteousness,
As a bridegroom decks himself with ornaments,
and as a bride adorns herself with her jewels.
Isaiah 61: 10 NKJV

It had been months since Sam had first proposed to Kate, and the wedding was scheduled for this next weekend. Kate and Granny were pulling out of the driveway in Granny's 1958 Chevy Bel Air. Her husband had taken meticulous care of the car and now that he was gone, Granny was carrying on where he left off. Its cream and surf green paint 'had nary a scratch on her', as Granny would say. The car glistened as the light of day reflected off its highly polished body and the women smiled from behind its windshield.

Kate and Granny were now on their way to the florist in the city to choose the flowers for the wedding. It would be a small wedding, but Kate was determined it would be beautiful. Their next stop would be Aunt Jackie's for the final fitting of Granny's vintage gown.

Kate's Granny and Granddad had raised her and the wearing of her Granny's gown meant the world to her. Of course, it didn't hurt the gown was made of the most exquisite hand-crocheted lace and that it had also been Granny's mother's before her, who had been married in Scotland back in 1892 before she and her husband immigrated to the United States. Kate was almost as excited about wearing the gown as she was getting married to the man of her dreams.

Kate's mind was racing as she thought of the day that was coming up quick. She had planned for Sam to go with her today, but he called and told her Police Detective Martin Jones needed his help in a local incident. Sam didn't say what it was, but that was normal. She had other things to think about today that would keep her busy.

Granny was more than glad to close the diner for the day and come along. She hadn't had much time with Kate since Sam moved to town and soon would have even less. As Granny drove, the two of them chattered happily about the upcoming wedding.

When Kate's phone rang, she pulled it out of her purse. Seeing it was Sam, she answered with a sing-song "Hel-lo!"

"Hey Sweetheart. How's it going?"

"Oh, we just pulled out about five minutes ago. Granny came with me. Well, I'm with her I guess as she's driving. Are you done now?" She waited for his reply. "Are you still there Sam?"

"Yeah I'm here, but I have something to tell you," he paused.

"Sam?"

"Kate, Chuck's escaped somehow."

"What? If this is a joke Sam, it isn't funny."

"It's not a joke Luv. He was being transported to the State Pen when he escaped."

"Oh no Sam! How is that even possible?"

"I don't know how yet, but there's more."

"What?"

"Deputy Sheriff Damascus has been injured, and he's...well it looks pretty bad, I guess."

"Paul?"

"Yes."

"Paul Damascus?"

"Yes."

"What do you mean you guess it's pretty bad?"

"That's what I hear, I haven't actually seen him yet."

"Where are you now?"

"I'm still on my way to the crime scene."

Kate had known Paul her whole life and he had always been a good friend. With a tear in her voice she said, "Pray for him Sam. Lay your hands on him and pray for him." The pain and emotion strangled her voice so she could say no more.

"I will Sweetheart, I will."

When Sam arrived at the crime scene, he stepped out of his patrol car to see a mixed group of paramedics, state troopers, trackers, and others. Official looking vehicles lined the side of the road while people were coming and going. Some he recognized and some were strangers.

Fanning off through the woods, the trackers lifted every leaf looking for something that would indicate which direction the escapee had gone. "I found blood!" Someone yelled and everyone moved toward the indicated spot.

"He must be hurt," someone stated the obvious.

"Hello, I'm Chief of Police Samuel Trusty," Sam said with a smile as he put his hand out to his friend.

"Police Detective Martin Jones, glad to meet you sir. I'll be overseeing this case," Martin jested as he took Sam's hand and clasped ahold of his arm with his other hand. "How's the simple life in the sticks working out for you Sam?" He raised his eyebrows when he said 'simple life' while looking around at the crime scene.

"Just fine up until now. Do you think I could see Deputy Damascus?"

"He's not conscious. He may not even come out of it from what I understand. Did ya..." he paused. "Do you know him?"

"Yeah, he's a friend of mine. Kate grew up with him."

"Well, I think they have him stabilized. If you hurry over, you might have a chance to let him know you're here before they take..." He stopped short as he watched the paramedics lifting the stretcher Paul was laying on with one harmonious movement and placed it in the back of the waiting ambulance. One of the two paramedics stepped up into the ambulance with Paul as the other closed the doors, ran around the vehicle, and jumped into the driver's seat.

Martin turned to look at Sam, "Sorry buddy."

"Lord go with him," Sam prayed as he watched the ambulance pulling away.

"Amen. He's going to need a divine touch from what I understand. Could I ask you some questions Sam about the escaped convict? I understand he's from around here?"

As Kate hung up her phone, Granny asked her, "Is everything alright?"

"No, Chuck has escaped and Paul Damascus is severely injured."

"Oh no!" Granny said as her face went pale just before her eyebrows drew down. "Was that Chuck's doin'?"

"Probably, they don't know yet."

"Oh Lord," Granny prayed. "Please be with Paul. Don't take him yet Lord. His sweet wife and precious babies need him."

"Granny, 'those babies' are in their early teens!"

"Sweet Jesus. That's when those baby boys will need their daddy the most. Trust me."

Kate gave up trying to make her point. There was no way of changing Granny's mind about Paul's boys ever being anything more than babies. She smiled as she looked over at Granny and gently shook her head in fond amusement.

"Well, what do ya' suppose this here's about?" Granny began to slow down as Kate turned to look.

In the road sat a state trooper's cruiser. The officer was waving them down as the car rolled to a stop.

"I'm sorry," the officer said as Granny rolled down her window. "I'm afraid I'm going to have to ask you ladies to take a bit of a detour this morning. We have an incident up ahead and I can't let you go any further on this road. So if you would follow the cones here, you can be on your way." He turned his head and pointed towards a less traveled road as he spoke.

"Is this about what Chuck done?" Granny spat out the name like it burned her tongue to speak it.

"Ma'am, I sure enough can't tell you that, not at this time. So if you would please." The officer stepped back and motioned again towards the detour.

Chuck moved through the underbrush. He had stirred around these woods often enough throughout his life.

He knew exactly where he was headed even though he had never been an outdoorsman. In fact, the only time he had even pretended to camp was when he wanted to keep his friend Leroy away from the 'Vacation Bible School' crowd. He growled to himself about Leroy in the end becoming a Christian anyway. "Leroy, you're an idiot," he grumbled under his breath, then pulled his thoughts back to the here and now.

Chuck had scraped a big chunk of skin off his left thumb and wrist as he pulled his hand free of the wrist tie. Now the blood ran down his hand and dripped onto the ground as he ran. Stopping to look at it, he pulled the chunk of meat connected only by skin back up over the gaping wound and pressed it back in place. He held it tightly with his other hand but the bleeding continued as he looked around for something he could use to wrap it up with.

When he heard water, he quickly moved toward it. He knew he could use water to throw off his scent, slowing down anyone who would be looking for him. When he reached the small creek, he stepped in and went down on his knees. He began to carefully wash his hands, but the bleeding continued. He rested his hands on his knees as he stared into the water. The water gradually calmed back down after being disturbed and he saw his reflection. His short, coarse, auburn hair was standing up because it had been tossed about by over hanging branches as he had run through the thick brush to get away. Across his red, hot face was a smudge of crimson where he had brushed perspiration away with his bloody hand at some point during his flight.

He leaned over and splashed cold water onto his face. It felt refreshing and he took some deep breaths. Looking at the sunlight through the trees, he knew it wouldn't be long now until his escape was discovered.

He took off his shirts and wrapped his undershirt around his hand, tying the knot taut with his teeth. He sat looking down at the orange jail shirt resting in the water.

"I have to keep my eyes peeled for something else to wear." Chuck said as he put his shirt back on inside out to hide the numbers imprinted on it. He washed the blood from his face and wet his hair, combing it back with his fingers. He then ran up the center of the creek, going as fast as he could until he saw a small bridge up ahead. Approaching it with caution, he made sure to stay behind trees whenever possible until he knew it was safe.

On the road just beyond the bridge was a man in a uniform, pacing back and forth across the road. As Chuck approached the bridge, he saw the man's pacing pattern was too short for him to slip under the bridge without being noticed. He slowly stepped out of the water and ducked behind a tree. Pressing himself against it, he paused to think. *'I have to get around that cop. But, I need the water to cover my tracks, so I'll just have to get back to the water as soon as I can.'*

He turned and peeked around the tree. When the officer's back was turned, he moved as quickly as he could from one tree to the next. It was working fabulously until he heard a car coming down the road and the officer turned abruptly towards the sound, almost spotting him. Chuck was certain the cop would have seen him for sure if it hadn't been for the car stopping his eyes from sweeping across the area where Chuck stood frozen in place.

Chuck moved slowly, sliding behind a bush to watch as the familiar car approached. "Well, what do you know? Here comes the bride!" He said under his breath as a smile of contentment passed over his lips. As he peeked out from behind a tree, he saw his lovely Kate sitting in the passenger seat. And a plan began to take shape in his mind.

9
New Slippers

*Therefore, if anyone is in Christ,
he is a new creation;
old things have passed away;
behold, all things have become new.
2 Corinthians 5:17 NKJV*

Later that afternoon, Sam and Kate stood in the parking lot at the hospital.

"Sam, why wouldn't they let me see Paul?"

"He hasn't regained consciousness yet. The only ones allowed in to see him are his wife, the doctors, and those investigating the case. I need to ask him some questions myself as soon as he wakes up."

"Did you pray for him Sam?"

"Yes, Luv." He stopped walking and pulled Kate into his arms, pressing her head to his lips, kissing her hair. "He's going to be alright Sweetie." Sam didn't know why he told her that; it just seemed to be the right thing to say. He stopped himself from saying any more as she took a deep breath and relaxed in his arms.

It was an unusually warm spring day and the smell of hot pavement rose in waves to meet their noses. The smell was whisked away by a cool breeze that accompanied the coming of evening. The trees stood around the parking lot waving their arms excitedly, like children on a playground waiting for the ball to come their way. The trees took no notice of the couple closing the gap between themselves and the car that awaited them.

Having walked all day, first in the creek and then the river Chuck was wet clear up to his waist. He was planning to slip into the laundromat on the edge of Ponder to find a change of clothes before finding a place to hide for the night. Pretty much anything dry would be acceptable he told himself as a cooling breeze began to blow, sending a shiver through his body that made his very bones shake. Even the small spring leaves in the trees quivered and trembled, seemingly from the chill in the air.

Chuck could see the laundromat from where he sat, waiting for the townspeople to move indoors as the night crept in on Ponder. Finally, Chuck made his move. The lights from the picture windows of the laundromat shone out onto the sidewalk as he slipped in the door. With one quick movement of his hand, he swept up an oversized hoodie that had hung on the same hook by the door for as long as he could remember. He slipped it on, slinging the hood up over his head. He pulled the jacket tightly closed to conceal his jail shirt. Chuck knew this laundromat well. With the large hood covering his auburn hair and hanging over his eyes, he scanned the place.

A young woman with a baby sat facing him not looking up from anxiously bouncing her infant as she spoke to it. "We're almost done here Sweetie. Then we'll go home and I'll feed you, I promise." She continued to talk as if she might at any moment convince the baby to be patient. Although Chuck thought the whole thing was humorous, he was actually grateful for the distraction; it was at any rate keeping the woman's eyes off of him.

Setting across from the woman, with his back to Chuck was an old man. The man seemed to be oblivious to the child's squalling or maybe he had turned his hearing aid off. He had a newspaper and was intently reading an article on the front page as he waited for his laundry to dry.

Chuck walked toward the restroom. As he passed a folding table, he grabbed a pair of the old man's unfolded jeans off the top of a basket and stepped inside the restroom. Locking the door, he struggled to pull off the thin wet county jail pants that seemed to be glued to his legs. Throwing them in the trashcan, he covered them with discarded paper towels and slid on the old man's jeans. The legs of the jeans were a little long but Chuck decided they fit pretty well. "Maybe that old man will forget how many baskets he brought in with him," he told himself as he stepped out of the restroom, picked up the basket of laundry, he had pulled the jeans out of and walked out the front door.

Meandering calmly down the sidewalk toward the edge of town he reasoned with himself, 'Who's going to pay attention to a man walking down the street with his laundry?' While passing a trashcan, he saw the newly changed out trash bag. Looking around, he stopped and pulled the bag out and quickly stuffed it into the laundry basket and continued on down the street.

With his stolen basket, Chuck waded along the bank of the river just inside the water line with his new jeans rolled up to his knees. It was getting increasingly dark and he was looking for a warm place to bed down for the night. When he came upon a pump house, he tried the door and found it was unlocked. He stepped inside.

Inside the pump house, he turned the laundry basket upside down emptying it of its contents. Going down on his knees, he checked out his newly obtained treasure. He found two more pairs of jeans and three flannel shirts. Never in Chuck's life had he owned more than two pairs of jeans. He also found a pair of red plaid, fleece-lined slippers among a few towels and rags. Chuck chuckled with delight. Slippers were a luxury he had only ever dreamed of having himself. He wasted no time pulling off his wet shoes and socks to put the slippers on his cold, wet, pruned feet.

He rolled the legs of his jeans back down and just sat there with his legs stretched out in front of him so he could admire his new slippers. For as long as a trace of light still came in the tiny dirty window, he sat looking contentedly. They were perfect in Chuck's view. Yes, the jeans were a little too long and one of the slippers had a small hole in its toe, still Chuck felt only contentment. He wiggled his toes inside his slippers as his feet began to warm against the softness of the fleece lining. He sighed as a tear of joy ran down his cheek unobserved.

Darkness crept into the small shed, bringing with it a chill that shook him. He pulled the large jacket tighter around himself and lay down on a towel, covering himself with the other towel. There he slept, still wearing his cozy warm slippers.

When the pump kicked on the next morning, Chuck awoke with a start and smacked his head into the pipe that hung over him. He cursed and struck out at the offending pipe, bruising his hand as well. Cursing under his breath he sat rubbing his head. The sun shone through the mud-streaked window of the shed, glaring into his eyes as he sat up. Scooting back, he sat against the plank board wall and looked down at his new jeans and his slippered feet. He smiled to himself when he thought of his good luck. But the smile soon faded as a feeling of loneliness swept over him. He was alone, all alone. The emptiness he felt made him want to lay back down and give up. But he had no time to feel sorry for himself. He would have to get moving if he were ever going to fill that empty part of his life.

Chuck had only one chance so he had to do it right. He jumped up and pulled off his jacket and shirt. In the corner of the shed, he dug a hole in the dirt floor and buried the county jail shirt he had just removed. As he dug, he could feel the dirt grinding it's way under the torn strips of undershirt he had wrapped around his wounded hand. Unwrapping it, he saw the darkening fold of skin he had laid back across the wound. "That's not going to work. How can I...?" He mumbled to himself as he slowly tried to pull off the flap of skin. He stopped as it began to tear the surrounding intact skin. "How am I going to get this off?" He said as he looked around for something to cut it off with. Then he remembered seeing a broken bottle along the side of the river. "I'll have to fix this later," he said as he wrapped his wound back up in the same dirty rag he had just taken off.

He moved faster now, knowing he needed to find a good place for him and Kate to hide out tonight if his plans succeeded. He put on one of his "new" shirts and then pulled his jacket on over it. He dropped back down to the floor where he slipped off the precious slippers and replaced them with dry socks and still wet shoes. Chuck put the remaining items in a towel, rolled it up, tied it shut, and threw it over his shoulder as he got up to go.

"No Sir, we haven't really found that much so far. Most of what we found was within the first hour of looking. We figured he made for the nearest creek and went upstream. Studying the rocks below the water's surface takes time."

"What can the rocks tell ya?" Detective Martin Jones heard his superior ask on the other end of the line.

"Well Sir, we're lookin' for rocks that have been kicked around a mite. That may tell us where he's been and in which direction he's headed. The problem is the longer they set in the current, the more they settle back in and the harder it gets to track him. In other words, the trail is getting cold and Chuck Atteberry is getting away. We have no other way of tracking him at this point."

"Isn't there something else we can do?"

"That's what I wanted to talk to you about, Sir. You see, if we bring in a tracking dog we might have a better chance of getting a lead on our man."

Martin's superior growled impatiently "I would of thought you'd have had a dog out there already."

"Yes Sir, the fact is someone did have a tracking dog in this area but a little over a year ago our man, Atteberry, shot him. He's all right, the dog that is, but after that he up and got himself a new master and moved somewhere up north of here. Truth be told Sir, we don't even know if he's being used as a tracking dog anymore. The only other dog we could get on such short notice was in the next county, but some fool got lost in the mountains there and the dog was sent out to find him. If he ever finds the man, we may be able to get him but I'm afraid it might be too late by the time he gets here."

"Well, get looking for another dog then! Why am I only now hearing about this? Why haven't ya been on this detective?"

"We have been Sir. That's how I knew about that other dog, but what can be done if no tracking dog is to be had? Our man, Atteberry, is keeping to the water and even the best tracking dog will be hard pressed to find his trail. Unless we know which direction he's going and the man steps out of the water now and then. This may take a while."

"Well, find someone local who knows where that other dang dog is. Get Samuel Trusty, he's had training and he'll know whom to contact or he'll know who will know! SO, GET HIM INVOLVED AND GET HIM INVOLVED NOW!"

Martin hung up the phone and in frustration breathed deeply several times, walking back and forth a step or two in order to clear his head, before calling his old friend Sam.

10

Lurking

Be sober, be vigilant;
because your adversary the devil
walks about like a roaring lion,
seeking whom he may devour.
1 Peter 5:8 NKJV

Chuck traveled most of the day before he finally found a broken bottle along the shore. He sloshed out of the water and squatted down beside the glass shards. Pulling the rag from his back pocket, he chose the longest, narrowest piece of glass and wrapped one end of it with the rag. He unwrapped his hand and found it oozing and sticking to its filthy white wrap.

"Oh, nasty!" He said as his face twisted with disgust. "This is gross!" He pulled at the wrap but it wouldn't release the flap of skin that was looking grayer and more gelatin-like than it had earlier. He was finding it impossible to keep the wound dry and couldn't foresee that changing in the near future until he was able to abandon the water altogether. He plunged his hand into the cold water in hopes of loosening the wrap as he began to wash the wound gently. Then he picked up the shard of glass and carefully cut the flap of skin away.

Chuck washed out the dirty wrap as best he could, wrung it out, and put it back on his hand. He wrapped a strip of towel around the wet bandage hoping it would wick away some of the water. Then he started off again, walking close to the shore as he went.

It was late in the afternoon by the time Chuck arrived on the outskirts of town. He wouldn't be able to get far with Kate tonight in the dark, but that couldn't be helped.

Casually he slipped into town with his hood pulled down over his hair and eyes while his hands were stuffed deep in the large pouch pockets in the front of the jacket, bandage and all. As he walked past the general store, he saw no one was in sight so he slipped in and stuffed his pockets with candy bars; anything with nuts as he needed the protein.

He could hear voices coming from the back room of the store as he tried to move quietly, the candy wrappers sabotaging his efforts at being silent.

"Did you lock up?"

"No, I thought you did."

"No, don't get up. I got it."

"Don't worry, I wasn't getting up."

"Very funny!"

One of the voices was getting closer as Chuck slipped out of the store and continued walking nonchalantly down the almost empty street. No one took notice of him as he turned and walked down the alley and around the back of McClure's Diner.

"This is the one I want. It's perfect, don't you think?" Mandy said as if she had never seen the dress before.

Kate looked at her with disbelief, "Yeah, I liked it the first time we saw it, but you didn't seem to like it this morning."

"Oh? I thought I did!"

"I think your words were more like, 'No, this isn't the right one. Let's try that new store out on Fifth Street. It will be fun'!"

"Oh well, it was fun wasn't it? Anyways, if I had said 'this is the one!', we would have bought it and headed back to Ponder right away. It was a lot 'funner' of a day the way we did it, don't you think?"

Kate just gave Mandy a playful scowl, "Oh you!"

"Oh, come on Kate. You have to admit it was 'fun'." Mandy stuck out her lower lip in a pout.

Kate put her hands on her hips in mock disgust and rolled her eyes. But she had to admit inwardly they did have fun, and she needed a day to laugh and enjoy her friend.

Mandy held up her phone to show Kate the time. "It's six o'clock, time for my feeding." She held her hands up in a 'ta-dah' motion.

"Wow, it's six already?"

"Time flies when you're having fun!" Mandy's smile took on a jolt of energy.

"I have to get home. Sam's going to be calling me soon!"

"Why don't you get yourself a phone?"

"Are you kidding me? You know I don't like phones."

"Oh, come on Kate." Mandy stuck out her lower lip again as she took Kate's hands and pleaded with her. "Sam knows you're with me. He can live one night without talking to you, can't he?"

Kate rolled her eyes again.

"Oh come on Kate, it will be fun."

Chuck hid in some bushes behind Kate's home at the back of the diner. He ate one candy bar after another while he waited for her to appear. It was quickly getting dark. "If she doesn't come out soon, I'll have to bed down in these bushes for the night," Chuck grumbled to himself. He lay back on the grass with his knees up, still concealed from view by the bushes.

He laid his forearm over his brow and thought. *"Being on the run is easier than I thought it was going to be. Maybe they're not even looking for me, or better yet maybe they have already given up. Maybe Paul's still laying out there on the road with the vultures eating on him."* A pang of sorrow passed over Chuck as he yelled out loud at himself, "Stop it! Why should I care what happens to that Christian freak?" But the more he thought about it, the more Chuck realized Paul had never been mean to him like most people had. He pushed the thought aside as it was too late to care about Paul now. He was most likely dead anyhow.

Just then, Mandy's car pulled up and Kate jumped out.

"No Mandy, I'm not going to open up just so you can have an ice cream. Come back tomorrow when we're open and get your ice cream then."

"Oh, come on Kate. It will be fun."

"No, go home!" Kate closed the car door while her hand brushed through the air and a smile threatened to give her away. "Go on!" Although Mandy was fun to be with, Kate was always exhausted at the end of any day in her company, and now she seriously needed to rest.

"Ok, it's your loss," Mandy said, winding up her window as she pulled away.

Kate let herself in the back door and put her bags down before closing it. As she was still chuckling to herself, someone knocked quietly on the door.

Chuck rushed for the door as he heard it lock and he stopped dead in his tracks. He growled to himself, hitting his head with his hand. He spun around, took a step, then spun back around to stare at the door in frustration. Stepping up to it, he knocked. *'If she asks who it is, I'm sunk,'* he thought to himself. But much to his surprise, the door swung wide open and there stood Kate as beautiful as ever. Her long dark brown hair tumbling over her shoulders in waves as her green eyes snapped with laughter.

"Oh Mandy, don't you ev-er...?" When Kate saw Chuck standing there instead of Mandy, her eyes got as big as saucers. She stepped back as Chuck followed her in, with Deputy Damascus's gun drawn. He closed the door quietly behind him.

"Grab yourself a jacket Kate. You're comin' with me," he said in low-hushed tones.

"What are you talking about? I'm getting married on Saturday," she snapped back.

"Be quiet. If you wake Granny, I'll shoot her dead Kate. I swear I will. You got that?"

Granny called down from upstairs, "Kate, who's down there with ya? Is that Mandy?"

Kate took in a startled breath and answered, "No, no, ahhh, I'm on the phone, I'm on the phone with Sam. Go back to sleep. Sorry, I'll try to talk a little quieter."

"How'd your day go with Mandy? Did ya find her a dress?"

"Yeah, it went great. I'll tell you all about it in the morning, okay? Good night, Granny, I love you!"

"Good night Sweetie. I love ya, too." Kate held her breath until she heard the sound of Granny's door closing again.

"Chuck, I can't go with you. I just can't." She pleaded in a whisper.

"I'm not asking you Kate, I'm telling. You can and you will go or I'll pick you up and carry you out. Now, let's get going!" He nudged the gun in the direction of a thin jacket hanging on a hook.

Kate slipped the jacket over the plum sweater she wore and stepped out the door.

"Chuck, where are we going?"

"Just you never mind that. Smile Kate, we're just out for an evening stroll." Chuck shoved the gun into her side. "I have this gun fixed on your rib cage, so don't try anything."

Kate looked at the pouch pocket in front of him and could see the bulge of the gun pointed at her. The thought of Chuck with a gun was more than she wanted to think about right now. Not only was Paul lying in the hospital near death because of Chuck's escape, but also he had already killed a man last year for being her supposed beau. Her heart fluttered with fear as her thoughts turned to Sam. The fear whipping them into complete confusion. All Kate knew for certain was she had to get Chuck and his gun as far from Sam as she could.

11

Till Death Do Us Part

For where two or three are gathered together
in My name, I am there in the midst of them.
Matthew 18:20 NKJV

Chuck and Kate had spent the night under an evergreen tree with low hanging branches. They hadn't walked in the river this time because it was late and he didn't want Kate to get a chill before lying down for the night. Anyway, he wasn't convinced that anyone was trying very hard to find him. Kate said they were looking for him but he wasn't sure if she was telling the truth or just trying to scare him. Either way, he figured he could lose them as soon as they started out in the morning.

Chuck woke a while before Kate, but stayed still so as not to wake her. When she finally stirred, he helped her scoot out from under the tree and sit up. He had tied her hands the night before with the towel rope he made by tearing a towel into strips and then braiding them together.

Chuck knew they needed to get going and move as fast as they could, keeping to the water. He thought to himself, *'If they weren't looking for me before, they will be now, because I have Kate in tow and that new police chief will be keen to find her.'*

From the moment he woke up he was aware of his hand throbbing with every beat of his heart. The bandage felt too tight but he left it alone, hoping the throbbing would stop after awhile.

"What did you do to your hand?" Kate asked as she stiffly struggled to stand up.

Chuck answered her question, brushing her off. "Took my skin clean off getting out of that zip tie, is all."

"What'd you clean it with?"

"Just water," Chuck said as he unwound it to show her. As he unwrapped it, he saw the swelling had extended from his wrist down his thumb, puffing out at the wrist where the bandage had not restrained it. The bandage also stuck to the wound. With one quick pull, Chuck pulled it away releasing both blood and puss to flow and drip onto the ground.

"Chuck that's bad, you need a doctor to look at that!"

He said sarcastically, "Oh yeah, thanks for your concern," in doubt of her sincerity.

"No Chuck, I'm serious! That looks really bad."

"I know but in case you haven't noticed there aren't any doctors out here so I'll be making do." He took a piece of the towel he had torn into strips and wrapped it around his wound. "We have to get goin'!"

"Chuck, just let me go. I promise I won't tell anyone where you are."

"No, I told you I'm not letting you go. We're getting out of this state and getting married, and that's that."

"I am not marrying you, Chuck Atteberry, and that is that!'" She said with disgust and irritation in her voice.

"You will Kate," he said with a sly smile. "There's no separating us now and this union will be 'until death do us part'. You got that?"

"Hello."

"Is this Shelly Wiley?"

"Yes."

"Good morning ma'am. This is Chief of Police Samuel Trusty from Ponder Tennessee. You may not remember me but..."

"Sam?"

"Yes, ma'am?"

"Sam, how are the wedding plans coming?"

"Uhhh, ma'am?"

"Sam, didn't Kate tell you we keep in touch?"

"I didn't ask her ma'am. This is official police business." Sam couldn't hear anything on the other end of the line. "Ma'am, ma'am, are you still there?"

"Sam, is everything alright?"

"Well, no ma'am. You see, Chuck Atteberry has escaped and we're looking for a tracking dog. Do you still have that tracking dog and is he still used for tracking?"

"Is Kate alright?" She spoke sharply with fear in her voice.

Sam was so intent on catching Chuck that he hadn't really thought of Kate being in danger. "She's fine ma'am. After having a long day yesterday, I imagine she's having a bit of a lie in."

"Does that mean she's sleeping in?"

"Yes, ma'am."

"Sam, please just call me Shel. And yes, as a matter of fact Duke and I just got back yesterday from another training course. It was more for me than Duke I'm afraid. Do you need his help? I would love to come down and help in any way I can. I was coming to the wedding anyhow so I'll just come down a couple days earlier instead. Didn't you know that I'm one of Kate's bridesmaids?"

"Oh, that's you." All of a sudden, Sam made the connection between her and the 'Shel' Kate had been talking about flying in for the wedding.

Shel continued with, "Well, actually I'm a bride's Matron. If you want to be technical about it, as I'm married."

"Well then Shel, how soon do you think you can get here?"

"Oh, by tomorrow morning or maybe sooner if I can get a flight out today."

"Good, let me know when you need picked up. Just so you know Shel, Chuck's already been on the run for over forty-eight hours so the sooner the better. The trail's getting cold and from what I understand most of it is under water."

"Under water? That's not good! Dogs can't track in water. If we know which way he's headed, Duke can follow the shore line and pick up Chuck's scent if he happens to step out of the water."

The office secretary stuck her head around the corner. "Excuse me Chief, but Granny McClure is on the other line. She sounds pretty upset. She insists on talking to you right now."

Sam put up his index finger, indicating she needed to give him a minute.

"I'm sorry Shel but I really have to go now, I have a call waiting. I'll see you when you get here. Thanks again, bye."

"Ok, bye Sam."

Sam sat the phone back in its cradle and stretched back in his chair, taking a deep breath then exhaling heavily. He really didn't have time for wedding plans right now. And even though he loved Granny dearly, her memory had been slipping a little, which meant he might have to hear the same question or request from her over and over again. "Ok," he said out loud and sat forward to pick up the phone and switch lines. "Good morning Granny. How are you this fine day?"

"Sam, he has her!" She spoke in a panic.

He sat up erect. "He who, has her who?"

"Chuck has Kate!"

"What do you mean? How do you know?"

"I heard her come in last night but now she's gone and her bed ain't been slept in."

He leaned back in his chair and released a sigh. He doubted that Granny heard Kate coming in. If she were in bed, she would have most likely had her hearing aids out. Plus, Kate spent the day with Mandy yesterday. When he called her last night, she wasn't home yet and Granny didn't answer the phone either.

"Did you call Mandy? You do know Kate was with her yesterday, don't you? Mandy probably talked her into spending the night in Bennington so they could finish up today."

"No Sam, it's Chuck. I know it's that boy!"

"Okay Honey, you call Mandy and if Kate isn't with her, call me back, okay?"

"But she never answers her phone!"

The secretary was back with another phone call. He put his finger up again to show her he needed one more minute to finish his conversation with Granny. "Then keep calling her. I have to go now. Give me a call back if you don't find her, okay? Bye now." Then he snapped impatiently at his secretary, "Who is it now? Can't one of the deputies take any of these calls?"

"It's the hospital. Paul's awake and wants to talk to you right away."

Leroy walked among the pews, picking up used tissues and bits of paper left from Wednesday night's church service. Picking up each small songbook, one by one, he shook them free of any scraps of paper left inside.

He replaced them neatly back into the book slot on the back of each pew.

He was now living in a small town near Ponder. Working for the pastor of a small community church, he hoped he could study for his own pastor's license, while he was there. He had never been so happy before. Even though he had only been there less than a week, he felt like he really belonged here. With a song of praise running through his head throughout the day, he found himself thanking the Lord over and over again for saving his soul.

After Leroy's trial, Pastor Hilby had taken him under his wing in order to help him along and give him a new start. He was thankful he hadn't been convicted of killing that man, but he was sad for Chuck. Sitting down on a pew, he dropped his head and began to pray for him.

"Lord, I'm never going to give up praying for Chuck. He needs You, Lord, especially now that he's in prison. My heart breaks for how lost he is and I know how it feels to be alone and lost. He doesn't know it's You that's missing in his life. Open his eyes Lord. Open his blinded eyes. Do what ever it takes to bring him to You before it's too late."

"Now Lord, You say in Your word that, *'everyone who asks receives, and he that seeks finds, and to him who knocks it will be opened.'* Now, I know that You're talking about 'things within Your will', and I know that it is 'Your will' that all be saved. I ask that Chuck be drawn to You, Lord. Come against the enemy of his soul that is holding him captive." Leroy drew in a deep breath and let it all back out before adding, "I won't stop praying for him Lord. I'll never let him go."

"Go on in Sam," the receptionist said as the police chief passed her workstation in the hall of the hospital. "He can't talk very well or long so make it quick. He seems desperate to talk only to you, no one else will do."

Sam opened the door and walked into the room where his friend Paul Damascus lay. His head was large with bandages with his eyes black in his pasty white face. Sam paused for a moment before gently laying a hand on Paul's arm.

"I'm here Paul. I was told you wanted to talk to me. Are you up to talking? I have a few questions for you."

Paul's eyes fluttered open. "Sam," he said with fear in his eyes.

"What is it Paul?"

"Chuck," he stammered, struggling to speak.

"We know Paul, he escaped. We're looking for him now."

"No!" He said weakly before taking a couple of breaths and attempting to continue, his eyes flaring as he tried desperately to communicate something serious. "Chuck," he flared his eyes again and raised his voice slightly as he tried to convey the urgency he clearly felt.

Sam pulled up a chair and moved in close, taking the man's hand while speaking in low tones to calm his friend. "Take it easy Paul, calm yourself down and tell me slowly, okay?"

Paul closed his eyes and began to take slower, more rhythmic breaths. There was a long stillness and Sam was about to get up and go, thinking Paul had fallen back to sleep. His eyes fluttered open and found Sam's as he began to say a few well-chosen words. "Chuck---------kid---nap--------Kate." His eyes pleaded with Sam to understand.

Sam was shocked to hear again what Granny had already told him. He stood so fast his chair flew back, hitting the wall behind him. Then he ran.

Sam beat himself up over and over throughout the day because he had failed to see or be warned that something was wrong. Why hadn't he followed up on finding her last night? Why didn't he listen to Granny when she called him today? She's a smart woman and not prone to exaggeration. And why, oh why, didn't he at least pay attention when he drove past Mandy's house this morning? If he had, he would have seen Mandy's car sitting in her driveway and would have known she and Kate hadn't stayed in the city overnight. 'Where's Kate? Is she ok?' The questions plagued him, but there were no answers.

When Sam arrived at McClure's Diner, Mandy was laying weeping in Granny's arms. Granny seemed to be calm as she patted the girl on the back with, "Now, now, everything's goin' ta be alright. You'll see."

As Sam drew near to the two women, he laid his arm over Granny's shoulder and said, "I'm sorry Granny, I should have listened to you this mornin'."

She wrapped her arm around his waist and pulled him into a group hug. "Now kids, the Lord is still in control and hasn't been caught off guard by this none. We need ta keep prayin' cause His word says 'where two or more are gathered in My name, there am I also'. Now that's the Word of God, so just you mind that."

12

Old Lem

*Though He brings grief, He will show compassion,
so great is His unfailing love.*
Lam. 3:32, NIV

Shel Wiley tied a blue bandana around Duke's neck. It made the dog happy to know he would be tracking someone again so the hound wagged all over.

"We need to get going. You'll have to ride in your crate part of the way."

Duke put his ears down and lay on the floor with his head on his paws as he looked up with pleading eyes. Maybe he could get his master to change her mind about the crate.

"Oh, stop it you sweet talker. It's not until we get to the airport and it's a fairly short flight. It'll be okay, you'll see." Shel knelt down and scratched the medium-sized hound behind his long ears. She ran her hand down the length of the dog's body, his auburn hair only giving way to the black saddle on his back. The white tip of his tail snapped in the air as his head turned and his black-and-white muzzle leaned into her next stroke, his nose rising, encouraging her to keep petting him.

"Shel, do you have everything?" Cody asked as he stepped back into the house.

"Everything but Duke here." She kissed the dog on the head.

Cody knelt down next to his wife and gave the dog a good scratching as he said, "you want your scritches, you want your scritches, don't you old boy!" Cody scratched Duke on his back and sides as the dog stood and eagerly licked his face. "Oh, stop that you mangy mutt!" Cody continued to ruff up the dog's shorthaired coat as Duke wiggled all over with delight. "Now you take care of our girl, okay buddy?"

"Our girl?" Shel stood and looked down at him in mock disgust.

"You are our girl whether you like it or not, right Duke?" He patted the dog once more before standing and giving his wife a kiss.

"Oh, I didn't say I didn't like it." She smiled shyly and batted her eyes at him.

"I need to get to work, but I'll call you tonight and I'll see you at the wedding on Saturday." Lifting his eyebrows up and down he continued, "and get us a nice room," followed by another kiss.

She pushed him back playfully. "Oh you!"

He patted his wife on the bottom then turned to go. "Love You!" He waved as the door closed behind him.

"Okay Duke, it's just you and me now. It's time to get going. You ready? Walk?"

Hearing the joyous word 'Walk', Duke ran across the wood floor, his nails clicking, as he slid to a stop under the hook that held his leash. He clutched the end that hung down in his teeth, pulling it until the other end slipped off and hit the floor. He ran back with the leash trailing behind him as he brought it to his master.

"Good boy," she said as she clipped his leash on and stepped outside. She struggled to get the key in the lock on the front door as Duke anxiously pulled on his leash. Then he dragged her down the sidewalk until they reached her car.

Re-examining all the neglected police reports filled out in the last couple of days, Police Chief Samuel Trusty hoped to find a clue where someone may have seen Chuck or something that would tell him where Chuck was or might be headed.

"Let's see," he spoke to himself, "first, a dog digging up tulip bulbs? Nope." Sam sat that report aside.

"Next, a cat in a tree? Nope."

"CD's stolen from a car? Nope."

"A drunk running over a garden gnome? Oh that's funny! Nope."

Sam paused as he stood up suddenly and looked intently at the next report. His eyes swung back and forth as they scanned the page, his mind spinning. "Laundry being stolen from the laundromat? Who called this report in?" Sam's finger traced the page until he came to the name, Lemuel Clayton. "Now, this isn't a frivolous report." He read it again before running out the door with the report still in his hand.

He couldn't help but feel an urgency to talk to Old Lem in person. As he drove up to his house, Lem stepped out to meet him by the front gate.

"Come on in Sam," he flung the gate open. "I been watchin' for ya ta come by. I got fresh coffee; it's just been brewed. Are ya here about my report? I been expectin' ya Sam. It just isn't right someone's laundry bein' stolen. I mean, who would want an old man's clothes? It isn't like I'm somethin' ta be lookin' at without 'um. If ya know what I mean!"

He chuckled at his own joke, causing a moment's pause, which certainly was not big enough for Sam to jump in before the old man began again.

"There really wasn't a lot in that laundry basket but some old jeans, a couple of shirts, and my old house slippers. Now, who would want my old house slippers? The dog done chewed a hole clean through one of the toes. Then I got ta thinkin' about Chuck escapin' and all, and well, it all made sense. The laundromat is on the edge of town and that boy is about my size. Oh, maybe a little shorter, but he's skinny as a rail just like me an' near enough the same size ta my way of thinkin'. The only thing I can't figure out is how he knew I would be there just then?" As he spoke, he poured the coffee and put some cream and sugar in it just the way Sam liked it.

Sam didn't get a chance to say anything about the coffee except, "Thank you." Instead, he just wrote notes best as he could, never having to add a word to keep the conversation going.

Old Lem talked for about five minutes longer before he began to talk about unrelated things. Sam had to cut in with, "Well, thanks a lot Lem. I do appreciate your help." He got up quickly and moved toward the door. Sam went down the walk and out of the gate, not losing any momentum.

"Anytime, anytime, I do hope ya find that boy soon. I can't afford ta be losin' any more of my clothes." The old man grinned, his eyes lost amongst his wrinkles as he closed the gate. Waving goodbye, he said, "Anytime Sam, I'm right good at figuring things out. Give me a call if ya need any more help."

Sam could still hear him talking as he drove away.

Lemuel Clayton had been right about being a good thinker. Sam had been so consumed with catching Chuck he had neglected the reports that lay on his desk. If he had talked to Old Lem yesterday, Kate might be safe at home right now. In the last two days, this case had gone from catching a man Sam barely knew to being seriously personal.

"I'm too close to this case to think clearly," Sam told himself. "I think I might just take Old Lem up on his offer to do my thinking for me."

The police chief pulled up to the laundromat and began to look around, starting with the trashcan out front. "That's weird, there's no bag in this can." He looked down the street to another can that still had its black bag. After looking over the few tossed soap bottles and soda cans, Sam stepped inside the laundromat to look around inside. First, he checked the seats and floor for anything left behind, and then continued with the trashcans. "Well, it doesn't look like the trash has been taken out for awhile. That's good." When he reached the bathroom trashcan he dug through the rumpled wet paper towels, soda bottles, and a few dirty diapers. Not expecting to find much, until his eye caught sight of something orange so he pulled it out. There in his hand was a pair of prisoner's pants! He froze for a moment as he thought of what to do next.

Lifting the pants from the trashcan, not touching them any more than he had to, he carried them with two fingers to his squad car. Pulling a large zipper bag out of the glove box, he carefully lowered the pants into the bag. "I have you now Chuck Atteberry! As soon as that dog gets here, you're mine!"

The crisp morning air blew its cold breath across the surface of the water as Chuck and Kate made their way down to the riverbank and stepped into the water. Its crisp, icy coldness lapped at their toes as they eased their way in up to their mid-calves.

"Do we have to walk in this cold water all day?" Kate asked, not understanding Chuck's reasoning.

"They haven't found me yet so I'm thinking it's working purdy good unless they haven't been looking for me at all."

"Oh, they've been looking. I know."

"Well then, there's your answer. You just keep putting one foot in front of the other and we'll do just fine." He pushed her slightly with his good hand to prod her along as Kate walked in front of him, her hands tied behind her back.

They walked on throughout the morning when Chuck began to feel sick with hunger. "Are you feeling hungry or is it just me?"

"Starved," came Kate's simple but angry reply.

He took no notice of her mood. He was too busy watching the minnows darting out of their way as they walked in the shallows along the shore. "I wonder if we caught these little fish if they'd be good to eat?" He stepped out of the water and moved downstream to find some minnows that hadn't yet been alerted to their presence.

"You mean if you can catch them, don't you?" Kate spat her words out as she stepped up on shore and sat down.

"Yeah, I guess you're right." Again, he didn't seem to notice the irritation in her voice.

He pulled his shirt off and began to sweep it through the water, catching sticks and dead leaves. He swept up some pebbles off the bottom of the shallow pool, but only caught one minnow.

"I got one!" He squealed at his first attempt ever at fishing.

"Wow, that's a big one," Kate said with disdain dripping from her lips.

"Do you want it?" He held it in the palm of his hand as it violently thrashed around trying to find an escape route. The water found its way out of his hand trapping the minnow inside the shrinking pool.

"No thanks, he's all yours," her face scrunched up with disgust.

"Ok," he threw his head back and tossed the fish down his throat. "I used to swallow gold fish in school to gross the kids out. It was the only time they ever paid any attention to me. They'd bring me earthworms, moths, and bugs just to see if I'd swallow them. It never helped, they still hated me, but I guess it's paying off now," he smiled.

The next swipe through the water brought up two small fish. Kate declined them also, but Chuck swallowed them along with the water, stopping only after catching and eating seven minnows.

"I don't know if you should be drinking that water. It might make you sick."

"I didn't get much water, but I hadn't thought of that. It seems to taste fine so it's probably okay. The fish aren't filling me up much anyways, so let's keep moving." He took her arm and helped her back up.

13

Jumpin' Bullfrogs!

*Do not be unequally yoked together
with unbelievers.
For what fellowship has righteousness
with lawlessness?
And what communion has light with darkness?
2 Corinthians 6:14 NKJV*

Stopping to rest, Kate sat on the bank of the river as Chuck moved among the scattered evergreen trees, finding one that had been scarred by a cougar or maybe a bear sharpening its claws. After the tree had been scored, it slowly bled out golden beads of pitch that over days, weeks, or even years had oozed down the side of the tree's bark, and stood glistening like jewels in the sunlight.

Finding the wounded tree, Chuck rolled the twigs he had collected in its amber sap, several at a time, and dropped them in a pile on the ground. Beneath the pine trees, the forest floor was covered with pine needles, so when he had finished coating each twig he knelt down and pushed the pile carefully into the needles. He then rolled the bundle until it was a soft mass about three inches in diameter. Taking a stick, he stuck it into the gooey mass and lifted it to carry.

Kate had been resting her eyes and when she opened them, she saw Chuck shoving a stick into a small brown blob and lifted it from its resting place under a tree. She stared intently at the mass that seemed to be growing longer as Chuck carried it toward her. "Stop! Stop! What is that?" she said with disgust, wondering what he could possibly want with a lump of... . Seeing it about to drop from the stick she scrambled to get away as Chuck drew near.

Plopping onto the ground, the mass spread out with a thud as the small twigs and pine needles inside jutted out, making it look like a porcupine caught in a mudslide.

"That's disgusting! You're crazy if you think I'm eating that!" She protested loudly.

Suddenly Chuck realized what she was thinking. He couldn't help but imagine the large stick-eating monster that would leave droppings like this one. Laughing out loud, he sputtered, "No Kate, it's fire starter! It's the pitch from a pine tree and sticks, that's all!"

"We're going to have a fire?" She asked hopefully. Her pruned feet cried out to be dry and her cold legs refused to be warmed by simply rubbing them.

"Why not? They haven't caught up to us and I personally don't think they ever will," Chuck said as he shoved the stick he had carried the sap with beneath the lump to elevate it from the ground. Collecting more sticks and broken branches, he stuck some of them below the blob and then piled a mound above.

"How are you going to light it?" Kate drew her face up with the question.

"By rubbing sticks together," he said matter-of-factly, as he went to get the two sticks he would torture all night long, as he tried to coax an ember from them.

After hearing the trackers yelling from up ahead, Martin and the others ran toward a pile of sticks on the shore. "Look at this! They were trying to start a fire!" He poked at the sap ball that ran in drips over the sticks as it found its way to the ground below. "What's this?"

Bringing a twig up to her nose Shel sniffed, "Ah, it's sap! That's pretty smart. Sap is flammable." She turned to look at Sam, "I think Chuck may be smarter than you give him credit for."

"Well if he's so smart, why didn't he get it lit!" Sam said with obvious disdain.

Shel dropped the twig and began to look around before picking up the two discarded sticks, rubbed nearly through. "I think he may have been rubbing these together to start the fire."

Martin moaned, he had heard of rubbing sticks together, "Why didn't it work?"

"I don't think you can ever rub two sticks together enough to actually get it to work. At least not the way he was doing it." Shel crossed the two sticks and showed how Chuck had been trying to do it. "'Rubbing two sticks together' is a reference to the hand-drill method or a fireboard. The point of friction has to stay stationary, and as you can see by these sticks the friction point moved all over the place from between five to six inches along the length of the sticks. The term 'rubbing two sticks together' is very misleading and I imagine there have been plenty of people who have died of exposure trying to simply rub two sticks together, like Chuck apparently tried to do."

Dying of exposure wasn't something Sam wanted to talk about while searching for his Kate, so he turned and walked away.

And once again, Shel knew she had gone too far with her wordy explanations.

It was late in the morning before Shel and Duke pulled into Ponder. The excited dog stood with his paws on the armrest of the car door, looking out the window as Shel slid out of the driver's seat and called him to her. She clipped on his leash and led him through the ally to the McClure residence at the back of the diner where Sam believed Kate had been abducted.

It was a clear and crisp spring morning with fragrances of new buds and blossoms drifting in the air. The clouds lay in pockets on the mountains surrounding the small township.

Sam stepped forward with his hand thrust out in front of him to welcome Shel and Duke. "Welcome back Mrs. Wiley. I hope you don't mind if we get started right away and deal with formalities later."

"No, I don't mind at all. Let's get started."

Sam opened a plastic zipper bag he already held in his hand and allowed Duke to sniff the prison paints inside. When the dog smelled Chuck he took several steps backwards before setting down. With his eyes fixed on his master, Duke raised his eyebrows as if to ask her 'why?' and let out a long piercing whine as his head tilted slightly sideways.

"What's the matter with him?" Sam questioned, puzzled by the dog's response.

"I don't know, but it could have something to do with the fact that he almost died at the hands of Chuck, when he shot Duke last fall."

"Oh, why didn't you tell me that?"

"I thought you knew." Shel paused and finished with, "he'll most likely still do the job."

"Would it help if we had him follow Kate's scent instead?"

"What? Kate's scent, why Kate's scent?" Shel's face went pale.

"Oh, I'm sorry Shel. After we talked yesterday we found out that Chuck had slipped into town, during the night, and kidnapped her. But when I finally thought to call you, there was no answer, so I assumed you were already in the air."

Shel whipped out her phone and saw on the display window, 'one missed call' and sighed, before thrusting it back in her pocket.

Sam turned when he heard a voice coming from behind, "Ya probably should have Kate's scent along with Chuck's just in case Chuck stashes her somewhere and runs off." Standing behind him was Lemuel Clayton.

"Ya need to be thinking that-a-way Sam." The old man continued, "Kate's life may depend on it."

"You're right," Sam said slowly, looking a little shell-shocked as he tried to put his personal fears aside. "I'll get something of Kate's." Sam stepped up to the back door of the residence and let himself in. "Granny!" he shouted as the door closed behind him. They needed to start soon if they were to make any progress today.

Lem patted Duke on the head as the dog's ears perked up, "I was out walking when I saw ya pull up out here. This here's a fine lookin' hound. Is he a tracker ma'am?"

"Yeah," Shel managed to say before the old man went on.

Lem put his left hand out to her. "Oowee, jumpin' bullfrogs! Ya sure are a pretty little thing. I'm Lemuel Clayton. 'Lem' ta those that know me, and 'Old Lem' ta those that know me best. And you must be the owner of this here fine dog." He patted Duke's head again.

Forgetting his manners, Duke jumped up to meet his new friend. Stretching his nose up as high as he could, the dog enjoyed another scratch behind the ears.

Shel smiled. She liked this old guy immediately. He was smart, friendly, and not afraid to say what he was thinking. "Yes, I'm Mrs. Shelly Wiley. 'Mrs. Wiley' to those that know me and 'Shel' to those that know me best." She smiled as she played his game.

"Well now, you're kinda ornery-like aren't ya?" He didn't wait for a reply; "I like that in a little gal! We're going to get along just fine." He chuckled at the playful banter. "Shel it is then!" He said with a nod.

"Then, I believe its 'Old Lem', too!" He put his hand out to her again.

"That sounds about right!" She extended her hand and he took it in both of his old bony hands, sandwiching it in as he patted it and said, "Well, how do ya do little gal?"

Sam came back out of the house, rushing toward the dog with a shirt of Kate's stuffed in another zipper bag. Once Duke had her scent along with Chuck's, he seemed to regain his focus and moved quickly to the back of some bushes, where Chuck had laid waiting for Kate the night before. The dog sniffed around some candy wrappers Chuck had left behind before moving to the back door. Pausing there, Duke headed toward the alley. Turning around the corner, he started down the sidewalk. The dog's head swung back and forth as his nose and ears touched the ground.

When they reached the laundromat, Duke turned and went inside moving straight to the bathroom just as Sam had guessed he would. Sam and Old Lem made eye contact with a nod of confirmation that said, "We're looking good so far."

"Your salad Madame," Chuck said as he laid a clean shirt full of greens before Kate.

"I can eat this?"

"Yep," Chuck felt proud of himself as he smiled at Kate. "They're not too bad either. I tried them when I was collecting them." He sat down next to her. "I like this kind the best." He held up the ugly, deformed looking leaf of the Plantain. "It tastes pretty good," he said as he shoved the leaf into his mouth.

Kate followed suit. "Oh, that is good!" She then tried a leaf of the bitter dandelion and miners lettuce. "These aren't too bad either." They both munched away at the pile of leaves that lay on the ground between them.

"Oh, and we can eat these now or later, I'll let you decide," Chuck said as he shoved his hand in his jacket pocket and pulled out a handful of tiny brown seeds along with some pocket lint. "Oh sorry," he said as he picked out the lint before placing them next to the salad.

"What are they?" Kate picked one up and crushed it between her teeth. "Umm."

"They're pine nuts."

She turned to look at him, "Pine nuts?" She fished up a few more.

"The seeds that fall out of pinecones." Seeing her eating them, he said, "So, I guess that means we're eating them now?" He pinched a few between his fingertips and placed them on his tongue.

14

Yellow Rock

*Be sober, be vigilant; because your adversary
the devil walks about like a roaring lion,
seeking whom he may devour.*
1 Peter 5:8 NKJV

Huge yellow rocks jutted up along the sides of the river as the sand extended up onto the bank. The water had pooled there less than a month ago, causing the ground to still feel cool in the heat of the day. Kate dropped with exhaustion onto the moist sand and laid back against a large rock as she closed her eyes.

"Come on Kate, we have to go up there to collect some greens."

"No thanks. I just need to rest. You go."

"Oh right! As soon as I'm gone you'll jump up and run off!"

"Sorry Chuck, but I won't be running anywhere." Her arms hung lifeless at her sides as her legs dropped unladylike in front of her. "Tie me up if you like, either way I'm not moving from here for some time."

Chuck stepped over, seeming disgusted with her unwillingness to cooperate and roughly tied her hands behind her and around the rock. Her fingers dug furrows in the sand as he pulled them back without a fight. "I'll be back in a little bit then," he stated before standing up in a huff and climbing the steep bank to the tree line.

Kate sighed deeply and felt as if she might just fall asleep when she heard pebbles tumbling from the cliff of yellow rock near where she sat. Opening her eyes sleepily she looked up, not expecting to see anything more than a bird pecking amongst pebbles. But she found instead a cougar's eyes fixed on her, leaning slowly closer on his haunches. He sat frozen, as if he were carved from the yellow rock he matched in color.

Forgetting her tiredness, she shot bolt upright and stared big-eyed in fear. Her once limp hands now drew tight against the rope that held her fast. Her legs pushed her back into the rock as she also froze like the big cat, not daring to move. Her eyes glanced up to where Chuck had disappeared on top of the steep bank, but he was no longer there. She croaked quietly, "Chuck." But as she did the big cat shifted as if he were about to pounce.

She sucked in her lower lip, swearing to herself to never speak again.

The cougar's head slid forward as if smelling her fear on the wind. His legs shifted below him as his hindquarters began to rise from the rock and he leaned towards her. His mouth opened and his teeth showed yellow and wet, surrounded by pink gums as he growled low and long.

Kate knew that with one leap this huge cat would catch her like a mouse with its tail caught in a trap. "Oh, sweet Jesus!" She whispered to herself, "Please Lord Jesus, please!"

The cat's monstrous head seemed to grow larger as he leaned ever closer. His front legs tensed as he readied himself to spring down on her.

Kate watched with terrified eyes as the cougar's mouth seemed to curl into a vindictive smile, exposing again it's sharp gleaming teeth. Just as she was about to scream, the big cat's head shot to the side.

"Kate, you won't believe it! I hit the mother lode!" Her head snapped around to see Chuck as he sat and slid down the bank holding a bundle in his arms. She quickly looked back to where the cougar had sat, but he was gone. Relief washed over her as her body went limp and she passed out cold, dropping over onto her side by the rock she was tied to.

"Wake up you lazy head," Chuck said as he shook Kate from her sleep.

Kate jarred awake and struggled to sit up. "Untie my hands now!" she shouted, startling Chuck as anger flashed across her face.

"You told me to tie..."

"I was just about to be eaten by a huge cougar!" She yelled intently, cutting him off.

Chuck said nothing but moved around her to untie her hands.

"Did you hear me? I said I was just about to be eaten! Don't you care?" Her eyes flashed with anger as she rubbed her wrists.

"Now Kate, calm down. There is no cougar. You were just dreaming." He swung around with one arm, palm opened to show her their peaceful surroundings.

"I was not dreaming. He was setting right there!" She pointed to the top of the steep rock cliff.

"Kate, there's nothing there. You were sleeping when I came back." He pointed to the place where she had been lying in the sand.

Kate faltered for a moment not remembering lying down to sleep, but still remembering setting up. "No... it was there, and I was just about to be eaten!" She snarled back, beginning to doubt herself, not knowing if it was actually true, but still trying to sound convincing.

She had felt defenseless setting there alone awaiting the cat's pounce. It made her feel like a slab of meat turning on the spit. She imagined the monstrous cat drooling in anticipation of devouring every last bite of her. She could see him then settling down to clean himself with tongue and paw, licking her blood from his jowls as it purred like a kitten.

Although brief, Kate's struggle to loosen her bonds had made her appear as if she were wounded, in the cat's eyes. If she had freed herself, and ran, the cougar would have been on her in a moment, without hesitation. And just as Kate had imagined, he would be licking his chops somewhere, before taking his catnap.

The river grew narrow where the water had cut through the soft yellow rock. The cliff stood tall on both sides of the river with huge rocks sticking out precariously as if they may fall at any moment. At the top, the rocks were fairly flat, leveling off onto the higher ground above the search party.

Duke's nose was to the ground as he moved toward a lone standing rock that appeared to have fallen from the cliff many years ago. As the dog approached the rock, his ears perked up. He walked around it and then sat waiting for his master. "What is it boy?" Shel asked, as she and Sam got closer. They saw footprints coming from the water up to the rock where either Kate or Chuck had sat. Beside the rock was a fragment of thread left from the towel rope that Chuck had used to tie Kate's hands. "Well I think it's safe to say we've found another place they stopped for a break."

When they heard Duke above them, they climbed the steep side of yellow clay slope to the top.

"What is it boy?" Shel asked the dog as he led them into the woods, stopping at some torn off low growing plants. "Oh, this was plantain, and this one," Shel stepped over to the next place the dog stopped, "this is miners lettuce. It looks like our man Chuck is feeding Kate salad at least."

Sam knew that should give him some comfort but he couldn't help but feel he wanted Chuck to fail in every way. But as Sam stewed in thought, Martin and his trackers moved away, following where Chuck had gone next.

Duke began to growl and, turning away from sniffing the plants, he moved quickly to the rock cliff that overlooked the river. There on the ground around a clearing were paw prints. "What is it?" Sam asked as he came up behind Shel.

"Cougar!" She said as she knelt down and touched one of the prints gently with her fingers then spread them out over the paw print and said, "a big cougar!"

"Do you think it's following them?" Sam asked with concern.

"If it is, we have more to worry about than... wondering if Kate is eating her salad or not. We also have to worry about whether this big guy is getting enough to eat."

❖ ❖ ❖ ❖ ❖

Kate lay silent, tied beneath the tree Chuck had chosen for them to sleep under. She listened as Chuck breathed deep and quiet. The soft repetitive sound was joined by a flock of geese sounding their calls from above.

She could see strokes of gold and violet splashing across the horizon through the boughs of the tree. The shadows grew long, stretching across the landscape, as dusk withdrew its sleepy rays, tucking them in for the night.

The wind moaned deep and long to wake the trees from their slumber as they stretched their arms and whispered up to the heavens. They swayed in unison as if caught in an unseen wave, the wind's breath passed over their canopy.

Near by, the water of the river ran babbling over rock and pebble until cascading over a falls, like a white crystal sheet. Striking the rocks below, sending ripples that radiated forth until they licked at the shore. Light reflected off the dark water with flashes, like sparks of gold.

Frogs and crickets began to slowly tune their instruments for a long night of attempting to woo a mate. At first, they crooned as if they were shy, then becoming more confident, they croaked and creaked ever louder.

But Kate was lost in thought. After being watched by that cougar as if she were a T-bone steak, she couldn't shake the feeling that those large cat eyes were still watching her, and she knew she would never look at a house cat in the same way ever again.

She was exhausted, and after what seemed like hours, she began to dream. She dreamt she was a mouse running from one hiding place to the next, only to be chased and rooted out again and again by that cougar. As she sat hidden in a shallow hole, she could feel the hair of her head being gently pulled, with trembling tugs as though the cougar was eating her hair. She shifted in her sleep, but the pulling and chewing began again. She shifted once again and realized she was only dreaming. Her eyes popped open and she sighed as she tried to replace the mountain lion's eyes with something less terrifying.

All of a sudden, she felt something gnawing and tugging at her hair once again. She knew that the hair part of her dream had been true. She screamed as she tried to sit up with no hands and banged her head on a low hanging branch, smashing back down again.

"What is it?" Chuck said groggily.

"Get me out of here! Untie me!" Kate fought franticly as tears streamed down her face.

"Stop fighting me or I'll never be able to get you untied!" Chuck shouted as she continued screaming, "Get it off! Get it off!" Chuck was starting to think Kate was losing her mind. With one last tug of the knot, it loosened enough for her hands to slide free.

She pushed him aside and shot out from under the tree. Standing, she franticly threw her head around as her fingers slapped at whatever she imagined was still in there.

Chuck just stood, helpless to know what to do as the dim light from the crescent moon lit this mad woman that thrashed about in front of him. She continued to scream about something being in her hair, but he couldn't see anything there. "Kate, are you alright?" he asked with resignation.

She leaned forward with a snarl as her hands dropped to her sides drawn into fists. Her eyes flared, glistening in the moonlight as her hair stood wild in tangled spikes around her incensed face. "Does it look like I'm alright?" she screamed.

He took a step back and wisely gave no answer.

Kate climbed a tree and sat crying in its arms as the moon slowly moved across the sky and beyond the hills, leaving the night much darker. No sooner had the crescent moon dropped from view than the light of day began to creep slowly up on the eastern horizon. The cobalt blue struck the black trees causing one's eyes to hunger for more light, but at the same time, desiring the moment to last a little longer, so they could feast on the blues depth.

Fog covered the forest floor with a white blanket that seemed to drink in the light and hold it selfishly in reserve. The distant lull of 'hoo hoo' was replaced with the sound of many cheeping songbirds, twittering in the trees. Kate sat still and alone as the birds flitted in and then away at the fall and rising of her breathing.

Kate felt at peace here and thought this tree would be the one place she could rest. And rest she must, but first she needed to make a comfortable spot to sleep. She looked from branch to branch and decided that if she could drag some long, strong sticks up the tree she could build herself a platform to sleep on. Silently sliding down, she began her search, wandering away from where Chuck lay sleeping.

15
Broken

The Lord is near to those who have a broken heart,
And saves such as have a contrite spirit.
Psalm 34:18 NKJV

When Chuck woke up, he had his arms wrapped tightly around himself. The blanket of fog did nothing to keep him warm as his teeth chattered from the cool dampness. Looking up, he saw Kate was gone. He stood and scoured the branches above him but she was not there. "Oh great, I slept too late and now she's run off!" He knew he couldn't go back to town to get her. They would most surely have someone guarding Kate both night and day. So he would have to go on alone. He could move much faster now and he knew exactly what he needed to do first, he had to cross the river to the other side.

Walking over to the tree they had started sleeping under before Kate had gone berserk, Chuck pushed the low hanging boughs aside to retrieve his belongings. But there on the ground where Kate had been laying, lay what looked to be a dead rat with a mouthful of Kate's hair. Chuck jumped slightly at the sight of it, then reached out and picked it up by its tail to have a look. Examining it, he decided it must be a mouse but it was a very big mouse. In fact, it was nearly as big as most rats he had seen.

Hearing something behind him, he dropped the rodent and grabbed his bag. Moving out from under the tree, he allowed the bough to fall back down behind him. Turning, he saw the cougar Kate had told him about. Being no more than twenty feet away, it glanced over at him for a moment before cautiously moving on.

Kate moved through the underbrush snapping branches as she walked. She was looking for thick branches she could build a platform out of so she could sleep up off the ground. She pushed over a small tree in hopes it would break off clean but instead it just creaked with discomfort as it fought to stand back up. Letting go, it snapped back so fast that it slapped her in the face as if to say 'how dare you!'

She knew she would never be able to break it off without a great amount of twisting and turning it from its roots, so she gave up and began to look around for something to chop it down with, but couldn't find even a sharp rock. Abandoning the young tree, she found some old dead branches she could easily snap off. Laying them out neatly side-by-side, she compared their lengths and when she felt she had enough she bundled them together with her hands and headed back, dragging them behind her.

Suddenly she stopped as the cougar she had seen the day before passed in front of her. She froze in her tracks as the big cat circled her slowly. As the cat moved, Kate turned to face it. 'What do I do?' She mumbled to herself, but heard nothing in reply. Fear gripped her as her heart pressed up in her throat and ears. She wanted to run but her legs didn't get the message and her feet only shuffled as she turned to face the predator.

When her foot caught on the branches, she grabbed one and raised it up, holding it over her head. She had heard somewhere that if she was ever confronted by a bear she should make herself look taller any way she could. Maybe this theory worked with the big cats too. At the time, she had thought it to be nonsense and maybe it was, but the cougar sized up the length of the branch and took a step back before he continued to circle her.

Seeing that the cat was not going to leave, she pushed the branch out towards it and yelled, "HAH, HAH," as she lunged forward. The cat stopped and looked at her with his large intense eyes, then stepped away and vanished into the woods.

Kate stood for a moment longer with the stick out in front of her, but when she heard the small snap of a branch behind her she spun around, the branch in her hand swishing through the air on it's way around. Nothing. She listened carefully but all she could hear was the twittering of birds, everything else was still. This was almost worse then the cat standing and looking at her, as she at least knew which side the attack might come from. But now she felt his eyes on her back no matter which way she turned. What seemed like an eternity passed before she lowered her branch, placing it back on top of the others. She began to drag the branches back to where she had left Chuck sleeping.

She knew if she told Chuck about the cougar he would once again not believe her. He would just think she was making it all up, therefore she was determined not to say a word.

So with her nose in the air and a look on her face that unmistakably said, 'Don't mess with me,' she walked back into camp with her branches dragging behind her.

Chuck said nothing but watched as she started to try and pull them up the tree behind her. "Here let me help you." He came and stood beneath the tree as he handed them up one-by-one. Once she had drawn them up, she laid them over the branches of the tree. "Are you going to try and sleep on that?" he asked as he looked up at her.

"Yes and don't you wake me up!" She snapped, looking down from her perch and appearing more disheveled and fragile then she had the previous night. In her hair twigs and leaves were sticking out and a fresh scratch ran across one cheek. Her dirty face was streaked where tears had slid down, clearing a path.

Chuck tried to assure her, "I won't. I know you need to get some sleep." He didn't know how well she could sleep on a row of branches but after seeing the big cat himself, he didn't question her reasoning. She hadn't been sleeping well and last night he was sure she hadn't gotten but a wink of sleep before being awakened by what he knew now to be, a rodent of unusual size.

As Martin and his search team crawled into the transport van, Sam turned and began to bark out orders. "Now as soon as we pick up where we left off yesterday I want you two to go upstream looking for other places where they may have gotten out of the water and made camp for the night."

The trackers looked at Sam in disbelief and then caught the eye of Police Detective Martin Jones in the rear-view mirror, but he said nothing. They knew their job well and had no intention of being told what to do by some small town police chief, so they turned to the map they had spread out between them and tried to ignore Sam as he went on. "And Mart, I think you should go with them, while Shel and Duke and I investigate anything new you might come up with. We have to get further today and every day if we are going to catch up."

Martin sat staring out the windshield saying nothing as Shel laid her hand gently on Sam's forearm and looked into his troubled eyes. "Sam, it's ok, we'll find her."

Sam looked at Martin as he drove and then looked back at the trackers who were notably avoiding eye contact with him. He sighed in frustration and turned towards the passenger seat window. He said no more to any of them until they got out of the van.

When they exited the van, Martin told the trackers much the same thing that Sam had before but they responded with "Yes Sir," as they started downstream. Martin grabbed Sam's arm to stop him. He nodded at Shel and she turned to lead Duke away. "Look Sam, I know you know this job as well as I do, but I'm in charge here and at the end of the day I'm the one who is going to answer for the things that are done."

"We're not moving fast enough and I know Kate better then any of you."

"Sam, if you were telling me that Kate was calling the shots we'd do well to listen to you. But, I'm pretty sure she has been kidnapped by Chuck Atteberry and he's in charge of where they're going." Martin paused for a moment before asking, "Sam, am I going to have to ask you to go home? Are you too close to this case?"

"No, I can't go home." Sam felt broken to think he might be ordered to go.

Martin put an arm over his friend's shoulder, "I know Sam, but you have to let me do my job and you know if I need your help, I won't hesitate to ask for it, right?"

"Yeah, I know."

"Well, let's get going then!"

As soon as Kate fell asleep and was breathing heavily, Chuck took off alone at a dead run, down to the river's edge. He knew he had several hours to kill as Kate would more than likely sleep most of the day. He and Kate had already taken too much time trudging along; and it was time to get serious and find a way to disappear from this side of the river and not leave a trail to be followed on the opposite shore.

As he ran, he could feel the cougar's eyes watching him. Whether the big cat was there or not, the fear of it urged him to run faster, with dread that at any moment he may be pounced on from behind. Reaching the river, he jumped in and swam hard for the other side, knowing that the cat most likely wouldn't come in after him.

The snowpack from the mountains above was melting quickly now and the river grew wider each day. Chuck's teeth chattered violently as he surged forward. Growing closer to the other side, he saw a small stream trickling down the mountain and headed for it. Stepping out of the river and into the stream, he climbed up the steep mountainside, staying to the middle of the stream.

Relentlessly, he trudged up the cold and slippery streambed. Soon, he saw a small waterfall a hundred feet or so ahead. Finally reaching the falls, he went to climb it, but found there was nothing behind the cascade to hold onto. Sweeping his arm through the current he found it was a cave hidden from view by the water that rushed over its opening. He stepped through the clear sheet of frothy water to find the cave walls dancing with the reflective light of the sun.

"This is perfect!" He exclaimed as he examined it and made his plans. When he jumped back through the falling water, he slid on the smooth rocks and mud in the streambed. He landed on his backside, sending a spray of wet pebbles skipping over the surface of the steep mountain stream.

But he didn't jump up; instead he sat looking back down towards the river. The stream twisted gently and peacefully down the side of the mountain. The river far below welcomed it into the flow of the larger body of water. The lines that divided where the river started and the stream ended disappeared, leaving only mere bubbles floating to the surface, bursting as they traveled on the shimmering current.

Kate made her nest in the tree lower then she had hoped to. Being exhausted, she slept soundly but not comfortably. The branches that she laid on were hard and knobby. No matter which way she turned, they poked and pressed on her back and ribs, cutting off her circulation. After some time, she rolled over yet once again, and as if in a dream, felt as if she were falling. Startled awake, Kate found herself really hitting the ground.

She moaned loudly as her breath was driven out in a rush. Looking up, she saw the rest of the broken branches coming down on her so she threw her arms over her head as she drew up her legs. Slowly, she caught her breath and carefully checked herself over for breaks, but there were none. "Thank You God!" She sat up and looked around, rubbing her now sore hip that had landed too hard on one of the broken branches.

Kate was trying to remember where she was when all of a sudden she saw the form of the cougar stalking her through the trees. She leapt to her feet and jumped for the lowest branch of the tree, scrambling up. When she saw that one of the branches still lay across the bough, she quickly lifted it and pointed it downward to fend off the cougar if need be. But when the cat reached the tree, he swiped at the branch, catching it with his claws nearly pulling Kate down out of the tree with it.

Kate scrambled up the tree as far as she could go as the branches swayed and trembled beneath her weight. She had seen house cats run straight up the side of a tree fifteen to twenty feet and catapult off in order to catch a bird in mid flight. Of course, the bird at times could manage to escape, but Kate was at a disadvantage because she could not fly to get away.

16

Conviction

But in accordance with your hardness and
your impenitent heart
you are treasuring up for yourself wrath and
revelation of the righteous judgment of God, who
"will render to each one according to his deeds."
Romans 2: 5-6 NKJV

When Chuck walked back to where he had left Kate high in a tree, she yelled out to him, "I thought you left me here to be eaten!"

Chuck thought he heard a tremble in her voice, so he called back, "No, I just went to find us a nice place to stay the night where you'll feel safe. I found a cave. I think you'll like it. I brought more to eat, if you're hungry."

Kate climbed down from high in the top of the tree and sat by Chuck. Picking up a leaf of plantain, she shoved it in her mouth as she said, "I can't believe you just left me like that! That cat just about had me this time."

Chuck, not wanting to add to her hysteria by telling her he had seen the cat too, just stared at her with concern.

"Don't look at me like that. Didn't you see him? He was right there." She pointed to the base of the tree where the branches she had collected earlier lay broken.

"Kate, did you fall out of the tree?"

"Like you care!" Kate unconsciously took note of the stiffness that was slowly creeping into her joints as she rubbed her hip yet again. "Chuck don't you know how to hunt? I don't think these greens are doing anything for me. I'm starving! Can't we have meat?"

"I never learned how to hunt or trap, but maybe together we can figure out how to catch something, somehow."

In silence, they ate the leaves Chuck had collected, but as they disappeared he knew Kate was right, he would have to get them meat to eat.

But first, he had to figure out how to get Kate to swim across that frigid river with him. He still had the gun stuck in the back of his pants, but he didn't like the thought of using it to scare her into submission. He had to use it to get her out of town quietly and that had been enough for him. Besides, he planned to put the gun in the black garbage bag he swiped out of the trashcan in front of the laundromat the night he kidnaped her.

'She might swim across without me threatening her,' he thought to himself. Kate puzzled him at times. She always seemed so calm and at peace, until recently that is. But still, under normal conditions, she had 'something' that Chuck couldn't quite put his finger on. Finally, he broke the silence.

"Kate, why have you always been so nice to me? You, Mandy, and Paul are the only ones who ever treated me like I was human."

She whirled around and looked directly at his face. *Was this some kind of a joke? She couldn't ever remember being nice to him. As far back as she could remember, she had been rude and meaner to him* than anyone she had ever known.' But still the question stood between them, awaiting an answer. And, the look on Chuck's face told her this was no joke. He was serious.

"What are you talking about? I've never been nice to you, Chuck. I have always done everything I could to push you away." She stopped talking, not knowing what else she could say to clear his obviously distorted vision of her.

He was not moved by her declaration and responded with a simple, "Everyone's done that." His shoulders came up in a 'so what' motion as his head shook slightly, accompanied by a confused expression.

Kate was struck dumb at the realization that everyone in this man's life had treated him worse than she had. She felt tears rushing to her eyes so she stood and began to walk away. "Which way are we going?"

Chuck jumped up and took the lead, "This way, down to the river."

Kate's thoughts churned inside her, 'How was it possible? She had been one of the many people in Chuck's life that had blown him off, never giving him the time of day and treating him like dirt. And still, somehow he had seen something different in her. What was it?' She asked herself. 'It certainly wasn't the likeness of Christ because she hadn't been Christ-like toward him; ever. She couldn't even remember witnessing to him as a child, let alone as a man.'

She now remembered telling him as a child, 'I'll never be your girl, Chuck Atteberry, because you're a heathen!' She knew at the time it had been too harsh but she never apologized for it. 'He was trash, everyone knew that, and she had gone right along with everyone else to make sure he knew it too. Why did she feel like it was her job to put him in his place and who had said it was his place?'

Tears rushed to her eyes and she fought to hold them back. 'Lord, help me to witness to this poor

unloved man. Give me the words to speak to him.
Lord, I know now You love him. Why didn't I see that
before? I'm so, so sorry, Lord. Please forgive me.
Give me the words and the opportunities to witness
to him now about Your love for him. Although I
haven't shown Your love to him in the past, please
give me that chance now.'

   'I know Lord that I'm to thank You for all things.
So even though this may end badly for Chuck or
myself, or maybe even for both of us, I thank You for
this time. I lay my life down before You Lord. Use me
how ever You will.'

   She wiped her tears away just as Chuck turned and
said, "Kate, if I don't tie your hands the rest of the day,
will you swim across the river with me without giving
me any problems?"

   Kate could feel her tears choking her as she said
with a trembling voice, "Yes Chuck, I will."

"Where are we going?"

   "Over there, do you see that stream?" Chuck
pointed to the opposite side of the river. "There's a
cave tucked in behind a waterfall up farther. You do
know how to swim don't you Kate?"

   "Of course I know how to swim!"

   "Ok then, don't you try anything, I still have a gun
you know and I'm not afraid to use it neither.

   Turning slightly, she raised her eyebrows. "So you
want me to just jump in and swim?"

   "First you're going to have to take off what ever
you can, to keep them dry. So I'll just turn around
until you're done." Chuck handed her the plastic
garbage bag. He already had one set of clothes to dry
tonight from when he swam across the river earlier, so
he turned around and pulled off his jeans and shirt.

   Kate quickly took her things off and shoved them
into the plastic bag. She then stepped to the edge of

the frigid water and jumped in, shooting back to the surface with a gasp, she cried out, "Chuck, I'm going across before I freeze!" She swam across the river as fast as she could go, followed by Chuck pulling the floating black garbage bag behind him.

Kate stopped just short of the other side as she shouted back to Chuck, "Don't look at me!" She jumped out and dashed for some bushes.

Chuck stepped out of the water. "Kate, where are you?"

"Don't look at me!" She squealed from behind some bushes. "I'm freez-zing!" Her teeth chattered, "Give me my clothes!"

Chuck opened the bag, removed his clothes, and sat the bag down near the bushes he knew Kate was hidden behind. "There ya go."

"Don't look at me!" She jumped back; being shocked how close his voice was to her hiding place.

"I'm not looking, I just sat the bag down here for you. I'm turning around now," he stated as he started to pull on his pants.

After they both were dressed, Kate stood wringing out her hair, "By the way Chuck, thanks for giving me some privacy."

Chuck looked at her for a moment, stunned that he had done something right and she didn't have a problem with telling him so. "That's quite alright," he finally said with a slight smile and then fell silent, thinking about how important it had been to her to have some privacy. His personal boundaries had been crossed so many times in his life that he didn't understand where they should be exactly. He knew not having boundaries made him feel out of control. Because of that, he desperately needed to maintain control at all times in order to protect himself.

Chuck now felt as if he needed to protect Kate from Samuel Trusty, her fiancé. *'Trusty', what kind of a name is that anyhow?'* The name 'Trusty' made him feel more leery of Sam than a name like 'Crook' or even 'Boozer' would make him feel. *'At least with a name like 'Crook' or 'Boozer', I'd know what to expect, but 'Trusty', really?'* Red flags went up for Chuck as he thought of the kind of man that would hide behind a name like 'Trusty'. His mind went back to the men who had convinced his Mom to marry them, only to see the monster come out of them shortly after the wedding bells stopped ringing. The one who had been the worst of them all had been named 'Christian', fixing it in Chuck's mind once and for all that no man was to be trusted, especially 'Christians' and men named 'Trusty'.

While they climbed, they both felt glad it was a clear hot day as they slowly warmed in the sunshine.

As they approached the falls Kate asked, "Did you say there's a cave behind these falls?" Her feet slipped on the small wet rocks but she regained her balance, being thankful that her hands were now free.

"Yep," Chuck pointed with his bad hand as his other hand helped him to climb.

"How did you find the cave? I can't see it."

"It's here, look," as he reached the falls, he stuck his hand through the water and into the empty space beyond.

"Oh, that's cool!" Kate said, coming up beside him and plunging her hand in as well. Stepping out of the water, Kate dropped to her knees and bathed her face in the cold water that bubbled at the bottom of the falls.

"This is where we'll be staying for a little while. I want to make sure we have lost them before we head out across country. And once we cross the state border, we can get married, change our names, and live happily ever after," Chuck said with a giddiness to his voice.

"You do know that I have to say 'I do' as well, don't you?"

Chuck stopped and looked at her. "Kate, you love me. You know you do. So why won't you marry me?"

"I do now Chuck, but not in the way you want. I love you the way the Lord tells me I must."

"You must? I love you and you love me so what's this MUST stuff?"

"It's more like I care about you, about whether your soul goes to heaven. I don't want to see you go to Hell, Chuck. It's Christ's love in me that makes me have compassion for you. Without Christ's love in me, I most certainly would not love you at all. I would treat you the same as everyone else has your whole life. That's why Paul, Mandy and I treated you differently in school. We're all Christians and even though I couldn't see myself as being particularly Christ-like," she choked up as tears threatened to show themselves again, "you still somehow saw Christ in me."

Chuck's eyes held deep pain behind them as he stared right through Kate and into the water that shimmered and danced in the sunlight behind her.

"Chuck, I'm so, so sorry. I should have treated you better in school. Setting a better example of God's love, not only for you, but also for those who were watching me. I can't tell you how sorry I really am. Please forgive me!"

Martin was frustrated at the end of a long day as he pulled Sam aside, "Look Sam, I know ya think that we're deserting you out here, but we have been walking around in circles all day long. And all we found are cougar tracks, some broken branches, and a dead mouse. Face it - we have lost them! You know my trackers found fresh truck tracks up by the road. And, that a fellow prisoner said he heard Chuck talking to someone on the phone about picking him up somewhere? So, what's the problem? If you were

Chuck, wouldn't you leave this area rather than staying to be eaten by some cougar?"

"I know they're still out here!" Sam felt strongly about his statement even though he knew he had lost the argument.

Martin shook his head slowly, "Sam, let's look at the evidence. First, we know they were here but are no more. Second, someone pulled a truck in very near to here and then went back out the way they came."

Sam snapped back "You know as well as I do those tracks could have been left there any time in the last two weeks."

"True, or they could have been made today. And thirdly," Martin continued, "we have a witness who said Chuck has someone working with him on the outside."

"Since when do we take the word of prisoners? You know as well as I do, that they like making 'The Law' look like idiots!"

"Which direction do ya suggest we go?" Martin spun around with his arms out. "There are no more tracks. The dog has lost the scent. I'm sorry Sam, I really am, but the trackers and I will not be coming back tomorrow. Ya can keep the dog, that is, if Mrs. Wiley wants to stay, as she's an independent. But the county can't pay for the dog's services from here on out. I'm sorry."

"We'll stay with you, Sam." Shel stepped out of the bushes and walked over next to Sam. Duke sniffed at Sam's shoes and then jumped up under his hand as Sam rubbed the dog's head.

Martin nodded as he reached out and laid a hand on Sam's shoulder, "Let me know if ya find anything new and we'll be back in a heartbeat. Ok?"

Sam nodded as he gave his friend a mournful smile. "Yeah, ok."

17
Black Shroud

Judge not, and you shall not be judged.
Condemn not, and you shall not be condemned.
Forgive, and you will be forgiven.
Luke 6:37 NKJV

Setting beside the falls, Chuck and Kate bathed their wounds, scrapes, and bruises. Chuck stared at the sparkling water as it slid over his numb wet feet. They looked like they were made of wax, cold and lifeless. Kate heard Chuck say under his breath, "And now he's dead."

"Who's dead?"

"Paul Damascus!"

"Chuck, Paul's not dead."

"He's not?"

"No, he's in intensive care with a pretty bad concussion but he may still make it."

He sighed deeply, not realizing until now how upset he had been thinking that he killed Paul. Chuck would never have admitted less than absolute hatred for the man. He hadn't wanted Kate to see past the tough exterior he had allowed to be pulled down. He felt like the scared little boy inside had been exposed and he quickly drew his mask back up again. "What kind of stupid name is 'Damascus' anyways?"

Kate had never thought about it before. "I don't know. There was a town in the middle-east called Damascus. I don't know if it's still there or not. Maybe the name's Jewish or middle eastern?"

"Humph, Jewish? With that blond hair and blue eyes? I doubt that."

"Chuck, not all Jewish people look like the Italian artist's depictions of them."

He turned and moving among the bushes quickly collected what he had spread out to dry. Laying them on a towel on the ground, he pulled the corners up and tied them into a bundle. Handing it to Kate, he said, "Here, hang on to this." Chuck continued, "I'm going to put this bag over your head. It will cover your body while you lean over the bundle and back up into the cave. I'll pull the bag off you when you're inside. You got that?"

"I think so, then what?"

"I'll be in after you with the bag over my head." He slipped the bag over Kate and aimed her in the right direction. Holding on to the top corners of the bag, he said, "Ok, step back."

Kate took several steps backwards into the cave as the water pounded on the surface of the bag. When she cleared the water, the bag slipped off over her head and disappeared through the curtain of water. She was amazed how well Chuck's plan had worked. She was fairly dry, with the exception of a little water that ran off the bag and down the middle of her back. She dropped the bundle on the floor and then turned to inspect the cave. She estimated the cave to be about seven feet deep and five feet across. The ceiling was about seven feet tall at the opening and dropped off as it went back.

As Kate stood looking around, Chuck came through the water and tripped over the bundle she had dropped on the floor. He flew forward defenselessly, ramming his hooded head into the back wall of the cave. Dropping one of the shoes he carried, he tripped over it and fell to the ground. He was still shrouded in the black bag that covered him from his head to just below his bottom.

As he lay on the ground, he fought wildly to get free or get up, it wasn't clear which. He cursed loudly as he finally escaped the black claustrophobic garb and yelled at the top of his lungs at Kate, "WHAT DO YOU THINK YOU'RE DOIN'? Are you trying to kill me, or...?"

"Sorry Chuck, I didn't think. Sorry," she pleaded as her face spoke of regret.

"You could have helped me out of that bag, you know?"

"Sorry, I..." but she said no more about it as she turned her face away to suppress a laugh that threatened to burst out of her from the slapstick comedy she had just witnessed.

"Oh, never mind." He calmed down after several moments of steaming in silence. He sat down and closed his eyes as he rubbed his head where a huge welt was already rising above his left eye and he cursed again. "That really hurt!" he grumbled.

"I'm sorry Chuck, I really am." But she remained turned away from him, busying herself with untying the bundle and folding the clothes that were inside. "Is this Old Lem's shirt?" Not expecting that it was, she went on, "he has a shirt just like this one."

When Chuck didn't answer, she turned to see him with a smile on his face as he said, "Was that Old Lem I saw at the laundromat? I didn't even recognize him. How's the old coot doing these days?"

"He's not an old coot! He's a good man."

"Good man? There is no such thing," he mumbled half under his breath as he sat still holding his head.

"Yes there is Chuck, there are plenty of men who seek to do good. Are they perfect? No, but they try."

He yelled, "Well, I've never met one, okay?" He lowered his hand and clenched it into a fist at his side, exposing the largest purple knot Kate had ever seen on anyone.

"Oh Chuck, are you alright?" Kate rushed to his side and dropped to her knees to examine the knot.

"Don't touch it," he grumbled but then allowed her access as he watched the compassion on her face.

"Oh Chuck, this looks really bad."

"Nah, you should of seen my mom when..." he stopped himself short, then pushed her away. "It isn't nothin', that's all. Now get back over there," as he pointed to the wall at the back of the cave. He got up and tied her hands behind her. He tied the other end of the rope to a root that had grown through the wall of the cave. Facing away from her, he held his head in his hands as his shoulders began to shake.

Concern for him caused her to pray silently. *'Lord please, help me to know how to pray for this man. He has been hurt so very deeply.'*

As he entered the room, followed by a tall ruddy-complected man, Pastor Hilby said, "Leroy, this young man is working in our community and would like to get plugged in at our church. He's volunteered to help clean up after Sunday services. Could you find him something to do?"

"Yeah, sure. I'm a little busy today, but if you can meet me here tomorrow, I'll get you started."

The man reached out and took Leroy's hand. "Ezekiel Bloom," he said.

"Leroy McCoy," he returned as he shook his hand.

Ezekiel hung on to his hand as his face lit up. "Leroy McCoy?"

Leroy's face sank with concern. *'How does he know me? Has my tainted reputation followed me here?'*

"I'm Zeke, don't you remember me?" He laid his free hand on his own chest.

Leroy's face still reflected concern.

"I lived next door to you for about three years when we were kids. Don't you remember me?" He held fast to Leroy's hand as his last statement began to sink in causing Leroy to take a deep breath.

Leroy's eyes popped open. "Zeekers?"

Zeke began to laugh. "No one's called me that in years!" He pulled Leroy towards him and encircled him in a bear hug matching his height. "So, you're a Christian now?" He stood back and slapped Leroy on the shoulder.

Leroy examined Zeke's face and said, "I just got saved not too long ago." His lips skeptically turned up as he continued, "You don't look anything like you used to."

"You don't either! We were only seven the last time we saw each other." Zeke laid his hand high on his own chest. "I thought I had lost my brother forever."

His statement caught Leroy off guard; he didn't remember Zeke ever having a brother. "You lost your brother?"

"No Leroy, you! I've been praying for you since we were small. I always felt like you were my long lost brother. Being from a family of sisters I can tell you, I missed you a lot man!" They both laughed before Zeke continued, "You better give me your phone number. I'm afraid I'm going to make a pest of myself! We have a lot of catching up to do, you know."

Leroy dug his phone out of his pocket, flipped it open, displayed his number and held it out to Zeke. Zeke entered the number into his own phone.

"So you're living here in town?" Leroy asked.

"For the time being. I'm here for work right now, then the wife and I will most likely be moving up north to be near our families."

"What kind of work do you do?"

"Oh, I'm into communications. Hey, I could get you a better phone than that old dinosaur."

"You'd have to teach me how to use it, too."

"Sure, no problem!" Zeke stated nonchalantly.

"So, how is your family?"

"Oh, Dad and Mom are great and all the girls are married except for Sarah. She's still living at home. She has her mind set on the Lord shaking the world to find her the right guy."

"Which one is Sarah?"

"She's just a year younger then me. You know, Sarah's the one who used to follow us everywhere!" Zeke raised an eyebrow and nodded when he saw recognition on Leroy's face.

Leroy saw a little girl with pigtails and smiled at the memory of the two of them trying to lose her.

"You know Leroy," Zeke said with a serious tone, "you're an answer to prayer! When you stopped coming to church with us, it tore me up inside." He paused before his countenance brightened, "It's good to see you again brother and welcome to the family of God!" Then he gave Leroy another monstrous hug.

Leroy choked down a tear that caught in his throat. He felt easy with Zeke as if they had not been separated by years on end. It would now just be a matter of getting used to him being an adult.

"What time do you take your lunch break?" He asked as he backed out the door.

"Today? About 12:30."

"Ok!" Zeke smiled once more before waving a hand, he turned and left.

Witnessing the whole exchange Pastor Hilby said, "Well, it looks like you do have family after all."

As Leroy faced him he smiled, "Yep, he called me 'his brother and an answer to prayer'."

Police Chief Samuel Trusty walked ahead of Duke, Shel, and Old Lem, staying within comfortable shouting distance.

"Lord," he prayed to himself as he walked, "what did Granny mean when she said this morning that Kate can't get away, but if she could, she probably wouldn't leave Chuck?" Fear, stress, and the lack of sleep were all wearing Sam down. *"Is she falling for him now?"*

Granny had said that, 'Chuck was in a bad way'. "I'll say Chuck's in a bad way! All of Chuck's ways are bad," Sam spat out the words with bitterness. Feeling a check in his spirit, he fell silent. Remaining still, he battled whether to obey his flesh or to give in to what the Lord might have to say to him. He knew the Lord died for Chuck's sins, too. But exactly how God could forgive someone like Chuck was beyond anything he could comprehend!

Sam had always had more trouble forgiving people who would hurt someone he loved than he had forgiving those who hurt him. All of a sudden, it dawned on him; *'If Kate can't get away, and Chuck dies, she may never be found... Or it may be too late for her by the time she's found.'*

"Lord, what can I do?" A new rush of fear washed over him as he stopped breathing for a moment. "Lord, what can I do?" he repeated. *'Pray for Chuck,'* Sam heard a still small voice answer. "But Lord, he... I..." he stopped himself again. "Yes, of course." He paused and took some deep breaths. "Yes Lord, thank you," he said out loud as he continued to walk. But still, he couldn't seem to open his mouth to pray for his enemy. The words stuck in his throat as rebellion, and hatred's strong hands strangled him; forcing him to swallow their bitter bile.

As they trudged along the riverbank, Shel grumbled, "Granny said Kate was trapped and couldn't get away. But she wasn't sure Kate would leave Chuck anyway, as he's in a 'bad way'." She made quotation marks in the air and rolled her eyes as she spoke to Old Lem.

"Chuck's in trouble? Is that what she said?" Lem asked.

Shel rolled her eyes before saying, "She said, 'in a bad way', whatever that's supposed to mean."

"That means he's in trouble. Ya sure that's what she said?"

"Yeah, that's what she said," she paused and then stated, "personally, I think she's just making stuff up as she goes. How could she possibly know what's going on with Chuck and Kate?"

"Well, I'll tell ya little gal. A lot of folks around these parts call her The Prophetess. Now, I've known Granny since way before she was called Granny by anyone and when she says she sees somethin', ya just best take heed. That's all I got ta say about that."

"So, you think she's heard from the Lord?" Shel said skeptically. "Is that what you're saying?"

"Yes 'um, I sure am."

"So what you're saying is she's a prophet and she has never been wrong about anything?"

"No, I didn't say that. Anyway, it takes years and a lot of obedience training for the Lord ta make a prophet. Just like your dog there. Someone saw he had the nose and the ears for trackin' before he received his trainin'. And without that trainin', he would just be a regular ol' dog."

"Prophets don't just fall out of the sky," Old Lem continued. "Perfect and never makin' any mistakes like some teach. No, they're folks just like you and me except they go through things that don't happen ta anyone else so the Lord can train them up. They're tested and tried. Sometimes they're turned on a spit for sayin' what they say and doin' what they do, just like the prophets of old did."

Lem took a breath before going on with, "The true prophet isn't on TV screamin' bout how ya are ta send them money so they can bless the world. All that is... is just pride and arrogance in my view. And prophets aren't folk that want ya ta follow them around, livin' in some commune where they can tell ya how and what ta do all the while they're drainin' your bank account. It's a sure indicator that they're a little off the mark. When they want you to hold them up as being holy, someone you should worship as 'god'.

"The prophets of old never claimed ta be God. The words they spoke weren't words to tickle the ear and they weren't words that would make everyone like them. These folks were considered outsiders, avoided, thought to be strange, and even a bit 'crazy' in their day. Most were killed by those they were sent ta help."

"So why does the Bible and the church warn us about false prophets in the last days?"

"Well, there will be false prophets to be sure, but I think by only focusing on the false prophets or by avoiding talking about prophets altogether, God-fearing pastors do the church an injustice. The body of Christ is going to be left with no help when they need it the most, making them vulnerable in 'the end' because of their ignorance. We need to know how to identify both God's prophets and false prophets."

"So how do you identify a prophet? By whether they have their hands in your pocket or not?"

"Well no, not exactly. The prophets did accept payment sometimes. Ya know, a place to sleep, bread, meat, and maybe a little money. They were human after all. They got hungry just like you and me. But they didn't become rich from bein' a prophet. No ma'am, they didn't want anything except ta serve the Lord their God.

"Ta see if someone is a prophet or not, we need ta learn ta see with our spiritual eyes. Does what they say line up with what the Word of God says or contradict it? Watchin' your pocket book is the world's way or the lazy spiritual man's way, it's not a sure indicator. Still, be careful. The Word says that the enemy 'comes as an angel of light and many will be deceived'.

"With all that in mind, take a look at Granny, Helen McClure. There are plenty of folks round these parts that think she's a mite crazy. They won't even grace her diner because she might have something ta say that they don't want ta hear, even if it may be the very thing that saves their souls from hell. They just want ta go on the way they're goin' with no one tellin' them they're wrong.

"Granny isn't any social butterfly, even though she sure do like ta dance. But she picks and chooses who she dances with and if she dances with ya, ya better plan on bein' ministered to in some way before the dance is over. Other then that, she mostly stays out of folk's way.

"She don't want nothin' from no one, ya see? Ya may not understand what she has ta say or want ta hear it. Like what she said about Chuck and Kate, but don't ya see that now ya have insight into what's going on with them so ya can pray. And if I might add, it seems ta me we need ta be prayin' for Chuck right now as much, or more then Kate. Somethin' isn't right and the Lord wants us ta be prayin' for that boy's soul."

Shel didn't know what to say because she knew he was right. She and her friends had prayed for Chuck before when they were being chased by him and Leroy, to be killed. Clearly, it was time to start praying for Chuck again. "One more question," she asked, "and please don't give me another sermon! I can't process any more."

"Fire away then."

"I'm still not sure I believe in prophets today. Aren't the days of the prophets over?"

"Do you believe were livin' in the last days?"

"Sure."

"Well, the Bible says in Acts 2:17 that 'in the last days the Lord will pour out his spirit on all flesh and our sons and daughters will prophesy'. So I guess ya ought ta start believin', don't you think?"

18

Amongst Filthy Rags

But we are all like an unclean thing,
And all our righteousness's are like filthy rags;
Isaiah 64:6a NKJV

Sam really didn't know too much about Chuck other than the fact he had murdered a man last year, whom Chuck had thought was flirting with Kate. But what really happened was Kate had been witnessing to that man and he had given his life to the Lord only hours before Chuck killed him.

It was a cold-blooded murder, but Sam had to admit that much of his distaste for Chuck had derived from the gossip he had heard after becoming the police chief of this small community. Even though Sam would never consider himself to be a gossip, he willingly swallowed each word, allowing them to become one with his new bitterness and ungodly actions towards Chuck.

Now even the thought of Chuck forcing Kate out of her home at night, most likely at gun point and carrying her off into the wilderness, burned in Sam like a hot coal dropped on dry grass. It was fear mixed with anger and hatred that drove him on. But out of obedience to God, he knew he needed to douse those flames and pray for Chuck.

It was hard at first, but as he prayed, he began to feel healing in his own heart and became aware of the bitterness he had been carrying around with him. Soon, he began to feel compassion replacing the bitterness, feeling pity for the man who obviously didn't know what love really was.

Sam walked upriver in front of the others for a little while longer before he decided he wasn't doing anyone any good. He knew he needed to be alone for a while to pray and seek the Lord before he could continue. So he turned and walked up the hill toward the road above them. He wanted to avoid any questions like... *'What's wrong?'* and *'Are you alright?'* When in truth, what the Lord was doing inside of him was all right. It was, in fact, very all right.

❖ ❖ ❖ ❖ ❖

"I can't believe we did that when we were kids!" Leroy said while still laughing at Zeke's recollection as they sat in the church kitchen eating their lunches.

"Well, we did. Do you remember throwing all the mattresses out of the upstairs window of that tiny two story house and then jumping out on top of them?" Zeke asked. He could hardly keep from bursting out, "that was great!" He laughed heartily.

"Now that I do remember!" Leroy thumped his fist high on his chest in an attempt to dislodge the food that refused to be swallowed. "And last, we threw Sarah's mattress out, not wanting to touch it until last. She was still wetting her bed. And those were the days before plastic sheets. Oh man! When I jumped out the very first time, I did a face plant right in it!"

"Ohhhhh nooooooo!!" Zeke threw his head back, holding his gut, as he continued to laugh.

"That was hideous!" Leroy croaked out as his face scrunched up in disgust.

"I can still see Sarah flying out that window after us. She bounced so high off the mattresses and landed on the hard ground, knocking the wind out of her."

"We thought she was dead for a moment before she finally jumped up and said," Leroy used his best child-like voice, " 'let's do it again!' "

"And when we were done, we had to wrestle all four of those mattresses back up that narrow bending staircase before my folks got home. That was even harder than pushing them out that window. Especially Sarah's because neither of us wanted to touch the wet spot in the middle, do you remember that?"

"Oh yeah, I definitely remember!" Leroy stared off into space as he saw it all over again. "If I remember right, when you stopped all of a sudden on the stairs, I did a face plant then too." Leroy glared in mock anger at Zeke.

"Oh man, were we ever stupid. Why didn't we think to move her mattress to the bottom of the pile instead of trying not to hit it every time we jumped?"

"Yeah, I had to strip down and take a shower when I got home to get that stink off!" Leroy scrunched his face.

"Oh noooo! Stop! Please stop, I can't take any more!" Zeke massaged his tired cheeks, "I have to get back to work anyways." He stood and picked up his mostly uneaten lunch, shoving it back into his lunch pail. "Same time tomorrow then?"

"Sure, same time tomorrow. I'll be here!"

When Shel saw Sam heading up the side of the embankment, leaving them to search for Chuck and Kate alone, she asked, "Where's he going? Do you think he found something?" She turned and looked at Old Lem inquisitively.

"Just follow your dog, Duke knows if the scent leads off in that direction. Stay the course missy, we're makin' progress here. It might not feel like we're gettin' anywhere, but we're right where we need ta be."

"Yeah, I guess you're right. I'm just getting tired. We haven't stopped for lunch yet and it has to be close to noon by now."

"It's nearer two o'clock to my way of thinkin'. I'm powerful hungry too and me out here with no lunch! Why don't ya call Sam on that fancy radio of your'n before he gets too far away and have him send back a van ta pick us up when we're through here in a couple of hours?" The old man settled down under a tree to rest.

"That's a good idea!" She sat down next to him and pulled her lunch out of her shoulder pouch. She handed it to Old Lem and then took out the radio. While setting on a grassy bank in the shade of the over-hanging trees, she called Sam.

"Sam, did you find something? Are you on your way back?" She took a bite of the half-sandwich Lem had handed back to her.

"No, I didn't find anything. I just need to go." He slid into the driver's seat of his patrol car and continued with, "Y'all seem to have everything under control here. I have things I need to tend to back in town."

"Oh, Okay. Hey, can you send back a van to pick us up in a couple of hours so we don't have to walk all the way back?"

"Sure, I'll have the driver sound his horn every so often so you can get up to the road to catch your ride."

"Sounds good. Thanks Sam."

Old Lem took a big bite out of the other half of the sandwich. He said, "Now, I been talkin' all day and I don't know anything more about you than I did when we started out this mornin'. How about you telling me about yourself missy?"

"Like what?"

"Oh, I don't know?" Just then, Duke laid his head down on the old man's lap. Lem patted him and broke off a bit of his sandwich and gave it to him. "Well, tell me how you came ta owning such a fine tracking dog like Duke here." He rubbed the dog behind the ears and went back to eating.

Shel liked to talk, but had her mind set on other things of late. She did miss talking and decided it might make her relax a little if she let some of her pent-up feelings out so she went into great detail as she began. "Well, as a child I was attacked by two big dogs. They were growling, snarling, and pinning me down," she paused and took a trembling breath before finishing with, "you get the picture right? Anyways, even though they didn't bite me, I've always been afraid of large dogs and I probably always will be. You know how fear is? It roots deep in our memory and we can't just uproot and throw it away easily. It stays with us forever."

"Well, after Duke was shot, the vet operated on him to take out the bullet and when he was healed, they sent him to the animal shelter here in Ponder. The doctor said he hated to put him in the shelter but he was sure someone would adopt such a smart dog." Shel scratched Duke's head and added, "Although he's not a large dog, Duke has helped me in a small way not to be so afraid of larger dogs. The fear is and will most likely always be there, but the longer he's with me, the more I can see the fear mellowing a little."

It had been the longest day of Sam's life as he lay sleeping on the cot of an open cell, behind the offices. The sun spilled into the small window above him, projecting images of waving branches being blown by the wind on the opposing wall. From the hall, he could hear his secretary's typing stop as the low rumble of voices worked their way into his dream.

When Shel brought Duke in, the dog immediately walked over and stuck his cold, wet, nose in Sam's ear. He immediately woke up. "What!? What!? What!?" He exclaimed as he jumped up, flailing his arms in the air, frantically swiping at his ear to free himself of whatever was trying to make its nest there.

Shel started to laugh and was soon joined by Sam as things began to make sense again.

"What time is it?" he said as he turned to look at the clock on the wall. "Oh man, I can't believe I fell asleep and slept for three hours this late in the day!" He straightened his clothes. "How'd you get back?" He walked over to his desk and saw two missed calls. "Oh, I'm so sorry. You didn't have to walk back, did you?"

She passed her hand through the air as if to say, 'No, don't worry about it.' "No, we didn't have to walk! My cell phone actually worked from where we were. So I called here but when you didn't answer, I called the church and they sent Mandy out in the church van to pick us up. It was nice to finally meet her. Kate talks about her all the time. I loved her immediately. She talks more then I do! It was like finding a long lost friend. And poor Old Lem just kept nodding off in the back seat, never saying a word."

Shel could see that Sam was trying to focus on what she was saying but his mind was somewhere else, probably on Kate. So she stopped talking, finishing with, "We're having a meeting over at McClure's Diner if you'd care to join us in about an hour."

"Oh, yeah I'll see you in a bit." He walked into his office and began to move things around on his desk, as if he were looking for something, or trying to find what he had missed. Clearly, he was still not quite awake.

"Ok, that sounds good, see ya! Heel Duke," Shel said as she began to walk out the door. Stopping short, she stuck her head back inside, "Oh, and Sam, it's okay that you fell asleep, really. Those dark circles under your eyes were starting to weird me out." She smiled and with that she was gone.

When Sam walked into the diner, Mandy, Shel, and Granny, were already there. Old Lem wouldn't be there as he had gone directly home to bed. Sam slid in next to Granny and she took his hand giving it a squeeze. When he looked up, she nodded with an understanding and compassionate smile. She patted his hand, "It's going ta be all right, we're all praying for him too, son."

Sam was caught off guard. "Who?"

"Chuck. We been sharin' with one 'nother and the Lord has been talkin' ta us 'all' today about prayin' for Chuck. Hasn't He been talkin' ta ya too?"

Sam wasn't sure why he was so taken aback by what Granny had just said. It was uncanny the things this old lady seemed to know. But somehow, he was hoping he had misheard the Lord and now that he had gotten some sleep he could get back to hating Chuck as normal.

Even as the thought passed through his mind, he was ashamed of the way he had convinced himself it had been okay to hate Chuck. As if God needed his help somehow to identify sinners amongst filthy rags.

19

A Statistic

If your law had not been my delight,
I would have perished in my affliction.
Psalm 119: 92 NIV

"Could you untie my hands?" Kate asked as she woke, struggling to sit up without the use of her hands. Her shoulders hurt from her arms being tied behind her. Her wrists hurt from the terry cloth rope that bound her. "I have to 'go', Chuck."

"Ok, but you have to promise me you won't run off?"

She paused for a moment before saying, "I promise I won't run away."

"Alright then." He moved in close and reached over her to untie the rope that fastened her to the gnarled root behind her.

She immediately brought her shoulders forward, pulling them in with her hands. She rubbed her wrists before diving through the surge of water. She didn't care if she got wet this morning as she felt grubby anyway and planned to wash in the stream after doing her business.

Chuck dove through the deluge after her. "I dug a hole behind those bushes over there for you." Chuck pointed as he rubbed his arm over his now wet face. "Just push the dirt back in over it when you're done."

She made a dash for the bush and disappeared behind it. Thinking of the cougar they had left on the other side of the river, she was relieved that she didn't have to think about him watching her any longer.

It was already warm outside and Chuck knew from living here all his life that it would be a hot and muggy day. Plunging into the waterfall, he came up combing his fingers through his short, auburn hair. He pulled off his shirt and wetting it, rubbed at the stink in his armpits. He sat on the bank and after pushing his face into a calm pool; he began to drink in the cool water. Sitting up, he watched Kate as she came back through the bushes, stepping into the water and going down on her knees.

Kate leaned forward over the water. Her pale slender face was framed by her dark waves of hair, mimicking the water over the falls. "I'm hungry, do you have anything to eat?" She asked as she threw some water on her face and hair.

"No, I'll have to find something out here in the great outdoors to eat, and if I catch a critter, I guess I'll have to skin it with my teeth." He chuckled as he threw her a smile.

She smiled back at him in spite of the fear that rushed over her. She knew the statistics on people who, after getting lost in these mountains, died of exposure or starved to death. Because of their lack of knowledge of survival, they walked in circles for days before sitting down and giving up, and then being found too late.

Behind her and Chuck the water fell in a clear sheet, springing over rocks as it sped down the stream towards the larger body of water.

Kate looked toward the river, hoping to see Sam riding in on his white horse. But all she saw was a mother duck swimming into the current as her ducklings dropped into the water from the shore line behind her. High from her vantage point, they looked like water drops running off an oiled surface. They followed their mother in a line, sending out waves that pressed against each of their tiny bodies. The ducklings were no more than specks in the water from where Kate and Chuck sat high on the side of the mountain.

The birds in the trees sang their serene songs as if all was well in the world, but all was far from well. Kate took in a deep breath and thought, *'Am I going to be one of those statistics?'* Surely, she would wake up from this nightmare soon and continue with her wedding plans. She wanted to put the last several days behind her so she could start her new life with the man she loved. But her thoughts were interrupted when she heard the sound of slurping and saw Chuck drinking from the stream. "Chuck, no! That water will make you sick! Drink from this small springs!" She pointed at a small hole in the ground where water bubbled out to join the falls.

"Oh, I'll be fine," he said. But he wasn't fine. An hour later Chuck began to moan, "Ohhh, I'm feeling so 'erpy'."

"You're what?" Kate asked as she passed her hand back and forth through the water.

"I'm feeling 'erpy'." He snapped back impatiently.

"I'm sorry Chuck but I don't know what 'erpy' means." She turned to look at him, seeing him turning green as the blood ran from his face and his hand rested over his mouth.

"I'm going to throw up! Alright?" Chuck took some deep breaths and slowly stood. He knew he had to get Kate inside the cave and tied up before whatever this was hit him full force. He also knew if it lasted long and or increased in intensity, he would be defenseless to stop her from running off. His eyes shot wide open as he turned toward the water and heaved. The bile, mixing with the clear water, sent up white foam that floated to the top and proceeded downstream.

When he had stopped vomiting, he rushed toward Kate and pushed her through the mouth of the cave. Getting her back against the back wall, he tied her hands in front of her and then to the root. But before he finished, he had vomited on the ground next to her while crooking "O'm sor-ry Ka..." then he plunged back through the water.

Kate sat inside the cave listening to Chuck retch his guts out for what seemed like hours. Her hands were tightly tied together in front of her. It was now late afternoon. The sun shone through the waterfall, casting reflections on the walls of the cave that looked like rain running down a glass window as the sun peeked through the clouds.

Kate was so thirsty but she couldn't even reach the water she faced. She needed a drink more than she needed something to eat right now. She felt desperate so she began to chew on the rope that tied her hands to free herself. But all she managed to do was make the braided towel rope wet and frayed. If anything, the rope seemed to be tighter and harder to pull against now.

She couldn't afford to waste any more of her strength on the rope, losing moisture she could never regain as water was out of reach. So she stopped gnawing and watched the reflection of Chuck bobbing up and down as he sat on his knees, dry heaving into the stream. "Chuck, let me go and I'll get help for you." She shouted over the sound of the water. There was no answer from the other side of the cascade. Kate didn't know if he just hadn't heard her or if he was purposely ignoring her.

Finally, he crawled weakly back through the shimmering curtain and fell like a water balloon sloshing everywhere as his limp body hit the floor. He looked terrible. His cheeks were hollow, his eyes had dark circles around them, and he had no energy left.

"Untie me, I'm going for help." Kate struggled to her feet, but Chuck pulled the gun out of the back of his pants and pointed it directly at her.

"Set down, you're not going anywhere!" He said weakly as he struggled to sit up.

"Chuck, you do know you can die from drinking unsanitary water, don't you?"

"I don't care. Do you think I'm looking forward to spending the rest of my life in prison?" He pulled the piece of glass, wrapped in a rag, from his back pocket and unwrapped it half way. Part of the shard fell off onto the dirt floor. Chuck cursed as he picked up the broken-off piece and threw it through the opening of the cave, making a hole in the crystal veil for an instant before it closed again. He moved the larger piece of glass on the rag, wrapping it again so one side stuck out. He began to cut away at her gnawed, wet rag 'rope'. Kate rubbed her wrist frantically as Chuck reached for more towel strips to tie her hands again. This time, he tied her hands behind her to the root.

As Chuck finished tying her hands, he sat back weakly on his legs. He stared blankly at her, sadness pulling his eyebrows up in the center of his forehead.

"Chuck please, at least let me help you," she pleaded quietly.

"You just want to get away from me. Just like everyone else I've ever known."

"No, I don't. I'll stay right here and nurse you back to health. I promise."

He slid sideways off his knees and collapsed again onto the floor. "Lies, it's all lies," he said blankly as he faced away from her, one arm draped over his head while the other hung limp over his sick stomach. "Don't think I haven't heard lies before or that I don't know a lie when I hear one," he muttered almost to himself.

Kate had to admit that she had thought of going to get help and then letting others come to get him instead of coming back herself, so she made no reply.

"Chuck, tell me about yourself. I'm sorry I never cared to ask you before. I'm so sorry Chuck, so sorry." Her voice was tender and sincere.

He rolled over on his back and turned to look at her. His face transformed into that of a little boy with his bottom lip pouting out. Tears began to run down his face and disappear into his ears. "What do you want to know?" His words came out strangled.

"Oh, I don't know? Tell me about your first memory." She grasped at the first thing that came to mind.

"My first memory? You want to hear what my first memory is?" His voice raised as his anger reappeared, drawing his face tight while his eyes and nostrils flared. "The first thing I remember Kate is my step-father beating my mom down to the floor and when I went to help her, he threw me up against the wall, kicked me, and told me to mind my own business. How's that for a first memory?" He swung his arm out toward her, but came short of where she sat. He then rolled back over and Kate could tell he was crying.

"I'm sorry Chuck. I didn't know," she choked up as she visualized the scene in her mind.

He remained turned away as he began to speak again quietly. "He left after that, my step-father I mean. And my Mom married another man just like him." His shoulders shook again for a moment and he finished with, "And his name was CHRISTIAN!" He spat the word out like it was acid that had burned through his very soul. The sound of the water spilling over the opening of the cave spoke of peace, but inside the cave there was only turmoil and pain.

She thought for a while as she watched him moving feebly on the floor. Chuck reminded her of a dying animal along the side of the road after being hit by a passing car. A tear rolled down her own cheek as she realized that's the way things had always been for him. Those who should have loved him as he went through life had struck him time and time again, with fist and words, and then left him writhing in pain. A long moment passed before Chuck spoke again, "I'm sorry Kate." His words were soft now. "I promised myself I would never hit a woman or a defenseless child. Not ever."

"But, you didn't hit me Chuck. It's ok, I'm ok."

He whispered back, "Well, I'm not okay and it's not okay with me, Kate." Then he fell silent.

20

Skippy

"But consider the joy of those corrected by God!
Do not despise the discipline of the Almighty
when you sin.
For though he wounds, he also bandages.
He strikes, but his hands also heal."
Job 5: 17-18 NLT

Seth worked with a neighbor man named Gray Mills, who had been teaching him the art of carpentry for the last nine months. Gray and his family lived close to five miles from where Seth lived with his dad and mom and his younger brother Micah. He loved taking the long walks through the woods and over the mountain. The Mills home was just outside of Ponder, so that gave him some much needed time alone to think and pray.

Seth walked down the dirt path that led away from his house, followed closely by a dog named Skippy. The little Jack Russell terrier ran around and around his feet, threatening to trip him. He had tried before to lock him up in the shed just to keep him from being under foot, but the little dog had squealed like a pig on a roller coaster until someone came and let him out. After being let out of the shed, Skippy followed

Seth anyway, catching up with him on the trail. The little dog had been more excited than if he had been allowed to go along in the first place. If indeed, it had been possible for Skippy to be any more excited.

Seth liked the little dog well enough, but he was certain he would like Skippy even more if he would just calm down a little. When the pup turned and ran down the steep side of the mountain, Seth just let him go. He watched him for a moment until he could see him no more. He could still hear him barking and was surprised when he heard another dog barking too.

"Well, I guess he found himself a friend!" He walked a little farther and turned to look down on the river, where he could see people on the other side. He stood transfixed as he watched them, "What are they doing?" He asked himself out loud. "They're probably vacationing here. They aren't gonna find a safe place to swim there."

Just then, he saw Skippy flying down to meet them. Stopping on the river's edge, the little dog barked frantically while he ran back and forth.

Turning suddenly, Skippy sped up along the stream and back down again. Seth put two fingers in his mouth and whistled so loud it echoed off the mountains around him. "Skippy, you get back here!" he yelled. The little dog turned and ran all the way back up the mountain, barking as he went.

Seth scooped the little dog up in his arms and said, "What do you think you're doing? You leave them folks alone, you hear me?" But Skippy just wiggled and licked Seth's face as he spoke, causing him to laugh. He couldn't help but love this small, ornery, ball-of-energy pest. He kissed the little dog's ear as best he could before being intercepted by another wet lick to the face. He set Skippy down and as the little dog ran back home, Seth continued on his way towards the Mill's house.

Kate suddenly heard what she thought to be someone sneaking around outside the cave, she yelled quietly, "Help! Help! In here!" trying to be careful not to wake Chuck. She did not want to wake him just to see him shoot her, Sam, or whomever it was that had come looking for them.

As the scuffling sound got closer, she heard a low growl accompanying it. She pressed herself against the wall behind her. The figure got closer, casting its monstrous shadow across the translucent water that covered the mouth of the cave. It was a bear! Fear rushed through her as her heart pumped faster and her breathing sped up for flight, but being tied she couldn't get away. The bear's paw swept through the water, reaching for what it might find and coming dangerously close to catching one of Chuck's legs.

Kate's heart sank as she realized Chuck might be pulled out and eaten alive within inches of where she now stood. She pressed herself against the wall. There was nothing she could do to save Chuck.

Just then, Chuck moaned and the bear answered back with another low growl.

"Chuck, wake up," she whispered hoarsely.

Chuck repeated his moan and again the bear growled back. Chuck moved slightly, moaning as he wrapped his arms around his middle, and once again the bear answered his moan.

"Shhhhh! Chuck. Please Shhhhh!" She pleaded in a whisper to the unconscious man.

The bear once again plunged his paw through the wall of water, sweeping it through empty space where Chuck's legs had just been. "Oh God," Kate whispered. When she heard her words, she began to pray, "Lord please save us!" She couldn't think of anything more to say as she trembled in fear. She repeated her prayer over and over again in a whisper.

The bear moved into the center of the stream and took another swipe through the waterfall, catching the back of Chuck's shirt and tearing it. As if in response to the cold air striking his back, Chuck rolled away from the opening of the cave and began to shake with violent tremors. Kate could now see Chuck's red face and realized he was running a fever.

Suddenly, her fear took a leap of uncontrollable panic as the bear plunged its enormous head through the surge of water and roared loudly, shaking the walls and those in the cave. Water and slobber flew, spattering Kate, Chuck, and the walls of the cave. With heightened senses, each drop felt like a knife striking Kate's skin. Responding to the roar, Chuck rolled towards the wall showing his sleeping face drawn into a grimace. He then lay silent and motionless once again.

The bear turned toward Kate as she huddled against the wall, pulling on the rope in hopes of freeing her hands. She fought to bring her arms forward to cover herself, but it was of no use.

All of a sudden, the bear stopped to listen. He backed out of the cave and stood to his full height, covering the opening of the cave with his enormous shadow. The bear let out one last low growl before dropping down on all fours and walking away, leaving Kate wondering what had just happened.

She heard a small dog yapping off in the distance. It came closer and closer until it bounded past in a white streak and then it was gone. The tension that had taken over Kate's body now let go of her, and as she fell to the floor of the cave, she slowly feel asleep.

Duke seemed to be lost as he searched high and low for some place where those he tracked may have stepped out of the water. Duke raised his nose in the air, sniffing for a scent, but found nothing. He again went back to the riverbank where he practically snorted the water up into his nostrils to pick up a scent, but there wasn't any. In fact, they had been going over the same ground for days now, with nothing more than he had smelt before. After awhile, Duke turned to go back the way he had come, his nose still to the ground.

Shel let the dog lead her. She knew he would only take her back the way in which they had already come, leading to nowhere.

Sam was growing more and more frustrated with the dog; with the situation... he knew Chuck and Kate were out here, but where?

All of a sudden, Duke raised his head and looked across the river just as Sam, Shel and Mandy began to hear a small dog barking off in the distance. The barking grew ever closer until the little dog appeared on the bank on the other side of the river.

The little wirehaired Jack Russell sprang up and down, running back and forth, trying to find a way across the water to his newly found friend. He never stopped his barking, but Duke stood listening before he barked back. With that, the little dog turned and ran up the mountain a ways and then back down seemingly running off his excess energy.

Hearing a high-pitched whistle and a man's voice calling out, "Skippy, you get back here!" The small dog bounded off towards the whistle, happily barking as he ran back up the mountainside and disappeared among the trees.

❖ ❖ ❖ ❖ ❖

Duke seemed to be unsettled now. *Had he become tired of the constant searching? Was he ready to give up and run off to play?*

Shel was discouraged too. It had been a long day and they had gone over and over the same spot, not finding anything. How could she know what Duke smelled? Was it worth going over and over again, hoping to find something more, something new? So even though they still had a couple of hours left before it started to get dark, Shel decided it was time to call it a day.

They stood looking out over the raging current. It was so strong now that the water crashed violently against the rocks that jutted out of the river's surface. The snow peaks that surrounded them were melting fast in this warm weather and the river became deeper and colder every day because of it.

Sam thought of a time when he had to have a river dragged for a missing woman. He swallowed hard and pushed the thought aside, still seeing her bloated, cold, lifeless body being pulled from the water. He fought the memory of it. What he needed now was rest and for everyone involved with the case to put their heads together and discuss what their next move should be.

But Duke was reluctant to go. He pulled against Shel as she began to leave. "What is it boy?" She said as she went down on one knee, holding the dog's gaze.

"What is it?" Sam repeated before coming up and kneeling beside her. Mandy stepped up behind them and stood as well, wondering what was going on. Sam looked into the face of the dog that just whined and shifted his eyes to the other side of the river. They all looked in the direction the dog was pointing, but there was nothing there.

Sam had already lost Detective Jones' and his search team because the trail had gone cold. They were now watching the freeways, security cameras at bus stops and airports, and anyplace that might show Chuck and Kate were headed out of state. Martin Jones figured that Chuck had used mass transit, or lined up a ride with someone, somehow. Or maybe, he just hitched a ride with a gun in Kate's ribs.

That left the small town Chief of Police, Samuel Trusty, on his own, to follow up on his suspicions that Chuck and Kate were still in the area.

"What's going on?" Mandy finally asked, staring at Duke before looking once again across the river. She scanned the other side in hopes of getting an idea of what Duke was thinking.

"I don't know. It seems to me as if he's ready to abandon the search." Being deep in thought, Sam's forehead drew tight. He rubbed a hand down his jaw line, over his mouth, and pulled his fingers off his face under his chin.

Mandy suddenly dropped down, "Well, I'm going back. I can hardly take another step. Could you call me a ride Sam?"

Sam stood up and stepped away from the two women to call for a ride for Mandy back to town.

Mandy laid back in the pea gravel with her knees up in front of her, "Do you think we're ever going to find her?"

"I don't know. Duke seems to want to give up and go play with that puppy."

"Oh, wasn't he just adorable? I think if I were a dog, I'd be a Jack Russell. Couldn't you just about hear him saying, 'Come play with me, it will be fun'!"

Shel laughed a little and then stopped short.

"What is it?" Mandy asked.

"Well, we know God uses all things for our good because we love Him. What if the Lord sent that little dog to lead us in the right direction?"

"So, you think we're on the wrong side of the river?"

"It's possible," Sam said as he stepped back over to them. "Why didn't I think of that before? We lost all new leads days ago when Chuck and Kate quite possibly crossed the river. That makes perfect sense."

"We have been going in circles so we need to go back to where Duke picked up the scent and see if he does something different."

Mandy sat back up and said in frustration, "I'm still going home. I'm not a Jack Russell after all and I'm not doing anything out here but getting sore feet. What can I do? I need to do something," her eyes pleaded.

Shel pulled out her phone and handed it to her. "When you get back to town start calling everyone you know who will pray. Then text or call all of my phone contacts and ask them to pray, too. We should have done this days ago." She looked at Sam and added, "I guess we thought any minute now we would find them."

They all fell silent for quite a while as they realized that it was true. Sam's head snapped up, "Get going Mandy, I can hear your ride coming!"

Mandy surged up the embankment and onto the road with a new purpose and a new hope. She loved to talk and now she finally had something she could do and do well. A call to arms, a battle cry of sorts, and she was already planning what she would say.

Leroy's thoughts were on Kate's wedding that was supposed to take place today. He knew Chuck would be having an especially hard time sitting in prison. *'Maybe I should have made a point to go visit him?'* he thought to himself. "No," he said out loud. He knew Chuck wouldn't see him but turn him away as he had in the county lockup so many times. He tried to put the thought of Chuck aside but with no luck. *'Maybe he should call Zeke and talk to him about it. Yes, that's what I'll do'.* He pulled his phone out of his pocket and dialed Zeke's number.

"Hello!"

"Zeke?"

"Yes?"

"Hey, I was wondering if we could talk?"

"Yeah sure, what do you want to talk about?"

"Well, do you remember my old friend Chuck?"

"Yes?" Zeke said hesitantly.

"Well, today is the wedding of the gal he thinks belongs to him. He shot and killed a man for moving in on Kate, you know that, right?" Leroy waited but Zeke didn't reply. "Hello?"

"Ah, Leroy, you do know that Chuck escaped the transfer van last week, right?"

Now, it was Leroy's turn to be silent.

"And that he kidnaped Kate McClure and is on the run, right? – Leroy, are you still there? – Leroy?"

"Ahhh, how? Why didn't anyone tell me?"

"I thought you knew! It's been all over the local news."

"I don't watch TV and my radio's broke."

"Be serious, you really didn't know?"

"NO, I seriously didn't know!"

Both men remained quiet for some time before Zeke continued, "Maybe God had a reason for you not knowing about it Leroy."

Still, Leroy said nothing.

"Leroy, I'm sorry, but God hasn't been caught off guard by this, even if you have!"

21

Old Screen Door

Run from anything that stimulates
youthful lusts.
Instead, pursue righteous living, faithfulness, love,
and peace. Enjoy the companionship
of those who call on the Lord with pure hearts.
2 Timothy 2: 22 NLT

Seth smiled with anticipation as he approached the Mill's house. Not because of the work he would be doing today, but because of Molly, Gray's sixteen-year old daughter. Just thinking about Molly caused his heart to skip a beat. He took in a deep breath and sighed out loud when he saw the screen door swing open and the young lady run out.

When Molly saw him, she shot out of the house and then remembered the screen door. There was a rule in their house that if someone let the screen door slam behind them, they had to put a quarter into the kitty to help buy something for the family as a whole. She did like the new flat screen TV they had bought and she had a hand in choosing the laptop computer they would be getting next. What she didn't like was being the one who had to fund them.

She dove back to catch the screen door, but she already knew it was too late. 'BANG!' The spring pulled the door shut angrily. Everyone inside and outside the house would have heard it slam. There was no hiding her offense this time so she went inside for a moment to contribute her quarter to the kitty. Then, in her haste, she repeated her action but this time turned and caught the screen just in time. Easing the door gently shut, she joined Seth out in front of her Dad's shop.

She was barefoot and wearing pale blue cut-off shorts and a sunny yellow T-shirt. Her strawberry blond hair rose and fell on her shoulders and trailed out behind her as she ran excitedly towards Seth.

"Hi Seth, did you come to help my Dad? He told me to tell you to get started on turning the balusters, whatever that means. Well, I'm sure you know, while I'm clueless! Anyway, he'll be out shortly." Molly prattled on with no set purpose in mind except to spend time with Seth. Whenever he was around, she didn't seem to be able to stop talking and in the end she would inevitably say something embarrassing and her face would turn red.

Seth knew he wouldn't be able to formulate a single coherent sentence so he remained silent as he just smiled. He took a deep breath of the same crisp morning air that blew Molly's hair gently, brushing it over her soft cheek. Molly's chattering joined the birds in the trees as they sang merrily, blending in harmony with her cheerful voice.

Seth's mind began to wander, remembering the first time he met Molly and how he went home and told his Dad, "I have met the girl I'm going to marry!" which brought on an onslaught of advice and counseling that could fill a book.

"Now Seth," his father had said, "that little gal isn't yet sixteen and it'll be two years before she's of marrying age. Two years is an awful long time! My point is, she isn't your gal yet and she may not ever be so you just mind your manners with her. You need to be honorable to that little gal as a man of God."

"You see men often think they're in love, when the truth is that their desire for a woman is just plain out and out lust. I hope it's not that for you son."

"No sir."

"Your Mother and I have been married for nigh onto thirty years now. So I know you know what true love looks like," Ken went on.

Seth had heard varying versions of this talk before, but never with this much fervor. And never had it been so real as when he was thinking of Molly. He had seen the way his parents loved each other at home. And he had decided long ago that he wanted a marriage just like his parents.

He wanted more out of his marriage than most people had. He wanted a lifetime of respect with the woman he loved. He supposed that the reason people give up so easily on purity was because they hadn't seen a real example of true love. One where two people cared more about the other than themselves and meeting their own selfish desires. It was going to be hard, but he was determined to stay pure because he knew it would be well worth it in the end.

As his thoughts came back to the present, Seth heard Molly still chattering on.

"They say he most likely has hightailed it out of the state since they can't find him round these parts."

Seth didn't want to admit he hadn't been listening for quite some time and had no idea who she was talking about so he just nodded his head and said "huuum!" as she went on.

"What I can't understand is how someone can just leave someone to die like that. And poor Deputy Damascus hasn't ever done anyone any harm that I know of."

That woke Seth from his wandering thoughts. "Are you saying Deputy Paul Damascus was left for dead somewhere?"

Molly put her hands on her hips and let out an exasperated sigh. "Seth Barnett, you haven't been listening to me at all, have you?"

Seth did his best to cover the truth. "I've been listening," he lied. "I just need you to clarify Paul's condition because I haven't heard any of this before."

"Oh, well, he's laying up in the hospital like I told you before. They haven't got but a few words out of him, but the doctor says he'll be making a full recovery. In his own time, of course."

"Yeah, I knew. I just thought you wouldn't want to talk about it. Sorry, Leroy." Pastor Hilby patted him on the shoulder. "Of course we can make do until you get back. When will you be leaving? Do you know?"

"I'll be leaving early in the morning. It should only take a couple of hours to get there. I don't know what I can do but I have to go and do something. Poor Kate, she's not what Chuck needs, he needs the Lord. Pray for him pastor and pray the Lord will show me what I can do."

"I'll do that son." He pulled Leroy in for a hug and prayed with him before slapping him on the back twice and releasing him.

As Seth walked passed the window in the shop, he saw Molly in the yard hanging laundry.

'Ok,' he thought to himself. 'There's no way around it. I know she's a mite young, but I'm going to have to make my intentions known.' Fear pushed his heart up into his throat, making it hard for him to breathe, pounding loudly in his ears. "I'm going to have to talk to Gray about this," he stated out loud as he set his resolve.

"You have to talk to me about what?" Gray said as he entered the shop, pulling the door closed behind him. "Ouuwee! It's going to be a hot one today!" He walked up behind Seth. "Is there a problem?"

"Well Sir," Seth snapped around to face Molly's father, then he looked down to the dowel he still held in his hands. "This dowel has a nasty knot in it. I don't think it'll turn very well."

"Oh, you're right! I thought I went through all of these. Oh well." He took the dowel from the young man and threw it into a scrap pile to be used for some other project, some other time.

It was later than they thought when Duke finally stopped and stepped into the water. Looking at his master and the police chief, they all turned and looked intently at the other side of the river. They knew it would soon be too dark to see anything.

Sam sighed, "We can't go any further tonight."

"It's alright, we'll get an early start tomorrow morning and I know we'll find her Sam, we'll find her."

Just then, Mandy blew the car horn as she had come back to get them. They turned from the river and climbed up the embankment to the road where she sat ready to blow the horn again. They piled into the car and headed back towards town. As they approached a narrow bridge ahead of them, they saw a young man walking toward them. He had a little Jack Russell walking beside him. The young man threw his hand up in a wave and Sam waved back.

"That's Seth Barnett," he told Shel. "He's one of the most respectful young men I've ever met." Sam had been in Ponder for a little less than three months.

In that time, he had met everyone who went in and out of town on a regular basis.

Duke's head shot up as he caught the scent of the smaller dog.

"Is that the little dog we saw down at the river?" Shel turned her head to look back as they passed the twosome.

Skippy ran after the car, barking excitedly as Mandy mimicked him, "Come play with me! Come play with me! It will be fun! Come play with me!" And they all laughed.

22

Delayed

Where can I go from Your Spirit?
Or where can I flee from Your presence?
If I ascend into heaven, You are there;
If I make my bed in hell, behold,
You are there. If I take the wings of the morning,
And dwell in the uttermost parts of the sea,
Even there Your hand shall lead me,
And Your right hand shall hold me.
Psalm 139:7-10 NKJV

The cave reeked with the smell of vomit and body waste. It had been a day and a half since Chuck had passed out. He finally woke up, and as he sat up he weaved back and forth as if he may fall over again at any moment.

"Chuck, I haf' ta haf' water," Kate said, her mouth dry from dehydration. "Please!"

Chuck turned to look at her. "Why o' you talkin' tho' weird?" but he already knew the answer as his tongue clung to the roof of his mouth from thirst. He clutched his throat, while looking at Kate, and felt bad about what he had done to her. Her eyes were red and her lips were cracking from lack of water. He turned onto his hands and knees and slowly crawled over to cut her free of the makeshift ropes. "Sorry 'bout that Kate."

When her hands were free, she quickly dove through the cascading waterfalls to the springs that shot out of the ground along side the falls. Cupping her hand, she slowly drank small swallows until she couldn't drink anymore. When finished, she slipped back inside and sat against the cave wall, "You ok, Chuck? You really should try and drink something too."

He sat up weakly and dragged himself toward the waterfall and drank deeply from it.

Kate said nothing, as she knew it would do her no good.

"Well, it's either good water or it will kill me," Chuck said. "I really don't care at this point, just as long as it takes me quickly. No more of this slow, miserable, suffering." He sat with his knees up and his elbows resting on them as he held his head in his hands. "We need to get out of here and go as far as we can today." He looked around and with a sour expression added, "Let's get going! " What had once been the most perfect place for them to hide had now become the worst.

Chuck stood in the stream and looked back at the falls. Slung over his shoulder was the black plastic bag containing his extra clothes, slippers, and both his and Kate's shoes.

"We need to stay in the stream awhile longer before we move onto dry land. Are you ready?" Chuck asked Kate as if she would have a hard time keeping up with him.

But she said nothing; she wanted to leave the cave, and standing in the cool water felt really good to her right now. She followed him as he began to climb. The water spilled over their hands and feet as they climbed almost ten feet straight up, to a point where the stream leveled off as they continued up the side of the mountain.

Granny walked over and reached into a cabinet for a small single-scoop ice cream dish. Opening the freezer case, she got herself a scoop of orange sherbet as Mandy walked in and leaned over the counter, tapping Granny on the shoulder.

"Ma'am, could I have a banana split with the works?"

Granny stood and said, "Now where did this Ma'am come from? I'm Granny ta ya- little girl." She put her hands on her hips in mock disgust as her gleaming white false teeth stood out like the smile of a jack-o'-lantern.

"I love ya Granny!" Mandy said as she scooted around the counter to give the old woman a big hug.

"I'm doin' fine. I have been prayin' like I ain't never prayed before. How're ya doin' little girl?" Granny said with concern.

"Oh, I guess I'm fine. Granny, ya do know I'm a grown woman now, right?"

"Oh stuff and nonsense! Old, young, ain't got nothin' ta do with it, 'cause I ain't plannin' ta be gettin' old any time soon.

"Oh Granny, you'll never get old."

"See, that's what I mean, it's not about years. It's all about your attitude toward what comes your way. That's why I'll never be old and you'll always be a little girl."

Mandy allowed herself to be wrapped in Granny's arms again as she giggled like she was still a little girl. After a long and much needed moment of soaking up the love Granny had for her, Mandy said reluctantly, "I know you told me to call everyone that was invited to the wedding, but I kept hoping Kate would somehow make it back!"

"Oh, you poor thing." Granny pulled Mandy back into her arms. "I think everyone must have figured out the wedding's off by now. Chuck's escape and Kate's kidnapping has been all over the news and I think half the nation is praying. So how's about you and I just call those we think maybe haven't heard about Kate bein'..." the old woman stopped and added, "delayed. Then you can help me figure out this new fangled coffee machine. What do ya say?"

Mandy curled her nose, "I like drinking the coffees and all, but I don't know anything about the machines. Besides, I don't feel like doing anything but crawling back into bed for the rest of the day."

"Oh, come on Mandy, it'll be fun!!!" Then Granny flashed an exuberant false teeth smile, using the girl's own catch phrase against her.

Mandy began to laugh and said, "I feel bad having fun while Kate's being dragged around the country at gun point. It just doesn't seem right somehow." Her smile turned into a frown that brought on tears she felt might never stop.

"Now that's enough. Kate wouldn't want us to stop livin' and havin' fun just because she's not. In fact, I bet if she knew you were carryin' on so, she'd stop and cry for you."

Mandy sucked up her tears and trembled slightly, "I suppose you're right." Another tremor struck her as she wiped her hands over her moist eyes, "Ok, where's that list of invitees?"

Duke had increased interest in tracking today as he led Shel and Sam on the search. They wished they had marked the spot where they had been the day before on the other side. A stick with a makeshift flag would have been nice, or a large odd shaped rock, because they couldn't make out any small dog's paw prints on this side. But Duke seemed to know where he was going as he pulled hard on the leash, dragging his master farther and farther throughout the day. Finally, he stopped and began to move in small circles, smelling everything along the bank where Skippy had been.

Duke seemed to move with a new urgency as they continued awhile longer. Sighting a stream, he turned and followed it up the steep mountainside. After several feet, he stopped and sniffed at something along the edge of the current.

"What is it?" Shel asked as she stepped up next to her dog and touched the yellow foam, then smelled it. "Oh gross!" She thrust her hand into the water to wash it off.

"What is it?"

"It smells like barf. It's stomach acid. One of them is sick."

Sam's face fell as he thought of his Kate being forced to go on while being sick. He felt driven to move faster. Approached a waterfall, he said, "They must be walking in the stream above the falls. It's kind of steep here but what else could they have done? Chuck's pretty smart and he seems to have a clear agenda of getting away with Kate in tow."

Shel was getting increasingly worried about Sam in his exhausted condition. She felt he wouldn't be able to continue much longer, not even another day, without having a total breakdown. "It's getting late Sam. We need to get back down to the river before it gets dark up here. We know where to pick up their trail tomorrow."

Sam knew she was right but wasn't ready to give up just yet. Every day that went by made the chances of them actually finding his Kate less and less, especially if she was sick and maybe even dying.

"We need to check out the stream above the falls." He placed a hand on a rock within the surge of water and then lifted his foot to find a step up, but found nothing behind the cascade.

Duke dashed between Sam's long legs, knocking him on his butt as the dog disappeared into the falls. Sam sat staring at the wall of water before him.

"It's a cave!" Shel exclaimed as she shot through the current. The water closed again in front of Sam, who still sat despondently looking on in disbelief. When he saw Shel disappear behind the falls, he stood and shot through the curtain. Quickly he brought his hands up over his face as the smell hit him hard.

"Sam, take a look over here," she pointed to a splattering of vomit near the back of the cave, next to a makeshift rope that was tied to a root. "Sam, she's sick!"

It did look that way and it confirmed Sam's worst fear. He couldn't stand the smell in the cave any longer so he shot back out through the waterfall and ran up the grassy slope yelling, "Kate, Kate!" But as he ran, his feet slipped out from under him on the steep incline and he landed on his hands and knees. "Kate!" He moaned in agony as his legs refused to move any farther. He lay back in the grass and wept convulsively as an overwhelming state of dread, exhaustion, and defeat overcame him.

Kate had been watching Chuck for the last half-hour, wondering if he would eventually just fall into the water and slip downstream with the ease of Jello slipping off a hot spoon. She had been trying to get him to stop and rest, but knew it was just stubborn will power that kept him going.

Mountain climbing hadn't been something Kate was prepared for when Chuck abducted her. She was at near collapse herself, with a lack of food, dehydration, exhaustion, and extreme worry. She couldn't leave Chuck now if she wanted to. It was all she could do to put one foot in front of the other. Her lips were cracked and bleeding, her tongue was dry, and her heart seemed to be laboring to keep her alive. She was sunburnt, covered in scratches, sick and weak, and yet she was more afraid for Chuck.

A couple of hours had passed and now Chuck's legs were starting to give way, refusing to carry him any farther. So, he stepped out of the water and collapsed on the bank, like a sack of rocks.

Kate stepped out and sat down beside him. "Chuck, you can't go on like this. It'll kill you, you're sick."

"Ya think!" He spat back angrily. His stomach and ribs hurt so bad he could hardly breathe without pain. The retching continued, causing tears to run down his face no matter how much he told himself to stop. He found it increasingly hard to even take a step without his bowels loosening in his pants. If this went on much longer, he knew what Kate had said about him dying was surely going to be true. That made him mad and more determined to go on. He hated to be told what to do, or in this case, what would happen to him. He couldn't let her know how weak he felt or she would surely leave him out here to die alone.

Just then, they heard a man's voice yelling, "Kate, Kate!" Chuck pulled the gun out of the back of his pants and had it pointed at Kate's head before she could scream out. "Now Kate, you best be still." Chuck knew the Law would soon be on top of them if it weren't for the fact it was getting dark. The police chief would have to turn back soon and start out again tomorrow. That gave Chuck some time to think. The law had obviously found their trail and was getting close. It was clear to Chuck that he and Kate wouldn't be able to outrun them now. He would have to outsmart them instead.

"Martin, they're out here after all! They crossed the river, that's why we lost their trail. They stayed in a cave for a while and at least one of them is really sick."

"Oh no, I'm sorry Sam. Do you think it's Kate?"

Sam paused before saying, "We do, but were are hoping to catch up with them soon."

"How's that dog doing now?"

"He's doing great now that we found the trail again."

"Good. Hey buddy, I'm going to be tied up a little longer here. I'm still afraid Chuck's going to try and slip over the border, so I'm making sure everything is taken care of before I come back to help you. Are you good there for a while?"

"Yeah, I'm pretty optimistic we'll catch up with them tomorrow." Sam was drawing energy from talking to his friend.

"Tomorrow, really?"

"Well, I'm hoping so anyhow!"

"Sam, you be careful. Remember he has a gun."

"I will. Thanks a lot, Martin."

"I'll see ya when I see ya."

Kate's hands were again tied behind her back, then tied to the trunk of a tree while she and Chuck slept. It was a chilly, damp night and even with pine needles mounded on top of them, along with the low hanging evergreen boughs, they both shivered and shook in the cold. Chuck lay with his arm wrapped around Kate's waist as he slept. She was certain he was still running a fever, but she welcomed the extra warmth. Still, it was another night of restless sleep as Kate lay awake listening to the night sounds and worrying about Chuck dying, Sam being sick with worry, her wedding being delayed, and so on and so on...

23

Dummy Trail

I will both lie down in peace, and sleep;
For You alone, O Lord, make me dwell in safety.
Psalm 4:8 NKJV

As the birds began to sing in the trees, the sounds of small animals scuffled through the brush around them and overhead. Chuck woke with a start.

"Ok, I've got it!" He said with conviction, "Kate, we need to go up to that little stream and do our washing this morning." He pointed to a smaller stream off to the left that fed into the stream they had been traveling up. He untied her, crawled out from under the tree, and stood slowly with his hands on his knees. His head finally stopped swooning enough for him to walk without feeling like he might fall over. He picked up his things and after putting on a good face, smiled at Kate. "Lets get going then!" He took a deep breath, while holding his ribs, and waited for her.

Kate shivered as she scooted out from under the bough and he untied her hands. She knew it wouldn't be long before she was wishing for a little of this morning's coolness. Right now, it was all she could do to keep from biting her tongue due to her teeth chattering. She wrapped her arms around herself and began to rub them vigorously, both for circulation and to warm herself. She wasn't sure she could stick her feet in the cold water, so she was relieved when Chuck seemed to be fine with her walking along the bank of the stream. In fact, it appeared as if he wanted them to leave as much of a trail as they could.

When they had gone several hundred feet, they stopped to clean up. Kate dropped to her knees, not wanting to go plunging into the water just yet.

Chuck said, "Now Kate, you turn around there until I get changed." Chuck pulled off his soiled pants, and then put on a clean pair. Then he washed out the dirty jeans and laid them over a rock to dry. "There," he said. "Are you going to wash, Kate?"

"Do I have to?" She asked timidly.

"No, you can wait until later, but you will need to roll your pant legs up and take off your shoes now."

"What, why?"

"Just do it Kate and let's get going."

Kate was surprised when Chuck, after stepping into the stream, pointed back downstream the way they had come. "We're headed back that way Kate, stay in the water, ok?"

Her mouth dropped open as a puzzled look passed over her face and Chuck laughed a little before saying, "it's a diversion Kate, a dummy trail. We can't have them following us, now can we?"

Last night at the diner, Shel had slipped a sleeping pill into Sam's decaf coffee before she handed it to him. She just wanted him to get a good night's sleep, but now she and Duke sat outside his house in the patrol car waiting for him. As the morning wore on, she realized that she would most likely have to go in and get him out of bed herself. "He's going to kill me if he finds out what I did!" She turned and said to Duke, "I'm not going to tell him until this is all over, if it's ever over." She looked deep into the dog's eyes in search of a response; Duke just laid his head down on his paws and glanced up at her as if he was thinking the same thing. She was about to get out of the car and go up to the door when Sam came flying out, pulling his shirt on as he ran down the sidewalk.

"Why didn't you wake me up? I can't believe I've overslept. Man, I feel like I've been drugged!"

She turned her face towards the window and cringed as he crawled into the driver's seat and closed the door.

Just then, they heard a tap on the window. It was the neighbor boy, Tad. Sam rolled his window down, "Good morning Tad. How can I help you?"

"Chief Sam, is that a dog in the back seat?"

"Yes it is, he's a tracking dog," Sam said with a smile, still working on getting his shirt buttoned up right.

Duke pressed his nose mournfully against the reinforced glass, feeling much like a prisoner, as the boy looked on with a sad expression.

"Do you mind sir if I ask, what he did wrong?"

Sam chuckled and said, "He hasn't done anything wrong, we're just taking him out to do a job."

The boy's expression remained unchanged.

"Don't worry Tad, he's a good dog and he's not in trouble. I'm just not allowed to have animals in the front seat of the patrol car. It's all right Tad, really. I'm sorry, but we have to get going now, I'll see you tonight, ok?" The boy stepped back from the car, a concerned expression still on his face and his eyes still fixed on Duke as he waved.

Pulling away from the curb, both Sam and Shel had a good laugh before their previous conversation resumed.

"You still should have woke me. Then we would have been ready at the same time at least."

"It was dark earlier. Anyway, you needed to sleep," Shel said in defense.

"Not that much, we should have been out at the crack of dawn."

"Well, I was just about ready to come bang on your door. Here, I brought you a coffee." She handed him a styrofoam cup with a lid.

"Is it one of Granny's coffees?

"No, sorry."

"Well, how long have you been out here waiting?" Sam said in disbelief as he eagerly took the cup from her.

She didn't want to admit she had been sitting in his car for close to an hour so she just said, "Oh, not that long!"

It was quiet in the car for a few moments before Sam spoke sharply, "This investigation is kind of important Shel. Maybe we can stop worrying about getting our beauty rest." He took a deep breath and released it, ready to move on to more important things. Taking a sip of his coffee he said, "Well, this is much better than the coffee you gave me last night. The coffee last night must have sat there for hours to get that bitter."

Shel turned away from him and stared out the window with a grimace as she knew the reason for its bitterness. "Well, Granny has been trying out new coffees," she said, trying to cover her guilt.

"Well, we'd all be better off if she didn't make that one again." Sam sat silent for a moment before stating, "Well Shel, here's how I figure it. If we take Willow Creek road up the back side of the mountain, we should come pretty close to where that waterfall is, don't you think?" He tossed Shel the map and she pored over it until she came to the same conclusion. Of course, neither of them were originally from the area so who could say whether they were right or not?

As they drove up the road in silence, Duke looked over the seat at his master. For a moment, Shel felt like maybe she should tell Sam about the sleeping pill. But in the end, she looked back at the dog and shook her head ever so slightly as if to say, "No, not yet." Duke just raised his brows and whined quietly.

Even though the day had been quite hot, Chuck shook with tremors that threatened to take him down.

"I... we... have to stop soon. I need a nap. How about you?" He asked as nonchalantly as he could.

Kate knew there was more to it than him just needing a nap. He had been taking such pains to cover up the fact that he was seriously sick and getting sicker by the hour. His face looked like it was made of wax, his eyes were sunk in with dark circles around them, and his cheeks were hollow. He looked as if he were already dead, which frightened Kate. But before whenever she would say anything to him about his needing to stop and rest, he would just say, "I'm not used to hiking in the mountains, the air's thinner up here you know!" He refused all the help she tried to give him so there was nothing Kate could do but hope he didn't fall down dead as they trudged onward.

She wasn't sure if he had accepted her help; what more she could have done other than lay down and die beside him. "Yes, I am tired. I could seriously use a nap too," she said as she thought to herself, 'Lord, don't take Chuck before he has a chance to accept Your salvation, please!'

As she looked around, she saw at the top of the ridge what looked to be a shed. "Do you think you can make it to that shed?" She pointed and added, "We could maybe spend the night inside." She dreaded the thought of sleeping under a tree again.

Chuck's eyes followed and a brief grimace passed over his face. But he pushed the dread aside and said,

"Of course I can!" taking on her question as if it were a challenge. Struggling to get to his feet, he took the lead.

Kate regretted asking now as she saw him staggering along trying to keep his legs beneath him. She knew at their present pace it would take them no less then twenty-five minutes to reach the shed.

"I'm sorry Shel for yelling at you. I'm truly grateful that you didn't leave with the trackers, when all traces of Chuck and Kate were lost." Sam looked over at her and waited for a response.

"I know it's hard to understand why everyone left when you were so sure Chuck and Kate were still here. You do understand why your friend Martin needed to follow up on those leads, don't you? He's still been on the case Sam, he just hasn't been here, and now he'll be back tonight."

"Yeah, I know," he said with resignation. Sam did know how investigations went, because he had been the police detective before Martin. When you lose the trail, it's best to move on to other tactics. But Sam had not given up here. And Shel had stayed behind to help him.

Sam drove as far as he could up the backside of the mountain until he ran into a narrow dirt footpath. He stopped the car and got out, and as Shel and Duke joined him, he said, "What's this? A hiking trail?"

"Or maybe a game trail," Shel added.

"Yeah, I suppose."

"Are we going to take it?"

"I think we have to if we're going to find the river and the waterfall."

"Well, let's get started," Shel said as she and Duke led the way.

After several more hours of working their way along the mountainside, looking this way and that, they ended up back at the river where they had started their search the day before. Neither Sam nor Shel said a word as they sat down under a tree. Words weren't necessary as discouragement filled the air and a sense of despair overtook them. They sat with heads hanging down in silence.

Finally Shel spoke in monotone, "We might just as well go home. If we travel the rest of the day, we won't even get as far as we did yesterday before turning back around and heading home."

"I should of stayed in bed this morning after all." Sam rubbed his forehead as if he was trying to make sense of the situation. "We were supposed to have been married yesterday. It's never going to happen now. I can't, I can't..." but he wasn't capable of saying what it was he couldn't do. Conflict stirred in Sam. He could never give up, but at the same time he couldn't go on this way. There had to be an end to it at some point, where he could say to himself, *'she is safe now, back in my arms, or... she is dead.'*

Shel placed a hand on his arm and sighed a sympathetic, "Sam..." the only word that would come out of her mouth. Her hand moved to his back feeling one with his pain. His despair seemed to travel up her arm and into her heart, causing tears to flow freely down her own face.

Shel had been told throughout her life that she was a cheerleader. She was able to cheer anyone on to any deed, but not today. Today, she felt like she had lost her pom-poms and forgot all the words that would bring about a victorious end. And all she could see at the end of this game was defeat.

She needed her husband Cody, right now, more than she had ever needed him before. Her good friend Kate was lost to her, and Sam had lost his beloved fiancé. There seemingly wasn't a thing she or Sam could do about it.

Sam clamped his hands around his head and rocked back and forth as he muttered, "Where is she God? Where on earth is she?"

As they approached the shed, Kate knew one or both of them wouldn't be leaving it alive, unless the Lord intervened soon.

Chuck opened the door to the shed and stepped aside as Kate walked in and sat down on some old gunnysacks. She spread a couple out on the floor for Chuck and he lowered himself onto them. "What are you doing Kate?" he said suspiciously.

"Just making a bed for you."

"Are you thinking if you're real nice to me I'll just fall right to sleep and forget to tie you up?"

"No Chuck, I was thinking you're really sick and if you don't get some help soon you're going to die."

"No, sorry Kate, I'm not buying it. You're just going to run off and leave me here to 'die' as you put it. Anyway, I don't have that kind of luck to just up and die and miss out on the pleasure of going to prison." He smiled slyly. "Come over here," he motioned to a bracket fastened to the wall.

As he tied her to it, she said, "All I have to do is yell out to whoever owns this shed as soon as you fall asleep. You've been sleeping like a bear in hibernation you know."

"Oh, is that right? Well, then I'll have to gag you too. I'm not going to prison Kate, no matter what. Regardless of whether I'm looking at the 'pearly gates' soon or not, I'm Not Going to prison! YOU GOT THAT?"

"Chuck, you wouldn't gag me!"

"Oh, yes I would. Open your mouth." He took a clean rag out and shoved it into her mouth, and tied a strip of towel around her head to hold it in place.

24

Tackin' Dog

Trust in the Lord with all your heart,
and lean not on your own understanding;
In all your ways acknowledge Him,
And He shall direct your paths.
Proverbs 3: 5-6 NKJV

Word had spread through out town that there would be a meeting tonight at the church. The problems the Chief of Police, Samuel Trusty, had been facing were to be addressed, along with what could be done to advance his search.

Pastor Smith unlocked the church door and stepped inside, along with Sam, Martin, Shel, Granny McClure, Mandy, and Old Lem. The church bell rang out clearly to summon all who would come. Prayer warriors and curious onlookers alike gathered in the sanctuary as Sam, Martin and Shel stepped onto the platform.

"I'm so glad to see you all here," Sam began, "as you may have heard, the state law enforcement efforts have shifted back to our area. The state borders, transportation terminals, and roads leading out of the state are still being watched. Our neighboring states have been alerted and are on the lookout, but we still believe that Chuck Atteberry and Kate McClure are up in these hills. But we have hit a wall and we believe if we are to go on, something will have to change."

"First of all, we must have someone along with us each day who knows this area. Mrs. Wiley and I," he gave Shel a nod, then turned back to the group and continued, "have done too much walking in circles because of our lack of knowledge in this area. We don't care if it's one of you, or if it's someone else, but we must have someone local to guide us."

"Second, we have wasted too much time running back and forth to town each night. We thought we would have found them by now, but that is clearly not the case. The plan is to spend the night on site at the end of each day. I also have a list of things we will need if someone would like to take care of collecting it for us?" Sam waved the list in the air and a woman put her hand up. The list was passed to her as Sam continued.

"Thank you ma'am, and third, and maybe this should have been first," Sam said but he had purposely put this last as he didn't know if he could go on after making this plea. "We most seriously need prayer for ourselves as well as prayer for Kate and Chuck. We have reason to believe one of them is very sick." He stopped speaking as his face tightened with the fear he was fighting with inside.

And as if on cue, Martin stepped up. "Ok, we have a lot to do. We have come up with some plans on how to proceed, but would like to hear any ideas you may have as well, especially from those of you who know the area."

Pastor Smith half raised his hand, "If you don't mind me asking, why did the state police think he was elsewhere?"

"Well pastor, we had a prisoner come forward who claimed to have overheard Chuck speaking to a friend that planned on helping him find a ride to a neighboring state. Plus, we found the tracks of a truck near the site where we lost Chuck's trail. So we followed up on those leads, but found nothing. Now that your good police chief here has found Chuck's trail on the other side of the river, I have gladly returned. Does that answer your question, sir?"

"Yes, thank you." The pastor smiled with a nod.

"No," a big man spoke up from the back of the room, "Chuck hasn't any friends. He's still out here, trying to make his way to the border on foot, for sure."

"Leroy!" Shel squealed, "Is that you? I would never of known you if you hadn't said something. The last time I saw you, your hair was longer and you were covered from head-to-toe with poison ivy." The silence in the room brought her back to attention. "We'll talk later! Ok?"

Sam stepped up feeling a new energy surging in his blood, giving him hope they might still find his sweet betrothed Kate. And their wedding, although delayed, might still come to pass. "Well then," he said, "If that is true, Kate and Chuck must still be in this area. So what can y'all do to help us?"

After spending as much time as he could behind the closed door of his office, Sam passed through the dark and empty reception area, stepped outside, locked the front door, and went home. He planned on spending the evening alone as despair had moved back in on him. But as he was pulling the patrol car up to the curb in front of his house, Tad approached him. "Did he get him Sam?"

"He who?"

"The bad guy. Did the tackin' dog get the bad guy?"

"No, sorry." The boy had no idea how sorry Sam was and he had no intention of going into it with a child so he smiled at the inquisitive boy. "Not yet, anyway," rubbing the boy's hair as he got out of the car and walked towards his door to shut himself away for the night.

"Hey Sam!" Mary yelled from next-door, "Come on over and have dessert with us. I baked Gil's favorite chocolate cake!" She turned and looked at her husband, who stood next to her in the doorway.

"Come on Sam, you're in for a treat. Her chocolate cake is amazing."

"Ok, I'll be over in a bit. I just have to take my things inside."

"Ok good, we'll be waiting." Gil turned and went in.

"Tad, it's time to come in now." Mary coaxed the boy in along with his siblings, who were playing tag in the back yard.

"Oh Mom, can't I talk to the Sam?"

"No, it's time for bed."

Tad wanted to be a police chief when he grew up, one of the occupations on the long list of things he wanted to do. "I'm going to get me a tackin' dog some day," he said as his mother ushered him in.

"A tackin' dog?"

"Yeah, like Sam has."

"What does he do with a tackin' dog?"

"He tacks men down, bad guys!"

Mary and Gil gave each other a smile that said 'he's so cute!', not wanting to correct the boy and to preserve this moment in time.

"Can I stay up and talk to the Sam too? Maybe he can get me a tackin' dog."

Just then, his older half-brother Markus walked by. "It's 'tracking dog' genius," he corrected Tad as his stepmother brushed him away.

"That's what I said! And I'm not a genius!" Tad said, irritated at the name his brother had just called him.

The older boy walked away with a smirk, "No kidding."

Most nights, Mary had Markus oversee Tad as he brushed his teeth because Tad had a tendency to eat the toothpaste when left alone. But tonight, she decided to let Tad set with the adults, granting the boy's request and avoiding the older boy taunting Tad's simple innocence.

"Knock, knock!" Sam said as he looked through the screen door.

"Come in Sam," Gil said walking toward the door to greet him, but Tad dashed past him to open the door first.

"Come on in Sam!" the boy repeated his father. "Can you get me a tackin' dog like you have?"

"Tracking dog!" they heard from the other room.

"Go to bed Markus!" Gil yelled.

Markus questioned, "Why doesn't Tad have to go to bed?"

"Go to bed. He'll be right up, he wants to ask Sam something first."

"Yeah, right!" The boy taunted once more before stomping up the stairs.

Mary said apologetically, "Sorry, he has a bur under his saddle about something."

Sam glanced at Gil and Mary and smiled, before putting his hands on his knees and speaking to the boy in hushed tones. "He's not my dog. He belongs to the lady who was with me this morning."

"Can she get me a tackin' dog then?" Tad boomed out.

"Well Tad, I'll have to ask her, ok?" Sam scooped the boy up in his arms and stepped into the house.

"He wants to be a police chief when he grows up, that's somewhat of a compliment to you," Gil said as he shook Sam's hand and patted him on the back. "Come sit down." He motioned him over to the table where they sat as Mary rushed off to the kitchen to get the cake and pour some coffee.

Tad peppered Sam with questions as he sat on his booster seat eating his small portion of cake.

It helped Sam to talk with the boy about simple things, rather than think about the hopelessness of getting his Kate back.

When the boy began to yawn, Mary took him to get his pajamas on. Hearing the men talking about the case, she sent him off to the bathroom to brush his teeth alone and she returned to the kitchen. As she entered, she said, "So you think it's Kate that's sick?"

"It looks that way. The vomit was all along the stream and near the center of the cave, next to the rope."

"Oh, that doesn't sound good."

"No, it doesn't."

The men sat in silence for a moment longer before Gil said, "Well you know Sam, the whole church has been praying and from what I gather from Mandy, half of Ohio. I've even heard some have prayer requests on the Internet for Kate and Chuck, too. God is in control and He has a plan Sam, we just can't see what that plan is yet. Just hold on Buddy. God sees the big picture and even if it doesn't work out the way we think it should, we have to trust that He is working all things for our good according to His purposes because we love Him."

Mary reached across the table and touched Sam's arm. "Would you like us to pray for you Sam?"

"Yeah, that'd be nice." They prayed one after the other, making their request known to their all-powerful God. The minutes of prayer passed along with the moments of silence, where they listened for the Lord to speak. When they had finished, Sam felt a peace that passes all understanding. They had sat back in their chairs and were drinking their last drops of cold coffee, when Mary realized she hadn't heard anything from Tad in quite a while. Calling out she said, "Tad, you should be done by now. What are you doing in there?"

And from the bathroom came a rushed and guilty reply, "I'm not eating the toothpaste!"

Seth lay in bed, ashamed that he hadn't had the nerve to talk to Gray about courting Molly. "What is it I'm so afraid of anyway?" He knew Gray to be a calm and levelheaded man, but then again he hadn't ever asked him anything concerning his beloved daughter before.

Truth be told, his biggest fear was that Gray would treat him disrespectfully, laugh at him or maybe brush him off as if he were just a stupid kid. It seemed so selfish to be thinking about himself at a time like this, but he couldn't help but worry about how Gray would react.

Seth knew he and Molly were old enough to be thinking along the lines of marriage in their future, but would Gray see it that way? It wasn't like they would be running off and getting married tomorrow after all!

The more he reasoned with himself the more confused and anxious he became. He pulled his pillow out from under his head and after covering his face, yelled a muffled, "I can't do this God! Please help me!" He stopped short, suddenly realizing he may have been heard as all was silent in the house. He slid his pillow down away from his eyes and nose, exposing all but his mouth, looking a bit like Kilroy looking over his wall. He listened for a moment for a responding sound but heard nothing but Micah in the next bed breathing soundly. He thought all was well until his door slowly began to creak open.

"Did you say something?" Ken said as he entered the room.

"Sorry Dad, I was just..." he paused, then finished with "praying."

"Are you alright? You seemed to be awfully irritable this evening. You care to talk about it?" He sat in the chair that divided Seth's bed from his younger brother's, where Micah lay drooling on his pillow.

Seth knew there was no use saying, 'No thanks, I'll be fine,' because once his father sat down in that chair he wasn't going to move until they talked.

Uneasiness pushed down on Seth's chest until it threatened to smother him. The tension filled the room as the two men waited to see who would bend first. When Seth could bear it no more, he turned away from his father's questioning gaze.

His father's eyes followed his as he looked over at his brother, not wanting the boy to overhear their conversation. The two of them looked at each other and chuckled together. The very thought of Micah being aroused from sleep, in the middle of the night by their low and steady voices, was humorous at best.

And while a smile still played on his father's face, Seth began, "Dad, I just can't stop thinking about Molly."

"Molly Mills?"

"Yeah."

"I thought as much."

"She touched my arm today and it took everything I had in me not to just grab her and kiss her right then and there."

"But you didn't, right?"

"No, sir."

Silence lay heavy in the room as Micah's steady breathing whispered of his carefree youth.

"Good. A man that can control his desires can take on what ever the world can throw at him."

"But, I don't feel like I can control my..." his face turned red as the dim rays of the moon spotlighted his embarrassment.

"Seth, controlling 'it' doesn't always mean you have to handle it by yourself. Sometimes it means being smart enough to know you can't do it alone."

The young man's chin raised. He knew he needed help, but from somewhere inside him pride rose up and hissed, 'I can handle this alone.' He took in a deep breath and set his jaw, then released it when he realized that it wasn't true, he couldn't handle it alone. Seth looked into the face of the man who had always been there for him in the past. His father had to know the battle that was raging on in his head; confusion, fear, desire, and a deceptive sense of pride. Finally he said, "Pride will lead you off by yourself so it can destroy you, right Dad?" How many times had Seth heard that while growing up? Still, he wrestled with his feelings, wishing he hadn't mentioned anything to his father.

Ken leaned forward, laying his hand on his son's forearm, "So tell me Seth, how can I help you?"

25
Search Party

*He who blesses his friend with a loud voice, rising
early in the morning,
It will be counted a curse to him.*
Proverbs 27: 14 NKJV

When Sam opened his door the next morning, he
found the church van sitting out front. Shel and her
husband Cody were standing talking to Leroy and
Martin as Duke sniffed at the grass along the
sidewalk. Old Lem sat in the van nursing a cup of
coffee as his morning paper lay across his lap.

Inside the back of the van sat five backpacks, no
longer would they be losing time running back and
forth into town. Small sleeping bags hung on the back
of each pack along with a canteen.

"Good morning sleepy head!" Shel sang out.

Sam grumbled under his breath, "A loud and
cheerful greeting in the morning will be taken as a
curse!"

"What?"

"Proverbs 27:14, look it up," he said flatly.

"Oops, grumpy this morning, aren't we Sam?" Shel
moved forward as Sam approached, took her husband
Cody's arm, and introduced the two men.

"Nice to finally meet you Sam."

"You too. Sorry, I've not been sleeping well so please give me a little grace until I wake up, please."

"Sure, I can do that," Cody said as he pulled Sam in for a reluctant hug. "I think we can give you a little grace this morning." he slapped Sam on the back before releasing him and stepping back.

Leroy spoke up, "We need to pray before we take off this morning." He took Sam's hand as Lem crawled out of the van and joined the circle. They began to pray, one after the other. Even Martin added a few words, and while he prayed, a set of small hands pulled his and Cody's hands apart and joined the circle saying, "and God bless this here tackin' dog. Please give him the nose to sniff out them bad guys."

Saying "Amen", they opened their eyes to see Tad standing there with them. Duke began to lick the boy's face as he squealed, "Stop!" and the boy pulled away from the circle and wrapped himself around the dog's neck, and then rolled to the ground taking Duke down with him.

"And who are you?" Cody said as he knelt down next to the boy holding Duke.

"I'm Tad and I'm going to get me a tackin' dog someday." The boy sat up burying his face in Duke's short auburn hair.

"Well, I hope you don't get your tackin' dog like we got ours."

The boy looked at Cody thoughtfully as the dog continued to lick and wiggle all over with excitement. "How'd you get yours?" he managed to ask as he tried to push the dog away.

"Well, we ran away from the bad guys for over two weeks before one of them shot Duke, and we took him home to heal."

"Did he get the bad guys?"

Cody looked over at Leroy and winked, "Well yes, I guess he did."

Leroy went down on one knee. "My name is Leroy and I'm one of the bad guys." Leroy awaited the boy's shocked response.

Tad froze as he pushed Duke aside and gave Leroy a long stare before smiling. "But you're not a bad guy anymore are you?"

"Nope, the Lord got ahold of me because these nice folks were praying for me and now we're praying for the bad guy we're chasing today."

Tad laid his hand on Leroy's shoulder and said, "He's going to be a good guy, just like you are."

"Out of the mouth of babes," Shel injected.

"Well, that's what we've been praying for. I'm afraid we're going to have to get going. It was nice to meet you Tad." Leroy put his big hand out for Tad to shake as he stood towering over him.

As the search party piled into the van, Mary came bursting out of her house and ran up to it. She handed Sam a brown paper bag through the passenger window. "I packed ya'll some bacon and egg sandwiches for your breakfast. We'll be praying for ya'll." She took Tad's hand and pulled him away from the van, stepping back onto the sidewalk.

As Sam said, "Thank you Mary," Duke moved onto his lap and sniffed at the bag in his hand.

"Oh, and I put some dog biscuits in the bag for Duke too."

"Well we need to get going. Thanks again Mary!" Martin said as he threw his hand up and pulled the van out and away from the curb.

Duke stuck his head out the window and barked as his ears flew up from the wind, waved goodbye to his friend Tad.

Seth felt a little better this morning knowing his father understood him and would also not only be standing with him to hold him accountable, he would be praying for him when he took a trip to town later today to talk to Gray Mills about his daughter.

He had made plans to meet Gray for lunch that day at McClure's Diner, being a nicer place to eat then Sally's Big Burger. Seth's family never went into Ponder, but frequented Bennington instead as it was closer to where they lived. Seth liked the smaller school in Ponder, so he walked seven miles there and back over the mountain each day. He never spent a lot of time in town and only occasionally did he and his friend Markus eat their lunch at Sally's, near the school.

Even though this would be a treat for Seth, he was extremely nervous thinking about going in to meet Gray. So as he worked on his morning chores, he moved like a robot, programmed by the memorization of each task. When he finished in record time, he turned to extra jobs to keep his mind on something other than his afternoon meeting with Gray.

Following him this morning was his little brother Micah and their Jack Russell Skippy. Micah asked Seth as he trailed behind, "What are we going to do next?" The little dog jumped up and down, running in circles around the two.

"Well Micah, I'm going to fix the latches on the shed door and windows while you move the rest of the firewood out. Then once you sweep it clean, Ma can start drying her herbs. She'll be pleased when she finds out you did the job without her having to ask you first, don't you think?"

"Yeah!" Micah was always happy to surprise his Mom.

"Then when we're done with that, we're off to school."

The younger boy wasn't all that excited about school so Seth added, "And maybe we can play catch tonight, if all goes well today." It had been an awful long time since Seth had time to play ball with Micah.

The boy of twelve held his excitement in check, not wanting to look like a child in front of his older brother. So as he ran off towards the shed, Skippy led the way, barking as usual.

When Martin dropped them off he said, "Call me with any updates, Sam. You've got my number and since you'll be on the side of the mountain you shouldn't have any trouble getting through. You sure you don't need me to come along?"

"Yeah I'm sure. You just make sure our man Chuck doesn't get across any borders. Believe it or not, it's a relief that you're taking care of that. Anyhow, the five of us and the dog are already a crowd. I'll call you, see ya!"

Sam waved goodbye to Martin as he and the others started hiking towards the small stream that Sam and Shel had reached yesterday before having to turn and go back to town.

Shel and Duke took the lead followed closely by Sam, Leroy, Cody, and Old Lem. Lem knew the area somewhat, at least enough to get by for today. Tonight, after they retrieved Seth Barnett from his home, the pastor would pick Lem up and take him home.

"Seth knows these parts much better than I do. In fact, he knows this whole area better than anyone." Old Lem told them about the nice young man even though they had heard it all before. "I reckon he'll be hikin' with y'all tomorrow. This isn't something I can do everyday." Old Lem continued to talk to Cody at the back of the procession.

Sam stepped back next to Leroy as he said, "I'm so glad you could come along Leroy. I'm excited that you're studying to be a pastor too. Tell me how you got saved and when you knew you wanted to be a pastor."

"Well, I gave my life to the Lord the same day that Chuck got shot. While I was at the hospital, Cody and Shel came in to witness to me and they answered some questions I had and they lead me to the Lord. I'll never forget that day. After I was saved and they went home, I told the jailer I wanted to talk to a pastor. Well, he sent Pastor Hilby in from a neighboring town to visit me and when I was released, I went to see him at his church. He met me at the door and asked me if I needed a job, putting me to work at the church as he discipled me."

"So, did you ever go to visit Chuck in jail?"

"Yeah, I went to visit him after the trial but he wouldn't have anything to do with me. Somehow, it didn't seem right to go to the jail without visiting someone, so I started visiting other inmates instead. As they brought the inmates in, they kept asking me if I was a pastor? By the time I left that day, I knew God had put it on my heart to be a pastor. I just hadn't put the pieces together until then." Leroy laid his hand on his heart, being moved by the memory of it, and said nothing more.

"That's wonderful Leroy!" Sam looked away for a few moments to give Leroy a chance to regain his composure.

"It is wonderful Pastor Hilby took me under his wing and I have experienced the love of a father for the first time in my life. Oh, and not just from the pastor, but from God who's love engulfed me, baptizing me, if you would, in His love. Oh, I don't feel it everyday, but I can draw on those experiences to bring me through the hard times. You know what I mean?"

Sam was smiling now with the thoughts of his own experiences of walking with the Lord. "Yes I do know Leroy, yes I sure do."

26

Critter Inside

The Spirit of the Lord God is upon Me,
Because the Lord has anointed Me
to preach good tidings to the poor;
He has sent Me to heal the brokenhearted,
To proclaim liberty to the captives,...
Isaiah 61: 1 NKJV

As morning wore on, the sun shone through the window. Kate continued to try and free her hands that were tied to the wall of the small shed. Her shoulders felt disjointed and her wrists were now raw from pulling at her bonds. Still, she felt no closer to freeing herself than when she had started this ordeal. Chuck lay on the cold ground, moaning and quivering with fever, while behind him lay his large black hoodie. Kate had tried to lay it back over him with her foot, but it slid off and now it was just beyond her reach.

When she heard whistling and a dog barking, she began to kick at the wall of the shed with her heel. She attempted to yell out but the gag in her dry mouth made her sound more like some kind of an animal than a human. As she struggled to free her hands, she could hear the voice of a boy coming ever closer.

The boy was asking his small dog as it barked excessively, "What do you suppose might be making that banging sound and how'd it get in the shed? Did one of the window latches not catch again?"

Micah stepped closer to the shed and walked around it, shaking the windows and door to check the latches. "Well, Skippy, I did them up right enough." He leaned down and patted the dog on the head.

Skippy continued to bark as he ran around the shed as fast as he could. Seth came up the path and asked, "What is it?"

"There's a critter inside I guess," Micah said. "I checked the windows and door and they're latched well enough, so I don't know how it would have gotten in there."

As Kate sat inside the shed, she heard the little dog barking as he ran repeatedly around the small shed. "That's enough Skippy," a young man scolded and then whistled sharply. When the dog stopped barking, the young man said, "What do you make of this Skippy?" The little dog stuck his nose under the door; his nostrils flared as puffs of dust blew up for Kate to see.

Micah pulled Skippy away from the door as the dog's dirty white muzzle raised to lick his face. Skippy sneezed twice before Micah decided to sit him back down. His tail swung back and forth so fast it could hardly be seen.

"Well, maybe the door blew shut behind the critter?" Seth said as Skippy started to whine. "No Skippy, I don't think you want to tangle with what ever it is. It sounds pretty big to me and I didn't bring my shotgun." Seth watched the small dog as Skippy looked back up at him. His little white and black tail brushed over the surface of the ground, swishing back and forth. Seth continued with, "but we'll have to let it out, won't we boy."

Skippy jumped straight up in the air, flipping head over heels.

Inside, Kate was frantic with thoughts of how she could let the boys know she was not an animal. She was afraid they would just fling the door open and run off, then come back hours later. She was sure it would be too late for Chuck by then. A tear slid down her face, cutting a path through the dirt that covered her cheeks.

She had never been musically inclined but now she knew she would have to try and kick out a rhythm on the wall that would identify her as being human.

Suddenly, the door flew open as she had feared. She heard the boys running away, laughing as they went. She kicked at the wall, but it was too late. Her energy was gone. She was defeated. What remained of the meager moisture her body still possessed began to reluctantly trickle down her cheeks.

'*Oh, Lord please!*' She felt the prayer wash over her despair as she suddenly felt a small wet tongue licking excitedly at her face.

Kate opened her red puffy eyes to see a wire-haired Jack Russell, wagging every muscle in his body. He dashed this way then that, taking turns running between her and Chuck. He was seemingly waiting for a pat on the head or an encouraging word, but neither she nor Chuck were in any condition to give him either.

'*If only the boys would come back!*' With that thought, Kate heard another sharp whistle and someone saying, "Skippy, you get out of that shed before you get yourself eet!"

The little dog dashed out of the shed, then back in over and over again, jumping over Chuck each time.

"Skippy, what have you got in there, a little squirrel or something?" Kate heard Micah say as his head came around the corner. The boy's eyes popped open and he stood staring as Seth stepped into the doorway.

"Micah, run and get Dad!" Seth spat out as he dropped to the ground next to Chuck.

The younger boy ran off as Seth felt Chuck's wrist and then his throat for a pulse. "He's still alive," Seth said as he stepped over the man on the floor and moved in next to Kate. "Now how'd you get yourself tangled up with a fella like this?" He said as he pulled out a pocketknife and began to cut away her gag. As the gag fell to the floor, she tried to talk but her tongue rolled around in her mouth making strange sounds instead of words. "Now that's alright little gal, you just rest your jaw and we'll get you a..."

Suddenly, Micah came running back. "Dad's coming!"

"Now you run and get this gal a drink," Seth directed Micah. But the younger boy just stood staring at the scene before him.

"Micah, get goin'!" Seth flung the wet gag at the boy as he turned and ran off again.

Just then, Ken came around the corner and stepped inside. "Oh my, what do we have here?" He kneeled down beside Chuck, repeating the actions of his older son. "We best get these folks in the house." Ken took over unwrapping Kate's hands from the now cut towel rope.

Seth lifted Chuck's emaciated body to a sitting position to help him into the house while saying, "We may have to get you to the hospital."

Chuck groaned loudly and then protested, "No hospital. No... " he trailed off before falling silent again.

Ken helped Kate to her feet but her legs were not capable of holding her up. So he carefully lowered her back down, then scooped her up in his arms and carried her like a child. He stepped over Chuck's legs and walked out of the shed, headed for the house.

Micah came running back, a glass of water in his hand, losing more of it than he was managing to keep.

"Go help Seth with that man!" his Dad demanded. Micah shot forward, losing the rest of the water in the glass, as he ran the rest of the way back to the shed.

The fear Kate had felt for days left her body. Her head fell to Ken's chest and she knew she no longer had to hold it together. *'We're safe now!'* She thought, *'these people will take care of us. Now I can sleep.'* Her eyes fluttered shut as her head slid back off of Ken's shoulder in utter exhaustion.

Micah dropped the now empty glass and stepped over to the side of Chuck, moving in under his other arm as Seth tried to manage him up off the ground. Getting Chuck upright, they moved together to take him to the house. Chuck's head hung down between them and on the side that Micah held up, Chuck's one leg drug behind him, leaving a single, faint furrow along their path.

Once they got Chuck and Kate situated in the boys' beds, Ken began to bark out orders, "Seth, go get me that old washbasin filled with hot water and bring some soap, a washcloth, and a towel. And Micah, go get the First Aid kit your mother keeps in the kitchen." The boys ran off to follow their father's orders and when Micah returned, he was instructed further. "Now Micah, you go find your Ma. She went to collect herbs and you get her back here as quick as you can, you hear me?"

"Yes Pa!" Micah said as he turned and sped out of the front door. The familiar sound of the screen door slammed behind him as his calls for his Mother faded in the distance.

When Seth came back into the room with the towels and soap along with a pair of old flannel pajamas, he saw his father holding Chuck's gun. Ken looked up at Seth for a long moment, exchanging concern, and then laid the gun aside. They would have to think about that later as there were more important things to do right now.

Seth assisted his Dad in carefully stripping off Chuck's clothes. Then he ran to get the hot water for his Dad.

After washing Chuck, Ken began to treat all his scrapes and cuts, cleaning them with alcohol. Chuck lay unconscious, oblivious to the pain he would normally be feeling. When Ken began to unwrap the bandage from Chuck's hand and saw the wound, he stopped for a moment. Carefully, he pulled the bandage free from the oozing, puss-filled wound that ran from his wrist down the side of his thumb.

Ken knew his wife would have a better idea of what needed to be done with the wound, having herbs she could use on it. After cleaning it as best he could, he laid a strip of gauze over it as he waited for her to come home.

The two men dressed Chuck in clean pajama bottoms, leaving the top off until Becky could treat the wrist. "I think you may have to cut that sleeve off a little so we can get it over the bandage once your ma dresses the wound," Ken stated.

"What now?" Seth looked up from giving Kate a drink of water, a spoonful at a time.

"Just wait for your mom. She'll know for sure if it's safe to treat them at home or not." Ken looked at his son and added, "I think we have done what we can. But, I think you have a call to make, don't you?"

Seth didn't need to be told twice as he glanced up at the clock, handing his father the dropper and water. He dashed from the room, having forgotten all about his meeting with Molly's father. Seth knew he couldn't leave with all that was going on right now so he would have to call off his meeting. He hated to do that but it couldn't be helped. He picked up the phone and dialed the Mill's house.

"Hello," Molly answered.

"Hi, this is Seth. Would you tell your Dad I can't make it today? Something..."

"Aren't you supposed to be meeting him at the diner in a half-hour?"

"I was, but something happened and..."

Molly cut him off, "I just passed him coming home for lunch and begged him to take me along but he wouldn't hear of it. Do you have any idea how long it's been since I've had an ice cream cone? Well, it must be nearly two weeks now."

Seth smiled, almost forgetting why he had called. As she chattered on, he tried to cut in with, "Some folks showed up in our..."

"Your folks know how to entertain guests better than you do, Seth Barnett," she scolded and then continued, "you should know my Dad's already in town and I can't get ahold of him. He'll be setting there waiting for you if you don't go!"

"I can't go Molly, my Dad needs me here. Mom is out and he needs me to..."

"Does he know you made plans to meet my Dad?"

"He knows alright, but..." Seth was getting frustrated and half expected to be cut off once again before he could finish what he had to say. So he sped up his speech to try and get as much in as he could before being cut off once again. "I thought I might be able to catch him still at home."

Just then, Ken started waving at Seth to hang up the phone and come help him.

"Molly, couldn't you call your Dad at McClure's and tell him I can't make it in today?"

Then Molly started to say, "Well sure I can, but..." Seth hung up and went to help his father.

"Ma, Ma!" Micah called as he ran through the woods, visiting all the places she frequented while seeking out herbs. Still, he couldn't find her. Calling out once more, he heard her say from behind him, "What is it? Is something wrong?"

He turned and began to explain excitedly, "We found some folks in the shed and they're both in a bad way. A man and a woman, and the man looks more dead than alive. Pa said you need to come right away."

"So how is he hurt?"

"I don't know. But he has a rag wrapped around one wrist and he looks like a bag of bones. But Pa said he's a fighter and won't give up liven' just yet."

"And the woman?"

"She doesn't seem to be as sickly. She was awake when we found them, but not for long. She's dirty and beat up a mite with scratches and bruises, but Pa says she's more dehydrated than anything. He said her heart is laboring to beat because of it. He thinks she hasn't slept much in a while too."

Becky looked at the herbs she had already collected. "I'm going to need some fresh Comfrey leaves," she said before telling Micah, "you run off and butcher me one of the spring chickens."

"But Mom!"

"A spring chicken I said. I haven't got time to be boiling one of them tough old things. Now get!" She slapped at his backside as he dashed off. Then, she cut through the trees to find the fresh herbs she would need before running back to the house.

Ken and Becky spoke in depth about the request Chuck had made about not taking him to the hospital. Becky knew the herbs she had would most likely soon set them both right. Ken and Becky both felt a peace about the situation, as if the Lord had laid these folks in their laps for some reason. They felt as if they had a part to play in the lives of these two people before this was all over. They were willing to wait on the Lord for an answer before they made any further decision about the hospital.

Ken had taken the gun and hid it from the man, so Chuck no longer posed a threat to his family. Ken now knelt down and began to pray with his wife Becky by his side. "Now Lord, I don't know why this man had that little gal tied up in our shed, but we'll be needing your guidance right about now."

"Use our hands Lord," Becky prayed, "to heal these folks physically as You give us the opportunity to lead them to You, especially this man that seems to have the worst of it. Lord, we pray that You save him." She laid her free hand on Chuck as they knelt between the beds of the two strangers.

Ken picked up the prayer with, "And Lord, I'm going to need to get our car fixed if I'm going to take these folks to the hospital. Now Lord, You know full well that my car's a reliable one so we have to conclude that causing our car not to run at this time is part of Your plan. We know You haven't been caught off guard by these folks showing up on our doorstep. If You want these folks to stay here for a while for some reason, then we will do our best to do as You direct us. Amen and so be it."

Becky leaned into her husband's embrace and asked, "Do you think we should call someone?"

"No, I don't think so. I think we're doing what God wants us to do right now. That may change tomorrow, but for right now we need to just listen for His leading."

27

Chicken Wink

In my distress I called upon the Lord,
And cried out to my God;
He heard my voice from His temple,
And my cry entered his ears.
2 Samuel 22:7 NKJV

Micah ran into the chicken coop scaring up the hens and sending them flying in all directions, including out the door. "Now that wasn't too smart," he scolded himself. The only hen left in the coop was Sadie. Sadie was the friendliest hen in the flock and Micah's personal favorite. He knew he would have no problem catching her today. Even as the other chickens were flapping and running across the lawn to get away from him, Sadie walked up to him. Her head bobbed forward and back with each step, clucking a quiet song of trust as Micah stepped forward and leaned down to pick her up.

"I'm so sorry Sadie, but you know how it is. This here's a working farm and that means you're going to feed us at some point. You know that, right?" he said to her as he was trying to be strong. "I was hoping you would be one of our laying hens that stayed with us for years and years but we need you for food right now, so come along." Sadie clucked contentedly as he kissed her on the head. He stepped out of the coop built in the corner of the shed. He pulled the hatchet from its place hanging on the wall of the shed and stepped around a bale of straw sitting on the floor. The other hens scattered as Micah came out of the shed. Carrying Sadie in his arms, he walked across the lawn and out of the gate.

He talked quietly to her as he walked, relaying to her what had happened, and then added, "Well Sadie, you do understand that I have to do this, right?" He stopped as he reached the end of the yard and stood beside the dreaded chopping block. He held her close to his face and began to cry, "It just has to be done. Do you understand me girl? It's really the noblest way to die, to lay down your life for another." He laid his face on her feathers as she turned her head and nibbled on his cheek lightly, as a kiss. Micah pulled away and looked her in the eyes and then she winked at him as if to say, "It's alright Micah, I understand."

Micah smiled a sad smile and said, "Good bye Sadie." He took her head in his hand and placed it between two large nails that stuck out of the stump. He then gently pulled her feet to hold her in place, and as he raised the hatchet, he felt something striking his foot. Looking down, he saw a young rooster intently pecking at something on his shoe. Micah instinctively pushed the rooster away before he gently released Sadie and scooped up the rooster as it came back again.

"How'd you get...?" He turned to see that the gate hadn't latched so he moved quickly to head off the chickens that were starting to wander out. He slowly coaxed the stragglers back into the run, along with Sadie, closing the gate behind them. Looking at the rooster he still held, he began to tell the story of Isaac and how the Lord had provided himself a sacrifice.

The rooster just looked at him, irritated, as if to say, "Ok, ok, can we just get this over with?"

Micah came into the house and handed his Mom a headless, plucked chicken. His eyes were bright with excitement.

"What, what is it?" Becky asked with a puzzled look on her face.

Micah went into great detail as he told his mother all about what had just happened "It was okay Ma, Sadie understood that we needed her help to heal these folks. I told her all about it and she winked at me to let me know it was all right. Really Mom, I haven't ever seen anything like it before. But then that rooster was right there, at my feet. I couldn't help but think of Abraham as the Lord told him to sacrifice his only son, Isaac. And as the knife was laid at Isaac's throat, how the Lord provided a sacrifice to take his place."

Becky took her son in her arms and held him to share the happy moment with him. "I love you Micah, but now I really need you to sit yourself down there," she pointed to the chair that sat between the two beds. "Talk to him Micah and tell him what happened. Read the Bible to him and tell him about the Lord, and how God loves him. I'm doing everything I can to heal him up physically, but I think he needs someone to care about him right now. He needs the Lord's love. Tell him everything you know about Christ's blood sacrifice, and how Jesus died in his place for his sins."

When Chuck woke early the next morning, he was disoriented. He sat up quickly and then thought better of it as his head swam around the dark, unfamiliar room. He laid back down in the twin bed, looking over at Kate laying in the other. *'Where are we? Why am I*

dressed in flannel pajamas and where are my slippers?' He thought to himself as he looked over the edge of the bed and saw them sitting there. Looking over the edge of the bed made his head feel heavy as if it might just fall to the floor, dragging his body along with it.

Exhaling loudly, "Where, where am I?" He rolled towards the edge of the bed and willed himself to slowly sit up. "I have to get out of here," he mumbled this time. Swinging his legs over the side, he slipped his feet into his slippers. He sat still for a moment longer before pushing himself up on his legs. He walked to the bedroom door and slowly opened it, stepped into the hall to find he was looking into a simple but very neat and clean living room. On the floor, a young man and a teen-age boy slept, their covers spilling off onto the floor on all sides.

Chuck walked cautiously through the room, opened the front door, and stepped outside. The sky was just starting to glow with warm light as he closed the door silently behind him. A cold morning mist hit him briskly in the face as he managed to take roughly twenty steps before collapsing on a bench in a pretty flower garden. As he sat there, he began to make a mental list of events leading up to now and decided someone must have found them in that shed.

'Well, obviously, I've thrown those that are following us, off our trail,' Chuck smiled weakly. *'Oh, how is Kate?'* He hadn't thought of checking on her before he left the house. Just then, his stomach growled and he placed his hand on his sore ribs. *'When did I stop retching?'* He asked himself as he held out his arm to inspect the now carefully bandaged hand and wrist. For the first time in days, he realized it didn't hurt too much. *'Well, maybe we should stay here for another day or so.'* Suddenly his eyes and mouth shot open as the thought hit him, *'Where's my gun?'*

Chuck was still feeling very weak and he felt compelled to lie down. He curled up as best he could on the hard garden bench and lay there shivering in the cold morning air, when he heard someone coming.

"What are you doing out here? You can't just run off like that. Now, let's get you back in your bed." Ken rushed over and swept Chuck up in his arms, carried him back into the house, and placed him in the bed.

Chuck liked that this man carried him so easily. It made him feel like he was a small child once again, except this time he felt like he was loved.

"Son, I think we're going to have to get you to the hospital."

"No," Chuck demanded, "don't take me to the hospital!" Chuck knew that going to the hospital meant he was off to prison next, so he was insistent about not going.

"You sure son?" Ken pulled the blankets up over Chuck's chilled body.

"No, no hospital, you got that?" His words slurred as he dropped back off to sleep.

Kate was still not awake when Chuck came to again. As he slowly sat up, a woman rushed into the room and began to spoon-feed him. Chuck was too weak to resist and, truth be told, he liked all the attention he had been getting. There was something about these people that made him feel welcome and special.

"The Lord loves you. You've been practically starved to death."

Chuck ignored the remark about the Lord loving him and eagerly opened his mouth. He felt like for the first time in days that what she fed him might stay down. He did feel like he was starving to death. So he hungrily ate the chicken broth. It tasted familiar and he vaguely remembered her feeding him before this.

"Now, you can't go drinking water out of a stream like you did and not pay dearly for it, you hear?" Becky scolded. "I want you to eat all of this good broth. Open up!"

Chuck took another spoonful.

"I've been trying to get you back on your feet, I'm pretty sure the parasites are dead because you've stopped throwing up and... well you know. But even though you're doing much better, there's still things I just can't do to help you because I can't test you here, like they can in the hospital. But, Ken said you won't hear of going in."

"No hospital!" Chuck held his stomach as it began to rumble with a now familiar sound.

"You sure son? Ken's been working on the car and feels as if he very nearly has it fixed."

"No hospital!" Chuck growled this time, turning to glare at her.

"Ok, ok, we'll see how things go, but I suspect you picked up a bit of a parasite in the water. I've been treating it, but there are all manner of problems that come along with something like that."

Chuck glanced over at her with a questioning look, but she didn't answer the unasked question.

"Now honey, I have some questions for you if you feel up to it." Becky didn't wait for his response before continuing, "First, why did you have that handgun on you?"

"Oh, we were out shootin' squirrels. You know what pests they can be and I guess we got a mite lost. " Chuck kept his eyes on her as he spoke to see if she was buying his lie.

She just nodded skeptically. "And why did you have that little gal tied up?"

"Oh, she was sick, too- and she was thrashing around something awful."

"She was gagged," she stated sternly, still not convinced he was telling the truth.

Making it up as he went, Chuck said, "Yeah, you know how those tremors will take a person. I heard of one fella who near chewed his tongue clean off before they got him gagged."

Becky cringed as her thoughts tumbled over each other. *'That woman didn't seem to be as bad off as this man, but then again, she is the one still sleeping.'* She turned and looked at Kate momentarily. She stood and placed a hand on Kate's forehead before sitting back down and saying, "Ok son, we haven't been properly introduced so," she put her hand out to him, "my name is Becky Barnett and may I ask you what your name might be?"

"Chuck At..." Chuck stopped short of saying Atteberry. "Well, it's really Charles, Charles Adams but you can call me 'Charlie', that's what I prefer."

"Charlie?" Becky asked unsure about it.

"Charlie Adams, yes Ma'am, that's my name, Charlie...Adams."

Chuck kept watching her face finding skepticism written there.

"And her name is?" Her eyes turned to the other bed where Kate McClure lay.

"Kate Knots, she's my fiancé, Ma'am."

"Kitty...Kitty Knots!" Becky exclaimed.

Fear rushed through Chuck, but it was soon clear his simple lie had accidentally done the trick to remove any suspicion.

"Well, Kitty did say she'd be coming to visit soon, but I thought it wasn't going to be until the Fall! And you're her fiancé, you say?" Becky looked at him for a moment as she thought to herself her cousin didn't have very good taste in men. She stood and went looking for her husband with excitement in her voice. "Well, we'll just have to take real good care of her then. I haven't seen her since she was a kid, but she does look familiar now that you mention it."

Chuck sighed with relief as he could still hear her bubbling over in the other room. There were no more questions from Becky, only the excitement of seeing her young cousin after twenty six years.

28

Talon

*...if you confess with your mouth the Lord Jesus and
believe in your heart that
God has raised Him from the dead,
you will be saved.
Romans 10:9 NKJV*

Molly had made plans to stay in Ponder after school
and go to a movie with her friend Pam. However,
when she arrived at Pam's house, Pam said that she
just got a call from the Tillman's and had to babysit
their three youngest. "Sorry, but you'll have to go with
Talon instead. He's been wanting to go to the movies
and has been looking for someone to go with him."
Pam leaned in as if telling Molly a thrilling secret,
"And you won't have to pay, he'll even buy the
popcorn."

"But I don't know him and he's eighteen. I don't
know him!" Molly protested, not wanting to say she
knew about him and his trouble-making friends.

"But I know you!" Molly heard a deep voice from
behind her. She turned to see Talon standing there,
tall and handsome. He raised one eyebrow and gave
her a pleasant smile. "I'd be honored to take the
prettiest girl in town to the movies."

Pam leaned in and whispered in Molly's ear, "He likes you!"

Molly's heart rose with fear but his flattery turned her fear into a nervous giggle. She was flattered and embarrassed. She was being put in an awkward position that she didn't know how to get out of. She thought of what her parents would say. She didn't want them to be disappointed in her. *Well, I am sixteen now, why shouldn't I date? Everyone else does after all. Plus they never said I couldn't date,* she reasoned with herself.

All of a sudden, a question furrowed her brow as she asked loudly, "Is this a date?" She was embarrassed by her own question and turned red.

"Yeah, sure it is. You'll be my gal. How's that sound?" Talon smiled again.

"Uh..." Molly struggled to come up with some response, but none came.

"What? Don't you like me?" Talon asked with a playful hurt look on his face.

"Uh... sure I do, but..." Again nothing.

"But?"

"Uh, nothing."

"Don't worry Sweetie, it will be fabulous just to have you hanging on my arm. All the other guys will be jealous." Talon put his arm out to her with a smile and said, "Shall we go then?" But as he walked past his sister, he whispered in her ear, "What's her name?"

Pam spat out, "Molly, you and Talon have fun now. And Molly, I'll expect to hear all about your first date tomorrow." Pam smiled at Molly and winked at her brother, giving them both a push towards the door.

But Molly didn't hear her last statement as her mind was turning over the last thing Talon had said, "All the other guys will be jealous." Thinking of Seth being envious caused excitement along with a confused sick feeling as Molly giggled uncomfortably.

Old Lem had been talking about everything he could think of for hours on many subjects. But Cody liked it and kept him going with questions about his childhood, all the way up to what it was like to be old.

When they came around a bend in the creek, there on a rock hung the pants that Chuck had hung there to dry. They were all excited to find another place where Chuck and Kate had obviously been. Duke sniffed around the rock and the footprints left in the soft mud of the bank. Being urged to quickly move on, he followed the stream up the mountainside. Even though there was no scent to follow, they assumed that Chuck and Kate had stepped back into the water as they seemingly continued upstream.

Old Lem didn't miss a beat. "It's gonna take some good strong soap ta get the stink out of these jeans. I guess I should burn them instead. That boy must be real sick. I wonder where he's got off to? It sure was a shock, a comin' around the corner ta find my old jeans just hanging over that rock like that."

Sam, Shel, and Duke were still in the lead. Leroy had dropped way back, walking as if he was waiting for Chuck to run out from behind some tree and say, *'Here I am! I really had you going, didn't I?'*

When they stopped for lunch Sam asked Leroy, "Are you alright?"

"Yeah, I'm alright but I feel like we're headed in the wrong direction."

"What do you mean? We're following the stream, there can't be much doubt they went this way." Sam snapped back.

"Well, that's what I mean. Chuck has been so very careful not to leave any traces, and then he leaves his pants lying in plain view for all to see! That just doesn't add up."

"He is awful sick so maybe he's not thinking clearly. Maybe he was planning on coming back and getting them when they dried."

"I guess, but..." Leroy was reluctant to say more.

Sam, irritated with his opposing opinion, spat out, "Duke still seems to be tracking him so I think we're good here."

"Yeah, I guess you're right," Leroy conceded, still not convinced of what he agreed to.

Talon bought two tickets at the entrance of the old-time movie theater. "Well, should we go in my dear?"

Molly loved being talked to like this. From the time they walked out his door, down the street, and entered the movie theater, Talon had not said one thing that wasn't absolutely perfect in every way.

"Oh, yes please," she said back in a playful tone. Talon wasn't the kind of guy Molly was naturally attracted to. In fact, she had avoided him her whole life and barely even noticed him. But now she found that he was charming and proving to be fun as well.

"Would you like some popcorn and a soda, Molly my dear?" He said with a pleasant smile.

"That would be lovely, thank you!" She smiled as she caught an amused twinkle in his eye.

"And your favorite candy is?"

"Oh no, popcorn and soda will be plenty for me, thank you!"

"Well, for future reference then."

"Well, my all-time favorite candy is Almond Roca if you must know!"

He stepped up to the counter and ordered a large popcorn, which they would of course share. He also ordered two sodas, and a large box of 'Good and Plenty' candy for himself.

As he paid for the items, Molly looked around the foyer at the movie posters on the walls. When a group of Talon's friends came in, Talon's best friend Brace shouted, "Hey Talon, why didn't you tell us you would be here?"

"Can't you see I'm on a date?" Talon said sharply as Brace slapped him on the back.

"Oooo! On a date are you? Well, who's the lucky girl?" He looked around but all he saw was a young girl standing beside a poster. "Well, did your date go to the can or something?"

"No, it's Molly here," he put his arm out to her and she stepped over along side of him. Then, he put an arm around her waist and pulled her in, kissing her full on the lips.

Her heart leaped as her stomach dropped and fire rose in her veins, blushing her cheeks. Talon held her firmly to his side, making her feel safe but confused. The other girls in the group stared at her with hostile eyes.

"Oooo! Alrighty then. Hey Talon, can I talk to you for a minute about a school assignment?" Brace nodded his head to the side to indicate where he wanted to talk. When the two of them left, Molly stood alone as the others abandoned her to go into the movie. She didn't mind though as their crude jokes and coarse talk made her feel out of place.

Brace glanced over and she knew they were talking about her, so she blushed again feeling as if she should run.

Sam's mind was now plagued with thoughts and doubts, some good, but mostly bad. *'What if Leroy was right and they were going the wrong way?'* No, he couldn't think that way, he had to believe they were headed in the right direction. Otherwise, he had to come to the conclusion that whole day had been wasted on a dummy trail and he was the dummy.

What he really needed was to get his mind off of the here and now.

"So Shel, how did you and Kate get to be friends?"

"Well, that's kind of a sad story. You sure you want to hear it?"

"Oh, I figure you met after Mac Ferrell's murder. So yeah, go ahead and tell me what happened."

"Well you see; Cody and I came into McClure's diner a little bit after you told Kate, that Mac had been murdered. Her eyes were puffy and she had a definite sniffle. So I asked her if she was all right. Shel raised the pitch of her voice slightly to indicate Kate answering, " 'Yeah, I'm okay. Can I take your order?' Kate had lifted her chin and struggled to smile in an attempt to put on a good face."

"She filled our orders as she tried to hide her tears. She handed Cody his ice cream cone and as he went and sat down, I just stood there. It seemed to me as if she needed someone to share with so I waited quietly for her to open up. Kate said so softly that I could barely hear her, 'He had just given his life to the Lord'. She had tears running down her face when I asked, 'Who, Sweetie?' "

" 'Mac.' "

"I didn't know who Mac was at the time so I just decided to listen and let her talk. This guy she was talking about had just given his life to the Lord. She said it took her forever to talk him out of that bar. He had apparently told her he was tired of living the way he had been. So, she called Pastor Smith and he got a prayer group together. They met her and this Mac at the pastor's house. They all prayed with Mac and he got saved. When he left them, he was hung over a little from drinking earlier, but she said he was free and so happy. Then she smiled at me and said, 'I had never seen him so happy'. After that, none of them saw him again and they didn't know what had happened to him until you came in to tell her he was dead.

"Suddenly it dawned on me. Kate was talking about the dead man that Cody and our friend Mike had found murdered in the gully wash. At that point, it all became very personal. I told her how sorry I was and I took her in my arms and held her for a long time.

"Kate continued with, 'you always hear about people waiting until the last minute to give their life to the Lord but I think it's the other way around. I think when your numbers up, it's up. But for Mac, God waited just a little bit longer'.

"I thought that was a really cool way to look at it. So I told her she was really blessed to know he gave his life to the Lord before he died. Anyways, she stepped back and looked at me for a second and I could tell she was wondering where she had seen me before and why she had just shared her heart with a complete stranger. Well, I guess the rest is history. We began to talk and became fast friends, and..." Shel threw her shoulders up, "Well, she's probably told you all about it herself."

"No, I've never heard any of this. So why did she think she knew you?"

"We stopped at the diner on our way to go camping a couple of weeks earlier. For two weeks, Chuck and Leroy chased us through the mountains. Chuck wanted nothing more than to sink his talons into us, being convinced we had seen Mac's murder. Which, we most definitely had not."

29
Good-Bye Chuck

"Therefore do not be ashamed
of the testimony of our Lord,
nor of me His prisoner,
but share with me in the suffering
for the gospel according to the power of God"
2 Timothy 1:8 NKJV

After a late afternoon nap, Chuck woke to the smiling face of a teen-age boy.

"Hi there, my name is Micah." He put his hand out to gingerly shake Chuck's as he continued to talk, "I've been reading to you while you were sleeping the last couple of days. I know you probably don't remember none of it but Ma said to just keep on reading to you. So I did."

Chuck didn't remember him reading but couldn't deny that the boy's voice did sound kind of familiar. He really didn't care this way or that for a story, but he wasn't ready for more questions and answers either. So he said, "Ok, then read on."

"Well, let me catch you up a mite first. This is a story about a man named Saul. Now this Saul was a bad man, he went around killing folks just because they were Christians."

Chuck smiled to himself, *'That sounds about right.'* He thought.

"Now, that just isn't right you know. Folks have a right to believe what they want to believe, don't you think?"

Chuck's head snapped towards the young man as he continued.

"Now this man Saul, he was taking himself a trip to Damascus to find more Christians to kill when God knocked him right off his horse and flashed a bright light in his eyes. Well, that made him blind of course. Then God asked Saul, why was he persecuting Him?" Micah interjected, "Now in case you don't know, that means God counted all them folks Saul had been killing as being part of Himself, you know, like family and all. Are you following me Charlie?"

Chuck's eyes were big as he nodded his head.

"Well, that's where I left off. So are you ready for the rest of the story?"

Chuck turned away from the boy and stared at the ceiling as he nodded.

Duke stopped moving forward and started to pull his master back the way they had come, Shel resisted his lead. Laying down, he looked up at her and whined with pleading eyes.

"What is it boy?" She asked, but the dog had no way of telling her.

When Sam saw the way the dog was acting, he puzzled over it. How could they have hit another dead end? As the fear and frustration he had been holding inside overwhelmed him, he became angry. "Make him get up, we don't have time for this nonsense! Let's get goin'!" He took a step toward the dog and began to pull hard on his leash.

"Sam, no! He didn't stop just to mess with you," Shel said, taking his hand and gently pulling the leash away from him.

Now Leroy stepped between Sam and the dog. "Sam, we are all on the same team here. Please, let's just set down and talk. We could all use a breather anyway." Leroy glanced over at old Lem, who plopped himself down by a tree and laid back to rest, and said, "And, this is as good a time as any."

Cody took Sam's arm and coaxed him to sit down in the grass. "Come on Sam, we need to figure out what's going on here and quick. Duke clearly doesn't want to go any farther and we have to assume he has lost the trail. Are we all in agreement with that?" Cody said with a tilt of the head and eyebrows raised, waiting for an answer.

They all nodded or responded with a simple 'yes', including Sam the reluctant police chief.

"So it's like this, we have lost the scent. Where is it and where has it gone to? Any ideas?"

"Um..." Leroy began, "I think we're going... the wrong way." He spoke in stops and starts, "I think those pants were maybe a decoy... to set us off in the wrong direction."

No one said a word for a few moments.

When Lem stated, "I think Leroy's right. I been thinkin' on it a mite and them pants layin' there on that rock just wasn't right somehow. And if we go back and follow that stream up the mountainside, we'll be lucky if we don't run right in ta Seth Barnett's house. He's the young man that's going ta be takin' over trackin' for me. His folks live at the top of that ridge."

Chuck lay listening to Micah for a long time, hearing the story about this man named Saul.

Micah kept reading, but Chuck stopped him as he asked, "How many stories are in the Bible anyway?" He continued to stare at the ceiling in deep thought.

"Well, there are an awful lot of them. I haven't ever had someone ask me that before."

Chuck lay silently for what seemed a long time. He was struck dumb by the similarity of this man Saul's story and his own.

Saul had hated folks just because they were Christians and he killed them. God changed Saul's name to Paul, just like Chuck had changed his own name to Charlie. Chuck couldn't help but feel that even the words, 'road to Damascus' were for him as the last time he had seen Paul Damascus - he was laying on the road.

Regret moved up his chest and stopped at his throat to strangle him as he choked back tears.

Also, Chuck remembered clearly being told this very same story by a woman named Shel last Fall, while being taken into custody. How was it possible all these things were lining up? Almost as if they had been planned out in advance? Far in advance!

Chuck felt a sudden driving need to see the man he had put in the hospital. Paul Damascus, the one man who had always cared about him, and in his own words had said, "I'll never stop praying for you, Chuck."

"I need to go to the hospital," Chuck spat out as he came out of his trance.

"You feelin' bad?" Micah finally asked. "Ma, Charlie's feelin' bad again!" The boy got up and ran to the other side of the bed and thrust a small bucket at him.

"No, I'm fine!"

"You feelin' sick Charlie?" Becky said as she turned the corner.

"No, no I'm fine. I just want to go to the hospital."

"Yes, of course, I think that's wise." Becky laid her

hand on his forehead.

"No, not for me, for a friend I want to visit."

Becky looked at Micah, "Go get your Pa." Micah rushed out of the room. She looked over at Kate who still slept. "Well, shouldn't you take Kitty in with you? Even though she seems to be fine, she's worrying me, sleeping this long."

"No, she's fine." Chuck waved her off, "She's just really tired. She'll wake up soon and you'll see."

With that, Ken came in and helped Chuck to the car he had finally managed to fix. "So this friend of yours is in the hospital in Bennington?"

"No, he's in Ponder."

"Oh, alright. We don't normally get into Ponder more than once or twice a year. It is slightly farther to Bennington, but Bennington's a straight shot, where as Ponder takes you on some small winding roads and it actually takes longer to get there. But that's no problem. I can sure take you there. I'll just stop in the hardware and pick up some things while you're visiting your friend."

Quiet tension held the two men captive as they drove down the long mountain road that led into Ponder. Finally, Ken broke the silence with, "Well, I do hope your friend's alright."

"I do too," Chuck said in sincerity.

"What's wrong with him?"

"He had an accident and cracked his head pretty hard." Chuck rolled down the window and rested his arm on the door.

"Oh, that's bad!"

"Yeah, it is."

Both men sat quietly for a while. Chuck was still feeling bad and he wanted to lie down. He wasn't ready to throw his hands up in surrender just yet so he did his best to sit up and act like he was feeling great. He leaned towards the window and took in a deep breath.

"Do you know the Lord, Charlie?" Ken asked.

"No sir."

"Would you like to know him?"

Chuck said nothing but kept his face turned away, not feeling like he deserved forgiveness.

Ken patted him on the shoulder and said, "Well son, if you're interested, you just confess that you're a sinner and ask Him into your life, that's all."

Several minutes passed before Chuck asked, "could you pull over for a minute?"

"Yeah, sure!" Ken pulled off the road and as Chuck stepped out of the car and moved into a grove of trees, Ken began to pray for him.

Chuck lay on the cool moist ground under a tree as the sun's going down cast long dancing shadows over the valley.

"Lord, I have no right asking you to save me but neither did Saul. I'm worthless. I'm a sinner, but here I am never the less, on the road to Damascus. Please Lord, forgive me."

Chuck's heart hurt so bad as the Lord massaged life back into it, making it into pliable clay, so He could mold Chuck into whatever He wanted him to become.

"Lord, I'm so sorry. Please don't let Paul die. Please, I don't want any more blood on my hands." Chuck laid his hands on his chest and gasped for air as tears threatened to drown him.

After some time, Chuck's tears dried and he smiled as he remembered Paul saying he could be *free indeed*.

"I am free indeed!" he whispered. "Thank you Lord that I am free indeed." A moment passed before he finished with, "No matter what comes!"

"I'm looking for my friend Paul Damascus. Can you tell me which room he's in, please?"

"Are you alright, sir?"

"I'm fine. Paul Damascus, please!" Chuck had his hoodie pulled up over his hair as he closed the unzipped oversized jacket, wrapping it tightly around him.

"Would you like a wheelchair sir? Are you a patient here?"

"No. Please ma'am, if you don't mind."

"Yes sir, he's in room seven. Can I help you in any other way?"

"No ma'am, thank you."

"They just moved him out of Intensive Care so you're in luck," she said as he walked away.

When Chuck reached Paul's room, he stopped to peek around the corner.

There sitting by Paul's bed was his wife Susan. She held his limp hand as she talked quietly to him. "Just everyone's been praying for you Paul, there're people all around the country praying for you."

Chuck moved away from the door and sat down in the waiting area. It was just slightly down the hall from Paul's room, giving him full view for when Susan left. After picking up a magazine, he pretended to read while fighting the urge to lay across the other two chairs that were connected to his own.

Ken had dropped Chuck off at the hospital, promising to be back in a half-hour to pick him up. Chuck was pushing it just by being here. The woman at the desk had been right to ask him if he needed a wheelchair. He was feeling much better but still not good and he was weak, so very weak.

As Chuck sat listening to the low murmurs coming from room seven, his eyes closed for what he felt was only a second as he whispered a quick prayer, "Lord help me, I can't do this. Please help me." His head lay back against the wall and soon his mouth dropped open, causing his pale wax-like skin to stretch thin. His eyes dropped into dark sockets that seemed to deepen under the shadow of his large black hood.

As Susan stepped out of Paul's room, she stopped and looked at him, "Are you alright sir?"

But Chuck didn't answer.

"Sir, can I help you?" Still no response, so she walked to the nurse's station and said, "That man in the waiting area is either dead or about dead."

The receptionist leaned out over the counter to look down the hall and then cringed. "I know, I tried to get him a wheelchair but he wouldn't hear of it."

"Well, I don't think he'll give you much of an argument now," Susan said, returning the receptionist's concern.

"Do you think I should...?" The receptionist paused before saying, "Oh, let me check him first." She stepped out from behind the counter and the two women walked down the hall together and stopped in front of Chuck.

"Sir, are you alright?" The receptionist laid her hand on Chuck's shoulder. "Sir, are you alright?" She shook him slightly and his head rolled back and forth on the wall as she drew her hand back fast. "Oh no, I think he's dead!" She turned and ran back to the nurse's station, swept up the phone, and said, "I have a problem here. I think the man sitting in the waiting area is dead. Can you send someone right away?"... "Yes... yes... Ok." She sat the phone down and looked at Susan. "They're coming to check on him."

"Ok, do you think I should stay or go?"

The receptionist just drew her shoulders up into a question.

The receptionist pointed towards Chuck as two men flew down the hall with a gurney between them. Reaching the unconscious man, they rushed around him, doing things the women could not see. Even though the emaciated man could have easily been lifted by the smaller of the two men, they lifted him together and placed him gently on the gurney. Rolling the gurney carefully down the hall, they entered the nearest empty room.

The doctor stepped arrogantly into the hall with his nose in the air and approached nonchalantly. He entered the room and closed the door behind him.

As the women stood staring at each other their eyes were big with questions, Ken came strolling in.

"I'm looking for a Charlie Adams. He came in to visit a friend."

"Ok, who's the friend he came to visit?" The receptionist asked.

"I don't really know."

"Ok then, what's he look like?"

"Well, he doesn't look like much right now as he's been real sick. He's wearing an over-sized black hoodie."

Both women's eyes popped open at the mention of the black hoodie. And Susan began to stammer, "Is he... does he look like... he's dead?"

30

Charlie Adams

You shall be called by a new name,
Which the mouth of the Lord will name.
Isaiah 62: 2b NKJV

"Do you mind if we all pray together before we retire for the night?" Leroy asked. But it was more like the gentle man was insisting, *'we need to pray and we're doing it right now!'*

They all pulled themselves away from their thinking, worrying, and just plain exhaustion to join together in a circle.

"Lord," Leroy began to pray, "we thank You for what You did today even though we don't understand why. We have all seen things we understood to be hopeless turn right around to be the best thing that could ever of happened. We thank You once again, Lord." He paused for only a moment and continued with, "Lord, we stand in agreement when we ask that You lead and guide us tomorrow. We pray You will give Duke a keen nose to sniff out and find Chuck and Kate."

Duke's head came up off Shel's lap as he looked at Leroy as if to say, "Thank you, I accept that blessing."

"Be with us as we sleep tonight Lord, giving us the rest we need so we can function well tomorrow." Each in turn followed his words by adding their own concerns, before agreeing together with a resounding, "Amen".

The next thing Chuck knew, he was looking up at Ken from flat on his back.

"What's going on?"

"The doctor said you have Leptospirosis from drinking out of the creek... animal urine and such." Ken winced. "Said you'll be alright though."

Chuck tried to sit up but Ken pushed him back down with very little effort. "Now you just stay put. I'm covering the cost of your care unless you have insurance or something. We couldn't find any records for a Charlie Adams anywhere so I'm guessing you're not from around these parts."

Chuck struggled to get up again as he simply said, "no," and fell back into the bed.

Just then Dr. Weaver came in, "Oh no, you don't! You need to stay put and get better." He picked up a syringe and inserted it into the IV catheter in Chuck's hand.

"What is that?" Chuck said with concern.

"Oh, it's a cocktail of things really. First, I have you hooked up to an IV to rehydrate you." The doctor pointed at the clear bag of liquid that hung by Chuck's bed, then went on, "The vomiting and diarrhea, plus the lack of clean water, dehydrated you like a raisin. Dehydration will kill you faster than hunger. Plus in this," the doctor held up the now empty syringe, "is an antibiotic. The parasites that are now dead left some nasty side effects. The antibiotic should take care of the problems there. Also, there is a painkiller and a sleeping aid in the injection. You need a lot of rest right now Charlie. The drugs won't take long to work so you'll be asleep in just a few minutes. You should sleep quietly all night." He patted Charlie on the arm, "so just relax. I'll be back tomorrow to see you. Now you stay in bed and get better, you hear?"

The last thing Chuck heard reverberating in his ear was, "Don't you worry abou-out a thi i i n g."

Cody and Shel sat up alone, talking quietly by the fire as everyone else slept.

"It has been really hard for me to watch Sam go through this without being able to comfort him," Shel said, looking worn out.

"Well, when I want to comfort you, I just take you in my arms and hold you," Cody said as he put one arm around her and slid the other under her legs, lifting her to sit on his lap.

"Well, that wouldn't have been appropriate," she said playfully, taking Cody's face in her hands and kissing him full on the lips. While yielding to his embrace, she whispered, "Oh Cody, I've missed you so much. It has been so hard doing this without you."

"So, is this the nice room you were supposed to get for us when you got here?"

"Shhh!" She whispered with a nervous giggle. "Cody no, not here."

Just then, they heard someone stirring in their sleeping bag and Leroy came walking out of the dark. Shel turned on Cody's lap and sat on the ground between his legs. Cody casually wrapped his arms respectfully around her waist as she sat back, leaning against him.

"Do you mind if I join you? I can't seem to sleep." The tall man sat down across from the couple and began to stir at the fire with a stick. His black hair fell forward over one eye.

"No problem, it's a little early for us to sleep, too," Cody said, a little disappointed to miss out on a romantic interlude with his wife.

"You know I can't stop thinking about Chuck." He turned to look off in the direction of the sleepers and then leaned closer to whisper, "he'd rather die than go to prison and that puts Kate in a particularly dangerous position. He's not going to let her go without a fight."

No one said a word for some time. Leroy spoke again with his eyes fixed on the fire. "I think we're all headed there soon."

"Excuse me?" Cody questioned.

"Ya know, to prison."

"We're going to prison? Why are we going to prison?" Shel spoke indignantly.

"Well, you might call it the 'last days prison ministry'. You know, when Christianity becomes illegal and we get thrown into prison just because we are believers." He paused for a few seconds then continued with, "Those are going to be some exciting days!"

"How's that?" Cody said, not liking the direction the conversation was going.

"Well, look at the stories in the Bible where Christians were thrown into prison and how revivals broke out during their imprisonment. As I read my Bible this morning, a verse jumped out at me. In 2nd Timothy 1:8, it says,

"Therefore do not be ashamed of the testimony of our Lord, nor of me His prisoner, but share with me in the suffering for the gospel according to the power of God."

"Did you catch that? He said 'share with me' as if it were a good thing. That got me to thinking," Leroy continued, "I know what it is to go through trials and to praise the Lord for bringing me out on the other side, but to look forward to the things to come with the attitude of, 'Bring It On!' I don't know if I could do that. But I'm clearly looking at it all wrong, I should be lookin' forward to seeing prison doors opened and captives being set free. To see the stories of the Bible come alive in our own lifetime would be amazing! Do you see what I mean?" But he didn't wait for an answer before he continued, "To see people's lives changed forever is going to be exciting. To stand as a witness with the glory of God shining on our faces like Stephen did, while those looking on see a glimpse of the peace that comes from knowing God.

"The world is going to recognize us as being His, reflecting 'His' Love." Leroy's voice cracked, as he was flooded with the joy of the Lord. "That is something I want more than life itself. Ha!" Leroy burst out with excitement as he clapped a hand over his mouth, then sat silent for a moment before leaning in and saying, "filling the prisons with Christians is going to blow up in the enemy's face! Oh sure, being in prison isn't going to be a party. But we'll get to see the hand of God reach out and touch the lives of folks that have, in most cases, never known the love of a Father before. And, the Lord is going to use us to introduce them to Him. Doesn't that just get you right here?" He thumped his big fist on his muscular chest.

The couple sat and stared at Leroy in his enthusiasm.

Then Cody said, "Well then, I guess we should be praying that God starts preparing their imprisoned hearts right now!"

When Kate woke up, she saw Becky pulling the bedding off the bed opposite her. What had happened to Chuck? She had woke up briefly last night to see him lying on the bed next to her looking quit dead, before she dropped off into unconsciousness once again. She knew without question that he was dead.

She had known he would die if he didn't get help soon, but she had hoped he would be brought back to health once they were found.

Despair washed over her like a flood as she lay on her side, her knees drawn up, and tears sliding over the bridge of her nose and plopping softly down onto her pillow.

Becky rushed over to her side. "Oh Sweetie, are you alright?"

But Kate couldn't speak. Her throat was too sore from dehydration and as she swallowed hard she cracked out, "Where's Chu..." then holding her throat, she put her hand up to stop any further questions.

"Now Kitty, don't you fret, we'll talk about what happened later. But right now, you need to concentrate on getting better.

"I've had you swallow as much liquid as I could, but now that you're awake you really need to drink more." Becky helped her to sit up and scooted in behind her to support her, as Kate sat back in her arms. "Here's some cold ice water, it's better for your throat if it's cold. I have some nice chicken broth I'll bring you. When you're done, and maybe if you're doing better, we can have some tea later and talk."

Kate nodded slightly, thinking that this woman probably wanted to break the news to her that Chuck was dead.

Becky pulled Kate's dirty hair back away from her face. "You'll probably want to take a shower soon too, I imagine." She paused to exclaim, "or a bubble-bath, now that's the ticket! I washed you up as best I could but, well you know, there's just nothing like a nice bubble-bath for us gals to get us back on our feet."

Kate had to admit a bath sounded really good right now but when she went to say, "That would be nice," all that came out was a *squeak*, followed by a *crack*, as she clutched her throat and decided not to try talking for awhile. She simply shook her head in agreement instead.

"Oh, that's alright Sweetheart. You'll be talking right as rain before you know it." Becky scooted out from behind Kate and ran off to run her a bath.

Kate sat against the headboard, surprised to find she was wearing a pink flannel nightgown. Her own clothes were now washed and folded into a neat pile, lying on the dresser by the door. She was still weak and exhausted, but wanted nothing more than to feel 'right as rain', as Becky had put it, so she took another swallow of the ice water.

When Becky came rushing back into the room she said, "I'm so glad you're here Kitty. I'm going to nurse you back to health. Just you wait and see if I don't. Then we'll catch up on the years we've missed."

Kate was confused by Becky's statement. It made her feel like she was this woman's possession or something. *'What ever could she mean?'* But she couldn't speak so she just continued to sip her glass of ice water.

"Now Kitty, I laid ya out a nice clean nightgown along with a towel." She helped Kate up off the bed and into the bathroom. "You need to drink as much as you can, ok? I set up a small table here by the tub so you can keep sipping your water and don't you worry about a thing, you hear? You'll be up and about before you know it. Well, I guess I'll leave you to your bath then. You take your time. My boys, Seth and Micah, are out hunting and my husband, Ken, took Charlie into Ponder. Charlie wanted to visit a friend in the hospital. They'll be back later so you don't have to worry about any men folk comin' banging on the door."

Kate just nodded out of politeness, not knowing why she should care where all the men in the family were and when they'd be back. Although, she did think it would be nice to have some peace and quiet right now.

"I never get any women folk up this way and family even rarer than that," Becky continued to prattle on.

It seemed to Kate the more this woman talked, the more confused and overwhelmed she became. So, she slowly started to close the bathroom door on Becky as the woman continued to speak on the other side.

"Okay, well, like I said, you take your time. We'll talk later."

Kate just pressed her back against the door and thought wearily, *'Oh, I just can't wait!'*

Chuck woke up in the hospital alone and sat up in shock. He remembered coming in to see Paul and recalled vaguely waking up when Ken talked to him. He had hoped it had been nothing more than a bad dream. But instead of being a dream, it was an awful nightmare.

Here he was, stuck smack dab in his own tiny hometown hospital, with nothing to stop anyone 'that might know him' from walking in and recognizing him. He hoped no one had spotted him yet, but how long could that last? He unplugged the intravenous tube and swung his legs over the side of the bed, jumping up so fast that his head swooned. Shuffling into the bathroom, he shut the door as he heard the nurse enter his room.

"Are you ok, Mr. Adams?"

"I'm fine, I just have to go."

Chuck hadn't lied even though he had gone into the bathroom to hide. He did have to go so he pulled the robe away from his bare backside and lowered himself onto the stool while he put his swimming head in his hands to think.

"Ok Mr. Adams, if you need anything don't hesitate to ask. My name is Nurse Stacy. I just came in to work. I'll be your nurse this afternoon."

Fear flooded Chuck's thoughts as his face swung up in shock. 'Oh no, not one of the Stacy girls!' He had gone to school with all the Stacy's and no matter which one it was she would know him for sure.

She asked, "Are you sure you're ok, Mr. Adams?"

"No! I mean yes! I'm fine, thank you!"

Chuck breathed hard as he heard her leave the room. He slowly stood to wash his hands. As he looked in the mirror, he had to clutch onto the sink to keep from falling over. Not only was he horrified with the situation he found himself in, but somewhere along the line he had exchanged his face for a mask of death. His yellowing skin hung on his face like melting wax and his eye sockets were dark holes. His once auburn hair was now dark brown because of two week's worth of oil and grime. Chuck scratched his head, pulling his hair out straight to get a closer look. He realized it was a good thing his red hair was now an indistinguishable color. His normally wavy auburn hair would have been a dead giveaway to his identity.

Maybe no one would recognize him if he kept his mouth shut as much as possible. But when he opened the door, there was Nurse Stacy.

"Mr. Adams, the doctor has asked me to make sure you take a shower as soon as you can. It will make you feel much better to be clean. Here's a toiletry bag with everything you might need in it. I could get a male nurse to assist you, if you would like help."

"No thanks!" Chuck seized the bag from her hand and stepped back into the bathroom as quickly as he could, shutting the door behind him.

"Well, just ring the bell on the wall if you change your mind or need anything," she stated before leaving the room thinking, 'Now who does he remind me of?'

31
Naïve

*Blessed are you when they revile and persecute you,
and say all kinds of evil against you falsely
for My sake.   Matthew 5: 11 NKJV*

"If we keep moving up this here stream, we should come right up on the Barnett place by this afternoon. It'll be a ways off to the left there." Old Lem pointed to the mountain and then to the left as if he could see the house nestled amongst the trees. "Then I'll grab Seth for ya and y'all can move on while Ken gives me a ride back ta town.

"I have ta say I'm more than anxious ta get back home. My old bones aren't used ta sleeping on the cold, hard ground. Not that I'm complainin' none. All this fresh air would make me feel like a young man if'n my old bones weren't complainin' so very much." Rambling on saved Old Lem from having to listen to his old creaking bones or falling asleep as he walked.

After awhile, the old man's voice had became background noise to the rest of the group. They were all lost in their own thoughts so as they failed to respond to him, he turned to the dog. Duke was attentive, giving him a thoughtful glance from time to time as if he understood each word. And of course, he agreed fully with the wise old man. The added benefit of talking to Duke was Lem could make up the dog's responses, which he gladly did as well.

Kate looked at herself in the mirror, gasping in shock at what she saw. There looking back at her was a woman with dark circles under her eyes. Her face had been sunburned and was now peeling. Her cheekbones stuck out as her hollow cheeks drew into shadow. On one cheek and across her forehead, there were deep scratches where she had not seen a bramble hanging from a tree until it was too late.

"Oh Sam, you'll never want to marry me now." And in her weakened state, she tended to believed that it was true. She stepped out of her gown and lowered herself into the hot, bubble bath, where she buried her face in her hands and wept bitterly.

Kate cried for some time and was still in the tub when she began to hear a male voice talking to Becky. She couldn't make out what was being said. She slid down into the water to try and escape from a world that, in her view, had drastically changed for the worse. When she emerged from the water, the voices had stopped.

Finally, when the bath had become cold, Kate felt it was time to get out. She raised her sickly body up out of the tub, dried herself off, and retreated back into the bedroom, closing the door behind her. Crawling back into bed, she pulled the blankets up over her head to shut out the light. The sun peeked in the window at her, pleading with her to share the beautiful day, but she didn't want it's cheerful intrusion.

No, she just wanted to be left alone. She most definitely didn't want the company of Becky Barnett, who she had only ever seen once in the diner a couple of years ago. Becky had been with someone else, so her and Kate hadn't even spoken, other than, "what can I get for you?" and receive her order. So, was it any wonder that Kate had no desire to, as Becky put it, 'catch up on the years they had missed'. Kate didn't remember ever hearing much about Becky, but in her view she seemed to be a little more than strange.

Kate couldn't bear the thought of hearing Becky say, 'your friend Chuck is dead.' She didn't want to know. She was tired and crushed. Not only had she been ripped away from her friends and family to miss her own wedding, but she felt certain she had lost the only opportunity she would ever have to witness to Chuck. She was supposed to have been a witness of God's love to his poor lost soul, but throughout her life she had been anything but Christ-like towards him. He may have been getting closer to accepting the Lord, but now it was too late, forever too late.

As Kate thought of Sam, she knew she could never call him to come get her, allowing him to see her looking like a hideous monster. She was weak, both physically and mentally, and couldn't think right. What she really wanted right now was a friend to talk with so she could sort things out. But even though Becky sat waiting for her to join her for tea, Kate lay in her bed and cried herself to sleep. Depression had overtaken her, causing her to feel like all was lost.

Molly didn't tell her folks she had gone to the movies with Talon instead of Pam and that Talon had asked her to go again today. She had fun and as long as they didn't find out, she was happy with the arrangement. But walking towards the theater after school, she stopped when she saw Talon's friends starting to show up. Even though Talon seemed very nice, Molly was uncomfortable with his friends, so she stepped back into the shadows. "Lord what am I doing this for?" She prayed not expecting an answer.

When Talon arrived, he spoke just as loud and coarse as his friends, and Molly decided she had seen enough. One by one his friends went in, leaving Talon pacing back and forth for a long while before he also went in. Molly waited a few moments longer before dashing out into the street and running all the way home alone.

The stream was getting smaller and smaller as they got closer to the top of the ridge.

"Now y'all set down and give yourselves a rest as I run up ta the house and get young Seth for y'all." What the old man was doing couldn't possibly be considered running by anyone but himself, and as he moved away, Duke followed happily.

Shel called him back, "Duke, come!" But he kept his nose to the ground as he walked around a shed, and then walked right up to the old man.

Old Lem had stopped to watch the dog but thought nothing of it.

"Do you think he found something?" Sam asked.

"Nah, the locks on that shed look new, Chuck couldn't have gone in there." Lem went down on one knee. "I reckon' he wants ta go with me, we're good friends by now, ya know."

The old man seemed pleased but at the same time concerned that he had somehow caused the dog to lose focus. "Duke, ya can't come with me. Ya have ta go back to your master. She's goin' ta need ya ta finish your job here. Now ya get on back there and I'll see ya back in town before ya leave ta go home. I promise ya that." He rubbed the dog's head roughly as Duke's ears flopped back and forth. Old Lem patted the hound once more before raising himself up off the ground with an effort.

Duke turned to look at his master who was already sitting on some soft grass. He sat down and put his head on the ground and whined one long sigh at the feet of Old Lem.

"I'm sorry missy. Perhaps if ya let him sniff Chuck and Kate's things, he'd be raring' ta go again?" Lem suggested.

Sam dug out the plastic bags containing the items of clothing for both Kate and Chuck, and held them out under the dog's nose. But it didn't seem to change the dog's mind. He still wanted to go with the old man to the Barnett's.

"Duke, Come!" Shel demanded.

Duke walked back to his master and sat with his head down on his paws and watched as the old man walked away. The hound seemed disappointed he didn't get to go along, releasing a mournful howl, but his friend kept going. The dog dropped his head down onto his paws and let out a long sigh of frustration.

Old Lem stepped up to the screen door and knocked. "Hello, is anyone here?" The door creaked as he stepped inside.

Becky peeked around the corner, then came and joined him in the front room.

"Hey! How you doing Lem, we haven't seen you out here in a coon's age. Come set down. I was just about to make some tea for my kin and myself. You want to join us?" She walked back around the corner as Lem followed her into the kitchen. She continued, "she showed up here unexpectedly, but I was still thrilled just the same to see her. I haven't seen Kitty since I was a teen-ager and she was around seven. She doesn't look the same as she did then, but she still has that familiar look about her. You know what I mean?"

"Sure, people change as they get older. I guess I could have some tea. I come lookin' for Seth, is he here?"

"No, he and Micah are off hunting. I don't expect them home until sundown or there abouts."

"Well, is Ken here then?"

"No, he went into Ponder with Charlie. Seems he had a friend in the hospital he wanted to visit."

"Who's Charlie?"

"Oh, he's my kin's intended. She's off taking a bath. They're hikers, you know. They hiked across country to get here. They've been awful tired and sick but they're doing much better now. I don't think I would have the stamina to do that kind of thing. But Kitty is several years younger than I am and that can make all the difference. She'll be out of her bath soon and you can meet her."

"Oh, I'm sorry Becky, but it's important I get back, since Seth isn't going to be back until dark. We had planned on getting here later, so I told him I'd be comin' by to get him tonight. But, here we are sooner than planned. Can I use your phone?"

"Sure you can! The phone's around the corner there on the wall."

He walked around the corner and picked up the phone to call the Pastor Smith. He told him everything that had been happening before adding, "we got here way too early and Seth isn't here, so I'll be going on with the search party so we can keep moving. We think we're getting close! Keep prayin' pastor. I don't know how much more of this mountain climbing an old man can take. See ya soon. Thanks a lot, bye."

"Becky, I'm goin' ta take off now, sorry about the tea. Could ya tell Seth I won't be by tonight? But, if he could catch up with us in the mornin' that would be great! We followed the creek up and will be goin' on to Ponder. We sure could use some help navigatin' these mountains and he knows them better then anyone." He turned to go as Becky followed close behind. "Sure,

I will Lem. I hope everything's ok," she said with concern.

"Oh sure, we're just havin' a mite of trouble trackin' down some folks and we could use his help, that's all. Don't worry yourself over it, if Seth could just meet us there tomorrow, we'll get this wrapped up."

"I'll tell him. Thanks for dropping by Lem. I'm sure Kitty will be disappointed not to have met you, but I guess that can't be helped. See ya later. Bye!" Becky threw her hand up in a wave as the old man disappeared down the path.

Pam showed up at the Mill's farm late in the afternoon and Molly led her off through the trees to talk privately. Pam seemed to be mad, but Molly didn't understand why she would be upset. All of a sudden, Pam clutched Molly's arm, spinning her around, and yelled in her face, "You were supposed to be my friend, but you humiliated Talon instead, and now his friend Brace will never look at me again."

Molly looked at her in disbelief. "Believe me, you're better off without Brace." Molly couldn't believe the transformation she was seeing in her so-called friend and now doubted every thing she said. "Were you really babysitting for the Tillman's or was that a lie?"

"Ha, the Tillman's don't call me when they want a babysitter. You should know that! Tess is the only one they'll trust with their precious babies." Pam's words dripped with sarcasm and bitterness as she laughed at Molly for believing her in the first place.

Molly stared in horror and her eyes flared as Pam continued, "You're such a simpleton Molly. How can you possibly think I'm better off without Brace? He's one of the coolest and cutest guys in school."

"Coolest, are you kidding me, he's a jerk!" Molly was madder than she could ever remember being. She hated to be laughed at, but most of all she felt like a fool for thinking this girl was ever her friend.

Pam spun around and stormed off, yelling back at Molly, "I don't have any more time to spend on you. You're a hopeless cause. Go back to your old boring, stupid, simple-minded friends, and stop messing up my life."

Molly just stood there staring after her in horror and disbelief. She was angry, but still she couldn't stop the tears from streaming down her face.

32

Out of the Dark

The wicked man does deceptive work,
But he who sows righteousness
will have a sure reward.
Proverbs 11: 18 NKJV

Chuck did take a shower but was careful not to wash his hair as he felt hiding the color of his hair was still important. His head itched after the steam of the shower so he scratched it fiercely with the comb provided in the toiletry bag. Then he combed his coarse wavy hair, flattening it out as best he could. After looking at himself in the mirror, he was content to know that no one would recognize him, at least until he started to look like he was alive again.

He was feeling somewhat better, although still weak. He hadn't been heaving or evacuating his bowels for he didn't know how long. He asked himself, "How many days has it been?" Time seemed to have gotten lost somewhere along the line. Clearly, whatever Becky had done for him had worked some and the antibiotics seemed to be finishing his healing.

Chuck put on a clean hospital gown and after slowly walking over to his bed, weakly, dropped down onto it. After eating the so-called meal, he covered his head and fell asleep.

Molly had been quiet all day, going off alone to walk among the trees on their Christmas tree farm. She found herself repeatedly sitting with her feet dangling in the water of a nearby creek, staring into its hypnotic sheen as the current worked its way around her hot feet before it continued downstream.

Late in the afternoon, she wandered home to help with supper preparations. She worked in silence and during the meal, just picked at her food. After finishing the evening dishes, Molly asked if she could go to bed early.

Gray and Maureen looked at each other with concern. "Yes, go ahead if you like," her mom said.

Molly went to her room and closed the door. But as soon as she crawled into bed, she heard a knock. "Come in," she said. Her mom entered and closed the door behind her.

"Molly, what's the matter? You haven't been yourself today. Is there something wrong? Do you want to talk about it?"

Molly did want to talk but she didn't know exactly what to say or if she should say anything at all. So in frustration, she began to cry as she reached out for her mother.

"Oh Molly," Maureen rushed to her daughter's side and sat holding her girl in her arms. "It's going to be alright Sweetheart. Please let me help you. Things seem so much heavier when you try to carry them by yourself."

Starting from the beginning, Molly told her mom how Pam had tricked her into going to the movies with Talon and how he and his friends had treated her. Then she told her about what had happened after school and how she ran home instead of meeting him again. Lastly, she related how Pam had come over to tell her off and now they were no longer friends. Molly buried her face in her mother's shoulder and shook convulsively.

"Oh Molly, we all make mistakes in life but if you love the Lord, He promises that those mistakes will work out for our good." She kissed the top of Molly's head and asked, "What ever happened to Rachel and Tess? They were good friends to you and they never tried to lead you into things that compromised your beliefs."

"I don't know. They didn't like Pam and she said I had to stop being the third wheel of their tricycle. It made sense at the time."

"But it doesn't now?" Her Mom asked quietly.

"No, I guess it doesn't. Pam was playing me for a fool from the beginning, wasn't she?"

"It sure looks that way."

"Mom, I'm so embarrassed." She pressed herself into her mother's arms once again and wept bitterly.

When Molly finally grew quiet, Maureen said, "You know, your Dad and I have had a hard time keeping up with you growing so fast. Maybe it's time for you to get some new clothes. How about you call Rachel and Tess and go out shopping with them this weekend? Would you like that?"

"How? None of us have our driver's license yet."

"Well, I was talking to Tess's mom at church last Sunday and she said Tess was going in this week to take her driver's test. She may already have her license!"

Maureen's head was coming down to plant another kiss on the top of her daughter's head when Molly shot up almost colliding into her, saying with enthusiasm, "Yeah! Can I call them right now?"

"Oh, I thought you were tired." Her mother teased her with a smile.

But Molly ignored her taunt and kissed her on the cheek saying, "I love you Mom!" She then flew toward her phone.

Maureen got up, "I love you too, Sweetie." She smiled and quietly left the room, leaving Molly to talk with her old and true friends.

A sliver of moon showed through the trees as a cloud cut across its dim light, scattering the light along the lines of its edges. The trees held their menacing black arms out over the heads of the group that slept beneath them. The fire had gone out long ago and now just emitted the slightest red glow. The cooling embers made a quiet ticking sound, like a clock without the sense of time, all while the springs babbled quietly in the background.

Old Lem lay facing up as he tried to get comfortable enough to sleep. But it was no good; something was bothering him about his conversation with Becky. He played it back in his head over and over again. What was it that troubled him about what she had said?

'The boys went hunting.' No, they're always hunting something. 'Ken went to Ponder with her kin's intended to visit someone in the hospital". No, of course Ken would take him to see his friend. 'Becky was going to have tea with her cousin'. No, that too was a fine thing to do. He would have joined them if Seth had been there. What else was there? "That's all Lord, nothing was out of place so why can't I sleep?" He grumbled to himself.

"What'd you say?" Leroy whispered as he had also been wrestling with the Lord in prayer most of the night.

"Oh, I'm sorry if I woke you!" Lem whispered back.

"No, the Lord won't let me sleep. I can't help but feel like we missed something yesterday."

"I know what ya mean, I've been recallin' back the conversation I had with Becky, but it all seems to be such a very average day, if you know what I mean."

"Well, tell me about it then. Sometimes you can't hear what's wrong until you say it out loud," Leroy stated.

"True. Well, I knocked on the screen door and then I stepped into the house as Becky came out of the kitchen ta meet me. She invited me ta have tea with her and her cousin. Becky said she was surprised that they had come as she wasn't expecting them and she hadn't seen her cousin since she was small. She said her and her intended had hiked there and that they had been tired and sick.

"I asked her if Seth was there, 'no' she said, 'he and Micah were out hunting'. So, I asked her if Ken was there. 'No', she said, 'he went in ta Ponder with her kin's intended ta take him ta visit a friend at the hospital'. Charlie was his name. Charlie and ahh... Kitty I think it was." Lem stopped all of a sudden and took a deep breath and held it.

"What's the matter?"

"That's it! Charlie and Kitty!" He yelled out in the dark.

Cody moaned from the darkness, "What are you yelling about in the middle of the night?" Then he gave a ginormous yawn that threatened to split his head from ear to ear.

"Charlie and Kitty!"

"Who in the world are Charlie and Kitty?" Sam spat out impatiently.

"Don't you get it? Charlie and Kitty... Chuck and Kate?"

Sam sat up suddenly. "What in the world are you talking about?"

"Becky said Kitty was taking a bath and that she was sick. While Charlie, her intended, had gone into Ponder to visit a friend in the hospital."

Shel rolled over, "It's the middle of the night Lem, please just spit it out. Who is Kitty and Charlie? And while you're at it, who's Becky?"

Sam was sitting, looking blindly in Old Lem's direction as Lem went on.

"Don't you see? Chuck and Kate. Charlie and Kitty are their alias names."

"You mean Chuck and Kate were at the Barnett's?" Leroy asked as he struggled to get out of his sleeping bag.

Sam stood, knocking something over in the dark.

Leroy stood up next to Sam. "Now Sam, the best thing we can do right now is to pray. If we try to start out now, even with flashlights, we'll all probably walk off in the wrong direction. We'll be worse off than if we had just stayed put."

Sam stepped around Leroy and tripped over Cody's feet, falling forward onto the hot coals. "OWW! Oh man," he jumped back, landing on both 's legs.

"Hey, calm down buddy, we'll find them." Cody yelled as he sat up to push Sam off.

"Sorry," Sam said, "I guess you were right Leroy, about hurting ourselves. There are a few hot coals still in that fire."

Now Shel came to life, having stayed put until now. "Did you burn yourself?"

"Yeah, I'm afraid so."

33
Fly on the Wall

...You shall be called by a new name,
Which the mouth of the Lord will name.
Isaiah 62: 2 NKJV

Chuck woke early the next morning and sat straight up. All was quiet in the hospital as he slipped out of bed and listened carefully. There was a distant sound of a rattling cart rolling down the hall and a few hushed voices as they spoke in passing. Chuck felt much better this morning and as he stepped into the bathroom and looked in the mirror, he noticed he looked much better too. He was starting to look like Chuck Atteberry again.

"I thought you were gone," he said to himself as he looked at his reflection and thought, 'I need to go see Paul before someone recognizes me.' He ran the comb through his hair and splashed some cold water on his face as someone passed his room. He grabbed a towel and dried his face extra long until whoever it was had passed.

"OK, ready or not, here I come." He started off down the hall towards Paul's room and then slipped inside behind the curtain. There, he found Paul lying with his head wrapped in bandages. Both of his eyes were blackened, fading into a sickening green color. Paul lay silent, not moving, and Chuck suddenly felt sick seeing what he had done to him. He dropped into the chair next to the bed and, after burying his face in his hands, said, "I'm sorry Paul! I'm sorry! I didn't mean to hurt you. I'm so sorry!" He had said what he had come to say but still he sat glued to his chair. When he suddenly felt a hand touch his arm, he sat up with a start.

"Paul, you're alright! Are you alright?"

"I'm alright Chuck or at least I will be."

"I'm so sorry Paul, I just wanted you to know that and to tell you I'm 'free indeed' now." Chuck grinned timidly.

A moment of silence passed between the two men before a broad smile spread across Paul's face. "I'm so glad Chuck, I can't tell you how happy I am for you."

"The name's 'Charlie' now."

"Charlie?"

"Yeah, Charlie." He told Paul how the woman named Shel had told him the story of Saul on the road to Damascus last fall and how, as he lay sick at the Barnett's house, Micah had told him the same story. In the end, God changed Saul's name to Paul. "At first, I changed my name so they wouldn't figure out who I really was," Charlie said, "but after being set free indeed, I decided to change my name permanently." Chuck continued, "Do you think that God might have had a hand in the changing of my name? I mean, like He had me hear that story twice so I would finally give my life to Him?"

Paul smiled slightly, "I'm sure He did Charlie." He squeezed Charlie's hand, "but what you're describing to me is called being 'born again'."

Charlie was silent for a moment before a smile began to turn up the corners of his mouth. "That's it... that's exactly what it feels like... like I'm new, like I've been... 'born again'!"

Mandy walked down the hall of the hospital with a vase of assorted spring flowers for her friend Paul. This was only the second time she had come to see him. The first time, he had been sleeping and still wasn't capable of talking. She had been told not to expect too much more today by the receptionist at the front desk.

"But go ahead and go on in, he'll be glad to see you! The doctor says it's good for him to talk so try and get him to say a few words."

But as Mandy approached the room, she could already hear talking. It was Paul speaking for the most part and as she got closer she froze as she recognized the other voice as being that of Chuck Atteberry. What should she do? Had he come to finish Paul off? Her mind spun out of control, stirring her into a frenzy.

Her hands began to shake and she decided to set the flowers down on the floor before she dropped them. As she leaned down to set them by the door, she ventured a peek inside. She saw Chuck sitting in the chair with his head down and his back to the door. Mandy looked at Paul and as their eyes met, he shook his head ever-so-gently and raised one hand slightly off the bed in a stop motion. Whipping his fingers down twice as if to say, "sit down ... stay there."

Charlie stood and walked to the window, looking out as he ran his fingers back through his dirty hair, only to repeat the action over and over again as he spoke.

"I'm so sorry Paul, I can't tell you how sorry I am. I wish I had given my life to the Lord years ago. What was I hanging on to? I've been so miserable." He fell silent as Paul began to speak words to comfort and encourage him. Mandy sat back against the wall in the hall as she sighed with a smile.

At the break of dawn, Sam pounded franticly on the door of the small house in the woods. Micah opened the door as Skippy, who had been barking excitedly, now sat back in silence and wet himself at the sight of the tall wild-eyed man.

"Can I help you sir?" The boy brushed the back of his hand over his sleepy eyes.

"Yes, we're looking for Chuck Atteberry and Kate McClure. Have you seen them? Were they here?" The police chief's rushed words made him sound angry.

"No, I can't say that we've seen them sir." The boy stepped back to make room for his Dad.

"We don't get many visitors up this way," Ken said as he looked around the chief of police to see the others coming up the path behind him. Since the Barnett's lived closer to Bennington, they had never met Chuck and hadn't seen Kate McClure since she was a small girl.

"Well, this Chuck Atteberry is a dangerous man," Sam continued, "he killed a man last year and he nearly killed another while escaping a transport van on his way to prison."

Ken stood with his mouth hanging open.

As he stood from wiping Skippy's puddle up off the floor, Seth asked, "What's that name again?"

"Chuck Atteberry!"

Seth's brow came down as he tried to remember an obscure recollection of that name. Maybe Molly had mentioned it while he was daydreaming the other day? He vaguely remembered the name but nothing more as he had been wrestling with other thoughts at the time.

Then Ken spoke again, "You can't mean that nice young man, Charlie Adams? I took him to the hospital in Ponder yesterday. He wanted to go see a friend there." Sam's eyes about fell out of his head as he heard Leroy say in a whisper behind him, "Paul." He whipped his head around to look at Leroy for a moment then back to Ken.

Ken just continued with, "But once Charlie got there he passed out cold in the waiting room. Sick as a dog he is. Becky tried everything she could to heal him up, but it just hadn't been enough. The doctor said he has side effects from the parasites..."

Fear rose as Sam finally shouted, "Where's Kate!?" as he began to falter and stumble back a step. Leroy clasped one of his arms to steady him as Cody stepped up on his other side to help support the tall man.

As Becky made her way down the hall, pulling her robe tightly around her, Old Lem moved around the police chief. Positioning himself in front of Sam, he calmly said, "Kitty? You said you had a woman named Kitty visiting?"

"Kitty? You want Kitty?" She asked then turned and called down the hall for her. They all turned to look.

Kate stepped out of one of the rooms in a full-length white flannel nightgown, sprayed with a delicate pattern of blue rosettes. Her dark hair tumbled in long waves over her shoulders. Her face was pale, with a kiss of pink that played across her cheeks and lips. Her eyebrows pulled up in the center as her mouth pulled down into a pout. Her lips moving as she said simply, in a hushed tone, "Sam?"

At that, Sam pushed Lem aside and ran to her, throwing his arms around her waist and lifting her up off the floor. Her toes stood on the tips of his shoes as she laid her head on his chest and let a low and mournful moan escape her innermost being.

"What is it Kate?" He pressed his lips into her hair as she moaned once again.

"He's dead Sam, he's dead...Chuck's dead."

245

Mandy sat for what seemed like hours, listening like a fly on the wall, as the two men spoke calmly to each other. Tears of joy slid down her face as they laughed and prayed together. And all the while, Paul's voice never faltered. Only once did she have to stand and put a hand up to stop a nurse from coming in to check on Paul.

"Oh, is he sleeping?"

Mandy nodded, not wanting to explain there was a criminal in the room with Paul. Not yet anyway. She, along with Kate and Paul, had grown up with Chuck. And, even though she and Kate had given up on him years ago, Paul had never failed to lift up a prayer for Chuck's lost soul. So it was only right that he was able to minister to, and encourage him now. Chuck would be off to prison soon enough and then who would be there for him?

As Mandy sat on the hard tile floor in the hall by the vase of flowers, the door at the end of the hall suddenly burst open and in ran the Sam with Leroy and Cody close behind. The police chief leaned in over the counter and spoke in hushed tones to the receptionist, who stood sharply as her eyes flew over the list of patients in the hospital.

Mandy stood and calmly walked down the hall towards the men. "Sam," she said as she stood at his elbow, "Paul's fine and witnessing to our new brother in the Lord."

Sam turned to look at her, trying to understand what she might mean, when Leroy said with a smile, "Chuck?"

"Yes, Chuck," she nodded and smile, "or as the hospital staff knows him, Charlie Adams."

The nurse's finger stopped on the name Charlie Adams and she looked at Sam there in his uniform, with apologetic eyes.

Paul didn't want to lie back down but he had no strength left in him to sit up any more. He had prayed for this day for so long and now that it had come, he didn't have the strength to keep up the conversation any longer. He began to shift in his bed but felt helpless to work his way back down into a lying position. He fell back on the hard headboard, which sent a sharp pain through his still bandaged head.

"Oh be careful", Charlie said as he stepped up beside him and helped him to slide down into the bed. Just as the police chief rounded the corner, Charlie slid his arm out from under Paul and began to pull the thin white blanket up around his neck. Sam leapt into action, whipping out his handcuffs. Taking Charlie down across Paul's legs, he snapped the cold metal around his wrists, one after the other, with speed and precision.

"Sam please, he was just helping me to lay back down, that's all," Paul said weakly as his eyes flickered before closing again.

Sam turned Charlie around to look at him and saw an expression of hurt in his eyes. Sam had dealt with a lot of different feelings for Chuck in the last several days but pity wasn't one of them. He didn't feel the least bit sorry for the man. Charlie didn't fight him, but instead seemed reconciled to taking that long ride to prison.

Leroy stepped in close and pulled Charlie into his arms, practically burying him in his chest as Charlie's laugh became muffled. But, he was defenseless now to push his big friend away.

"You're going to smother him you big galoot!" Mandy said as she pushed her way between the two men and wrapped one arm around Charlie's middle. "Welcome to the family of God!" She said as her head came up to look him in the eyes, laughing merrily. "I'm going to make myself quite the pest, I'm afraid."

She nodded energetically as she continued, "I'll send you Bible studies or whatever you need. Oh, Oh, I know! Care packages, that would be fun!" She threw her hands up in her excitement as everyone in the room laughed except for Sam, who was not amused, and Paul, who had fallen back to sleep.

When Kate walked into the room, Charlie only looked at her for a moment before he found his eyes back on Mandy. He had always seen Mandy as being an obstacle that stood between him and Kate. A ridiculously excitable girl, but now her exuberance made it feel like there was still a glimmer of hope in the world. He swallowed hard and with a trembling smile said, "Thank you, I would like that."

34

One Of Us

So God did what the law could not do.
He sent his own Son in a body
like the bodies we sinners have.
And in that body God declared an end
to sin's control over us
by giving his Son as a sacrifice for our sins.
Romans 8: 3 NLT

Charlie lay in the hospital bed being poked and prodded by the doctor to determine if he was well enough to be moved to the state prison. Chief of Police Samuel Trusty sat outside the hospital room along with Leroy. Sam was clearly agitated, his face drawn into a sneer as he got up and began to pace back and forth.

Leroy, watching him, began to speak. "Why are you so mad Sam?"

"I just want him to leave. I don't know why he has to stay here. I shouldn't be expected to deal with him after what he did to Paul and Kate."

"Sam, Chuck has repented. He's a brother in the Lord now and both Paul and Kate have forgiven him." Leroy tried to reason with him. "Besides, he was extremely sick when he came in and he may not be able to be moved yet."

"Well, I can't forgive him. What if it's all an act? What if he gets out and does it again?"

"So, you're afraid he'll escape on your watch?"

"No, but what if..." Sam spun away in frustration, walking to a window to collect his thoughts. When he turned back around he said, "It's just that, how can we ever trust him? How can we believe there has been a true conversion? Has..." Sam turned back to the window.

Leroy finished his thought. "You want to know if God has really forgiven him?"

"Yeah, exactly! Aren't we supposed to judge each others fruits?"

"But, are you judging his fruits or trying to be his judge? There's a difference Sam." Leroy looked Sam in the eye as silence passed between them.

Sam turned back to the window and became lost in his thoughts.

"Ya know Sam, I've always been a fan of the futuristic type Sci-Fi's. In one of my favorite movies, there is a scene that has always stood out to me as having a deeper meaning. Each time I watched the movie, I would think on that scene in the back of my mind for hours, but I never saw the parallel until recently.

"In the movie, a man in black comes in trying to find the robot guilty of a particular crime, and for illustration purposes, let me call the crime 'sin'. All the robots in this large warehouse look exactly the same, lined up in rows, one beside the other. They all have the same face, legs, arms and chest. There are 1001 robots, 'one more than was accounted for'.

" 'The Accuser', the man in black, points his gun at one of the robots standing in the front row and says, 'Which one of you is the sinner?'

" 'One of us'," Leroy said, using a monotone voice to depict all of the robots responding in unison.

"Which one?"

" 'One of us'," Leroy repeated. "Ok, we know the Word says that 'all have sinned and fall short of the glory of God'. So picture it, can you see the row upon row of robots, each one looking like the next?"

"Sure," Sam said not knowing where Leroy was going with his illustration.

"Well, you know Sam, this is exactly the way God sees us. We are all the 'sinner' in the room. The murderer is standing next to the boy who steals an extra bite of the cookie before sharing it with his brother. We all have the same filth on our hands, 'sin'.

"Now in the movie, the accuser points a gun at the head of one of the robots in the front row and shoots him in order to flush out the 'sinner' from among them. How would it look, when 'the Accuser' comes and says, 'which one of you is the sinner?' if 'One of us' stepped out and points a finger at the brother or sister next to him? Does the one being pointed at look different as he holds his stance? No!" Leroy continued, "the 'One of us' doing the pointing looks different! In fact, the 'One of us' doing the pointing looks more like 'the Accuser' that points in order to kill and destroy. He doesn't look like the One who came to stand in our place, paying the penalty for our sins, giving up everything, even heaven, to become, - 'One of us'."

Kate fell into her Granny's arms as the two came together, both clinging to each other for a long time.

"Oh Granny, I'm okay now," Kate said.

Tears slid freely down the old woman's face, into deep ravines, only to reappear at the ends of her wrinkles and drop down onto Kate's shoulder.

"I knew you were going to be alright, you had the Lord with you after all. I just didn't know if I'd ever see you again." With that, a new surge of tears spilled down her aged face.

"Well, I'm awful glad to be back, but I'm going to need some fattening up." Kate smiled slyly with fond affection at the dear old woman she knew would rise to the challenge. "And I still feel like I could sleep for a week."

Granny took her hand as if she might never let it go and ushered her into the kitchen to get her started on the fattening up. "I made some chicken soup when I heard they found ya. Ya just set right down here while I get ya a big bowl of it."

Kate didn't tell her she had eaten so much chicken soup in the last few days that she was afraid she might grow feathers and start clucking soon.

Granny walked over to the stove where she had the soup heating and scooped out a generous serving. "Now, tell me what happened with Chuck. We've all been prayin' and-a prayin' for that boy, so tell me, what's the Lord's done?" She sat the bowl of soup down and pulled up a chair across from Kate.

Kate smiled and as tears welled up in her eyes she said, "He got saved Granny! I'm so happy! I've been praying for him since he kidnapped me, more than I ever had before, much to my shame. You can't know how much I've grown these two weeks. Forgiveness is such a powerful thing, Granny! How could I have ever thought I was acting Christ-like when I had such a hatred in my heart for Chuck?"

They both sat in silence for a few moments as Kate sipped at the hot broth.

"Well, you'd think bein' old like I am, there wouldn't be anything left for me ta be learnin', but I've been askin' myself that same question."

"You should have seen him Granny, he's a changed man! Just like the scriptures say, 'a new creation'."

"I'm happy for him. He's had himself a hard life but because of it he'll rest better in the Lord's arms than you or I could ever imagine being possible. Like the scripture says in Luke 7:47,

"Therefore I say to you, her sins, which are many, are forgiven, for she loved much.
But to whom little is forgiven, the same loves little."

"I've been thinking more about forgiveness lately. I mean, I want folks to see I have forgiven Chuck and that he's a new creation. He's so deeply repentant Granny," Kate looked up with tears in her eyes. "I just want everyone to see the love and forgiveness of Christ, I want to make everyone see that it..." Kate's voice cracked and then failed her all together as tears ran down her face unchecked. She sat looking longingly at her Granny, wanting her to understand the depth of what she was feeling.

At long last the old woman spoke, "Kate, I see your heart Sweetie." She sat forward and extended her hand toward her granddaughter. "That's the way things ought ta be, especially amongst brothers and sisters in Christ. I'm so proud of you." The old woman patted her hand and added, "You can't make people see good when they want ta see bad. They'll believe what they want to believe, that's just the way we are as human beings. It's our sin nature ya know and no one is exempt from it, not even Christians I'm sorry ta say."

❖ ❖ ❖ ❖ ❖

It had been decided that Charlie would stay in the hospital for a few more days. After that his condition would be evaluated again before a decision would be made on whether he was ready to be moved to the prison. He had already been placed in a more secure room and was now being guarded by the state police.

As Sam sat in his office catching up on his backed up paperwork, his Secretary Pauline opened his door with, "Ralph called again." She rolled her eyes and continued, "He said that the dog next door dug up his flowerbed again. He wants to talk to you this time, so I told him I'd have you call him back when you're available." She threw a hand up in exasperation and backed away from the door as Kate came strolling in. Pauline gave Sam a nod as she stepped forward and pulled the door closed behind her, leaving Sam and Kate alone.

"Police Chief Trusty, do you think you could take a little break and join me for some coffee?" Kate sat two steaming cups down on the coffee table across the room, then sat down on the worn leather couch against the wall and waited for a response.

Sam stood. "Well, I don't know ma'am. You see, I've been out scouring the county looking for a little gal who got herself kidnapped and I haven't had a minute to finish up my paperwork. So how's about you tell me what this is all about?" He meandered over and sat next to her on the couch.

She fell into his arms and said, "I love you Sam."

"Well!" His eyes popped open, "If you're going to put it that way ma'am, I guess there's nothing I can do but to accommodate you!" She laughed as he pulled her head closer, running his fingers through her hair and held her for a moment.

"Sam, you have to try this coffee. I had been thinking about adding a coffee bar to our diner to bring in the morning crowd."

Sam chuckled at the word 'crowd'.

"Oh hush!" Kate said as she handed him his cup. "Anyway, while I've been gone, Granny went and bought a fancy espresso machine and has been keeping herself busy trying new coffee drinks. I think this is really good! What do you think?"

Sam didn't tell her he had already been one of Granny's guinea pigs. "Mmm, this is good!" He had to admit she was getting much better at it.

Picking up her own cup, and staring at the steam that rose around a dollop of whipped cream, Kate said, "Well, Pastor Smith says Saturday at the same time will be just fine for the wedding. Everything is falling into place just like nothing bad has happened and..." she paused as she looked into his eyes.

"And?" He stated after her pause.

"And, I don't think anything bad has happened. I mean plenty has happened but I choose to look at the good that has come out of this." She watched his face intently to see his reaction.

Sam's eyes got big. "Kate, are you crazy? Chuck kidnapped you for crying out loud!"

"I know he did, but he didn't hurt me. He came in on his own to ask Paul to forgive him and most importantly, he's given his life to the Lord, Sam. Are you telling me you don't believe in forgiveness?" She snapped back.

She sat her cup down, stood up and walked over to the window to look out, with arms folded over her chest. "Sam, I have come to understand Charlie this week. He needs us to forgive him. He needs us to love him like the brother he is."

Sam got up and walked over to her as she stood by the window, wrapped his arms around her and held her. "You're right Sweetie. Leroy told me pretty much the same thing."

Saying no more, she just stood there enjoying his embrace.

35
Dark Tongue

And do not be conformed to this world,
but be transformed by the renewing of your mind,
that you may prove what is that good and
acceptable and perfect will of God.
Romans 12: 2 NKJV

After calling too late to cancel his last meeting with Gray, Seth set up another meeting at McClure's Diner. So now, he had to start all over trying to find things to keep him busy until 9:30 this morning. He was glad McClure's would be closing early today for Sam and Kate's wedding, having their meeting earlier made his day more bearable.

Again this morning, Micah and Skippy followed him everywhere he went. "Why can't I go? I want some ice cream!" Micah begged.

"No, you can't go. I have business to talk over with Gray, man talk."

"Oh, I know," Micah, said with a taunting tone, "Seth and Molly, sitting in a tree, K-I-S-S-I-N-G..."

"Stop it, go away! Believe me, sitting in a tree is the last place I would want to be." He stopped himself short of saying, "with Molly." His mind had put him in a lot of places with her, but never in a tree. "Go away! You don't understand."

The day of the wedding had finally come and Kate stumbled groggily around her room, trying to remember all she needed to do today. She looked in the mirror at the evidence she had not slept well, her green eyes blinking behind heavy lids that seemed to belong to someone else. "Well, what are you looking at? You have a lot to get done today missy, so you better get started," Kate said to herself as she pulled a comb through her dirty hair. She needed to get a shower before going into town later in the day, but for now she tied it back out of her face and went to get dressed.

Mandy and Shel would be meeting her at the church this morning and when they were done decorating, the three of them would be off to the city to get their hair and makeup done.

Kate looked at the clock on her nightstand and said with a start, "Oh, I'm late!" She was supposed to meet Sam this morning so they could have breakfast together, and pray a blessing over each other and the day. They both felt it was ultimately better than hiding from each other, in hopes of it bringing them some false sense of 'good luck'. They chose instead to look to God for His blessing.

She sat putting on her sneakers by the door when Granny called out to her, "Good morning Kate! I'll be closing up the shop as soon as Gray and Seth finish their meeting."

Kate sat up from tying her shoes and took the coffee Granny handed her. She drew in it's deep rich flavor and held it in her mouth for a moment, before swallowing slowly, feeling the warm rush that flooded her senses. "I have to go Granny. I'm late to meet Sam." She took another mouthful of coffee and repeating the action of the previous swallow, sighed deeply before handing the cup back to Granny. "I love ya. I'll be back around two, bye!" She kissed the old woman on the cheek, grabbed a jacket, and ran out the door while scolding herself, "Get going girl, being late isn't a very good way to start your big day!"

Talon felt certain Molly had been influenced by her friends to stay away from him and he wasn't yet willing to let her go quietly. As he saw her walking down the street with Rachel, he approached her. "Molly, can I talk to you?" he asked.

"Yes," she said as Rachel took her arm and stepped in close with a protective stance.

"Alone?" he said impatiently.

"No, you can't talk to her alone. She's never alone; she has friends and she has God on her side." Rachel sneered at him.

With that, Talon took Molly's other arm and jerked hard, trying to free her from Rachel's grip. Molly cried out as Talon's fingers wrapped around her arm, causing considerable pain. "Let go of me!" she cried out and she pulled herself free.

Talon had invested time and money in her and felt she owed him something in return. She had humiliated him in front of his friends and he felt like the whole town was talking about how she stood him up at the theater. "Why won't you even talk to me?" he whined, with a pout that was meant to shame her into submission.

"What do you want Talon?" Molly said in a much softer tone.

Just then, Tess came running across the street yelling, "Leave her alone!"

"Oh, that's all I need!" he said, before turning and kicking a large metal trashcan. Pain shot through his foot and ankle. As he tried to put his foot down casually, he winced and began to curse Molly and her friends vehemently.

Molly's eyes grew big at the vile words he used to describe her and her friends. Tess took Molly's other arm and turned her from him, leaving him there to scream after them, "I'll get you back for this, just you wait and see!" Then he turned and limped away, muttering as he went.

Seth walked toward Ponder alone, praying as he went. He tried to slow his pace several times, not wanting to arrive at McClure's sooner than scheduled to meet Gray. But he found himself, out of nervousness, flying along once again. *'Stop!'* He said to himself as he stepped off the path and sat under a tree to breathe deeply.

He wanted to be respectful and honorable, and at the same time, let Gray know how he felt about his daughter. Fear gripped him as he searched for the right words to ask Gray if he could court Molly.

"I can't do this," he said out loud as he imagined Gray glaring at him in contempt.

'If I don't say this just right, he might just laugh at me and say you're just a kid, you don't even know what love is.

'This is going to be hard. No wonder most fellas take the easy way out. Maybe I could just...' He stopped himself, 'No, this is not about me and what I want right now, it's about forging a relationship with her father based on mutual respect. It's about having a better married life because I won't have to battle with her family, but instead I'll become an accepted and respected member. It's about a love that will never be cheapened, where I can honor her and she will respect me.'

Seth knew these things were true and he had practiced saying them over and over the last several days in order to encourage himself to stay focused on the end result. He stood and brushed himself off and, after taking a deep breath, stepped back onto the path and headed toward town again.

'Calm down, Gray's going to respect you for asking his permission to court Molly.' His pulse pounded like horses running a race in his chest, up his throat, and back down again as he swallowed hard. Somehow, he couldn't convince himself that Gray would see him as anything more than an eager boy, who only wanted to play the dating game with his precious daughter. Seth knew what he wanted from a relationship, but would Gray be able to see that?

He felt so vulnerable, like such a liar. Would he be able to push his flesh down far enough that Gray would see what was in his heart? He knew it would be easier to just go on day by day without making any declaration of love and intent, but along with the lack of commitment would come a slackness that would threaten his relationship with Molly. So with that, he set his resolve and moved forward toward his goal, Gray's approval and ultimately, Molly's.

Entering Ponder, he could see McClure's Diner about a block down the street and Gray going through the front door. His heart jumped into his throat once again, pressing against his windpipe, shutting off his oxygen supply when he needed it the most. "Lord please," he gasped, "give me a peace that passes all understanding." And then he felt it, a peace that washed over him as he took a deep breath. Seth knew the Lord was with him and that gave him a measure of confidence and comfort he couldn't explain. And, it most certainly did pass all understanding. "Thank You Lord!" he whispered as he opened the door to the diner and stepped inside.

Charlie looked out of the hospital window at the street below where he saw two young women standing together as if they were waiting for someone. A young man came up to them and began to demand an audience with one of the girl's. Charlie felt a need to defend the young woman. He knew how to identify someone with abusive roots so as he stood watching he quietly spoke to the girl through the glass, "Get away from him missy, you're too close, back up!" But it was too late as the young man grabbed her, trying to pull her free of her friend. "Lord help that girl!" he prayed as she shook herself free. Just then, another girl appeared on the other side of the street and quickly came running. The young man turned and kicked a trashcan that stood nearby. When the he began to scream profanities at the girls, they turned and walked away. The young man then lunged toward them. Charlie placed his hands on the window and leaned in to yell through the glass, but stopped short as he saw himself in Talon's actions - limping away, red faced, and angry.

That was him just a couple of days ago! He stepped away from the window, walking slowly backwards until the back of his legs felt his bed. He sat down on its edge. "Lord help that young man!" He laid a hand on his heart as it trembled and continued, "Lord protect that little gal and let that young man see it. Show him You are real and You have Your eyes on Your people to protect them." He paused for a moment longer before saying with a distressed whisper, "Your people."

Charlie felt sick as he played the ugliness of that young man's anger in his head, actions that showed him what he had looked like. "Your people," he whispered again, then laid back on the bed and curled up in a ball, covering himself with the sheet to hide his shame from the Lord. "I don't deserve to be called one of Your people, Lord. How can You forgive me? You just can't!"

As he lay deep in thought, he saw something before his watery eyes-

In a courtroom, he saw a gavel in the hand of what he knew to be God -The Judge. The gavel came down hard, striking a spike that was driven through the wrist of Christ. As it pierced His flesh, His blood ran over Charlie's head, covering his sin. The spike struck and sank into the rough wood under the wrist of Christ with a 'Thud', then Charlie heard the word 'FORGIVEN!' spoken with such authority it was clear that it was final.

Charlie drew in a deep breath and held it; he lay frozen and silent with large eyes. Slowly, he began to praise his Lord as tears of joy replaced those that had been bitter.

When the girls stopped hearing Talon's cursing, Rachel asked Tess in a bubbly tone, trying to cover the anxiety they all felt, "So did you get it?"

"Oh yeah, I got it alright!" Tess held up her new driver's license. "You should have seen it, it was great! You know how I hate to parallel park and how I had to practice it over and over again, right?"

Molly and Rachel said, "Yeah."

"Well, you won't believe this! Out of nervousness, I hit the gas too hard and the car whipped right into the parking space as I franticly turned the wheel. I nailed it like some kind of stunt driver! I mean, wow! My heart was pounding, but there I sat in the parking space just wondering how in the world did I do that?"

Tess was laughing hard as she continued with, "The instructor was so impressed, he just said, 'Wow!

That was a little faster than I would have done it, but you did it perfectly'."

"I just smiled nonchalantly at him, I didn't bother to tell him that that was the last time I ever planned on parallel parking! No, I just raised my chin and nodded as if I did it on purpose!"

They all laughed together.

"Now, let's get going, Molly's wardrobe awaits," Rachel smiled.

"I have to get a dress for the wedding too!" Molly added.

"I think we all do," Tess sneered, "the only dress I have to wear is about three sizes too small, and if I could get it on, it would make me look like a thumb sucker."

Molly and Rachel laughed again at Tess's blunt humor as they ran across the street arm-in-arm to her waiting car.

❖ ❖ ❖ ❖ ❖

Gray Mills sat with a shocked expression on his face as the young man across from him poured out his declaration of love for his daughter. This wasn't what he had expected to be talking about today. No, instead he had thought a new opportunity had come up for Seth, and he would be moving on soon. Or maybe, he wanted a job with him once he graduated? But not this!

'Molly is only sixteen years old for crying out loud. How can Seth want to take her away from us already?' Even though that wasn't what Seth had asked, still that's what it felt like to him.

Gray looked down at his hand as his ice cream had melted and began to run over his knuckles. But how could he start licking his hand now? He needed this young man to respect and maybe even fear him a little. So instead of licking his hand like some sort of child, he set his ice cream cone down in the now empty burger basket. He needed to come up with some sort of a dignified answer for this boy, a way to say *'go home and grow up first'*, but his tongue seemed to be tied.

"Sir, what I'm asking for is your blessing and a measure of accountability."

An awkward silence filled the room as Gray wiped the ice cream from his knuckles and sat thinking.

"Sir?" Seth began to grow nervous again from the lack of response from the older man.

Gray looked up with a stone expression and said, "Yes, I see you are sincere, but Molly is only sixteen."

"Yes sir," he awaited more.

"And you are seventeen," Gray said as if his point was clear for all to see.

But, Seth didn't see his point. "Sir?"

"Well, I guess it's only two years before she," Gray began to sort through his thoughts out loud. A pang of fear and anger passed through him as he thought of his precious little daughter being old enough to marry in two short years.

Just then, the bell rang over the diner door and Mary Tillman walked in with her kids. Stepping up to the counter, she was met by Granny, who stood waiting for their order.

When Tad saw Seth, he came running, "Hi Seth! What kind of ice cream did you get? I want to get the same kind you got."

Seth reached out and rubbed the small boy's head, ruffling up his light blond hair. "I had licorice, it's always been my favorite flavor." Seth stuck out his dark tongue, impressing the small boy with the color the ice cream always left behind.

"Licklish?"

"Yes, licorice."

"Cool!" Tad wrapped his small arms around Seth and Seth squeezed him back. The boy squealed with delight and turning away from the brief hug, ran back to his mom, "I want licklish! I want licklish!"

Gray was thankful for a moment to think. As he watched Seth with the small boy, he knew he could search the world over and not find a better man for his beloved Molly and possibly someday, the daddy of his grandchildren.

Seth had approached him respectfully, just as he would have wanted any man to do on behalf of his daughter. Seth was a gentle man and clearly good with kids, to the point where they sought him out. So, as he watched Seth with Tad, Gray made a decision, *'Yes, this is the young man I would be proud to call my son-in-law.'*

36

Anything Green

But the time will come when they Will not endure
sound doctrine, but according to their own desires,
because they have itching ears,...
2 Timothy 4: 3a NKJV

Bart was a cousin of Kate's who had come in from out of town for her and Sam's wedding. He was somewhat handsome with dominant features that matched his overbearing personality. Kate had a lot to deal with today and so between everyone else's questions of, 'How many dishes have to be kept hot?' and, 'How do you want these flowers arranged?' Kate had to also deal with Bart, who wanted to catch up for the past fifteen years.

Shel and Mandy had been working side-by-side with Kate all morning. As Kate's frustration with the situation grew, the two women exchanged looks of concern and tried to run interference, with little success.

"Oh no," Shel finally said, "I think we're going to run out of greenery before we even get to the sanctuary. What are we going to do?" She looked pleadingly at Mandy.

Mandy's eyes brightened as she caught her meaning. "Bart," she blurted out, "you're not doing anything, how would you like to go collect us some greenery?"

"But, where? What do you mean?" Bart's world began to crumble as he knew nothing about plants, or decorating, or what would look good. He looked at the flower arrangements around the room in desperation.

Mandy came back with, "You just drive out into the country a ways and when you see some pretty green vines or branches, you stop, cut them, and bring them back here. Take your time, we won't need them for quite a while and - it'll be fun! You'll see, and you'll be helping Kate out ever so much!"

Kate nodded, finally catching on to what her friends were doing.

Shel had a box she forced on Bart along with hand clippers. Not giving him the chance to refuse, she said, "Fill this box with anything green. There's another box there by the door, you can use it too." She pointed towards a box that had just been emptied of crystal candlesticks and still held a few crumpled pieces of tissue paper.

He speechlessly took the box she handed him and turned to go, passing the other box on the floor, and continued on out the door.

"Was that mean?" Kate asked.

Mandy chuckled, "No, this is 'Kate and Sam's' day, not 'Kate and Bart's'."

"But I haven't seen him for so long," Kate began to argue.

Shel slid an arm over Kate's shoulder saying, "So drive to town with Sam and meet Bart at a restaurant some day." She pushed her free hand away from her slowly to indicate sometime in the distant future and they all laughed.

"There is a time and place for everything Kate, and your wedding day is not the time to catch up with

Bart! Just saying..." Mandy nodded as she spoke to make her point.

"You're right," Kate said as she turned to answer a question that was shouted from the kitchen.

Sam and Cody walked through the alley and around to the back of McClure's Diner. Unlocking the garage door, they stepped inside to look over Granny's 1958 Chevy Bel-Air. The plan was to sweep Kate off in it after the wedding and take her to Sam's secret destination for their honeymoon. Stepping up to the car, they both ran their hands over its smooth surface.

"Oh man, this is perfect!" Cody exclaimed, adding his oh's and ah's as he walked the length of the car, never taking his hand off its body as his fingers slid over its cream and surf green paint. "When were you going to show me this?"

"What do you mean? I'm showing you now!" Sam spat back in a playful manner.

"Whoa! This definitely rivals Mike's Mustang." Cody pulled open the driver's side door and scooted in on the green and cream vinyl seats. Then putting his hand out, Sam handed him the keys. Cody put the keys in the ignition and turned, ruuuu...ruuuu... ruuuu. The car tried, but never quite started; dying each time he'd try. "What's the matter with it?" He tried it again with the same result. He pushed the gas pedal again and tried once more.

Ruuuu...ruuuu...ruuuu...

"Don't flood it," Sam said impatiently.

"I'm trying not to, but it just won't start."

"No kidding. Here, let me try." Sam smacked Cody on the shoulder with the back of his hand and Cody slid across the bench seat. When Sam had positioned himself, he put his foot on the pedal and turned the key.

Ruuuuu...ruuuuu...ruuuuu...ruuuuuuu...

"We've been so concerned about the wedding that no one came in to see if the car was running right," Sam said as he slid out.

"Do you have any starter fluid? I've heard you can spray starter fluid in the carburetor to start an old car like this." Cody looked at him with his eyebrows raised as if posing the question, 'Well, what do you think?'

"That sounds dangerous."

"Do you have a better idea?"

Sam had to admit he didn't. "All right, let's see." The men walked over to the workbench and began to scan the shelves that hung behind it on the wall. They moved tools and polishes until Sam picked up a spray can of starter fluid. "Bingo!" he said, turning and opening the hood of the car.

Cody slid back into the driver's seat and said, "Tell me when you're ready."

Sam pulled off the air filter and began to spray the starter fluid into the carburetor while holding the automatic choke open. "Ok, go ahead and try it now."

Cody turned the key.

Ruuu...ru...

Sam leaned in to see if the fuel was injecting and BAM!! the car backfired out of the carburetor, shooting a flame right in Sam's face. Sam yelled as he jumped back, holding his hands over his eyes.

Cody jumped out of the car and ran over to Sam, "Are you ok! Did you get burnt? Let me see!" But when Sam pulled his hands away, Cody began to laugh.

"What, what is it?" Sam touched his face again as he tried to adjust his eyes after the sudden flash that left him temporarily blinded.

"You're fine, you just burned off your left eyebrow, and a little of your hair in the front. What were you thinking, sticking your head in there?"

"What does it look like?" Sam ran a finger along the stubble that was once a full blond brow.

"Well, it isn't pretty if that's what you're going for, but if you knock off the singed hair..." Cody stopped as he began to laugh again and Sam joined him.

It didn't take long for Bart to drive out of town. He was a little put out at the whole situation but was determined to do a good job and get back as soon as possible. He would have to pick up the story he had been telling Kate, when he was so rudely interrupted.

As he drove along, he looked out at the countryside. The trees, grass, mountains, everything was green. "Anything green, yeah right!" He grumbled, "Everything is green out here!" But he drove on, looking at everything like he had never really seen it before.

Somehow or somewhere he had formed the opinion that enjoying simple beauty was a feminine thing to do so he had avoided it. Not that living in a city had encouraged him to look around in any way. But now that he was doing a job that required him to look too for beauty, he began to enjoy it.

He slowed his car to a crawl, pulled over to the side of the road, and got out. Leaning back against the car, he took in a deep breath as his eyes feasted. The mountains rolled with wave upon wave of bushes and trees in varying shades of green, while an occasional spear of evergreen shot out along the skyline to point to the heavens. The sun's golden orb was directly overhead in the clear blue sky. Shadows fell at the trees feet while the breeze blew their branches gently, causing them to wave serenely while whispering inaudible calming words in Bart's large ears.

"Anything green," he said again out loud, but this time with a smile pressing his full lips. He began to hone in on the plants closest to him. He didn't want a little of everything. He thought it would make the arrangements look messy and random so he decided to pick a lot of one or two things. But whatever he picked, it needed to flow like vines that could be woven throughout all the arrangements to complete the look Kate was going for.

He could see it now in his mind's eye, and he liked it. "I think I may actually be good at this kind of thing," he spoke to himself, imagining the pats on the back he would receive when he returned with whatever he harvested.

He walked toward a grove of trees and there he found what he was looking for. Green vines ran along the ground and up the bark of the trees. "That's it!" Bart said as he began to cut the vines, laying them in long streamers over his bare arm. He moved along until he noticed some of the leaves had a slight blush about them, as if they might turn red in the fall.

He smiled, looking once again over the scene before him and imagined it in the fall. Like a red blanket, the vines would lay on the ground, then spread up the trees holding them in their delicate embrace. The orange and gold leaves of the maples and oaks would fall, floating down to rest amongst the red ivy.

❖ ❖ ❖ ❖ ❖

Sam felt a little self-conscious about his now missing eyebrow. He wondered what would their wedding pictures look like? What would people think when they came up to shake his hand after the wedding? He looked in the rear view mirror for only about the hundredth time. Having only one eyebrow gave him a very wry, snide looking expression.

"Stop worrying about it Sam," Cody injected into his thoughts, "it's not that noticeable. Now, if you had dark eyebrows, one missing would be something else.

But, no one is going to notice one of your almost invisible eyebrows missing, that is, if you don't tell them it's gone."

Sam felt nervous, wondering if Cody was telling him the truth or just saying what he thought he wanted to hear. Sam glanced over at him and noticed an ornery smile spread across his face.

"You could just face Kate so the photographer only gets your good side," Cody injected. "That is if you have a good side? Of course, that won't stop people from pointing and laughing."

"Oh thanks a lot!"

"Sure, any time," Cody snorted.

"Here we are," Sam said as they pulled into the Tillman's driveway.

"Ok then, here's the test. Don't say anything about it being gone and we'll just see if Gil notices, ok?"

What choice did Sam have? It wasn't like there was anything he could do about it now. He had to face someone sooner or later, so he rolled his eyes and said, "OK."

"Hey, there you are. What took you so long?" Gil said as he stepped out of his house.

Cody turned and looked at Sam as if the explanation might just burst out of him like a crazy monster at any moment, but Sam shook his head and gave him a threatening look. Cody's orneriness sparked to life, as his eyes got bigger and the corners of his mouth turned up into a smile, but much to Sam's relief Gil didn't seem to notice the exchange. He was too busy looking at the car he had agreed to tastefully decorate for the newlywed couple. He would bring it up to the church at just the right moment, when the happy couple exited the building. He spoke as he walked over and pulled the garage door up, "You can pull her in here so no one sees it." Sam drove the car forward and Gil pulled the door back down behind them. "Now, let me show you what I have here Sam."

Sam and Cody stepped out of the car and followed Gil to a box on the floor. "Mary found this paint that won't hurt the cars paint job," he lifted a bottle from the box. "But I'll use it to write on the windows of the car, just in case. And, here I rigged up a string of cans that will clang-bang well enough. I weighed them down so they won't fly up and chip your paint, if you don't go too fast that is. Then once you get down the road a ways, you can just stop the car and flip them into the trunk and be on your merry way."

Gil turned and looked at Sam for the first time and said, "You look a little skeptical Sam. I promise if you keep your speed low, say below forty-five, those cans won't be flying up. Now, I wouldn't take her on the freeway that way so just put them cans away like I said and you'll be good." Sam's expression became more concerned as he seemingly drew up one eyebrow. "Ok Sam, I'll tie them on my car and try it out for you, if you like, would that be good?"

Sam finally said, "No, no, that's alright Gil, I trust you. It looks like you have this end of things tied up, so I guess we ought to be going." Sam walked toward his car, which was parked in front of his house next door, while Cody stayed put a minute longer.

"Is he ok?" Gil asked, "He seems a little out of sorts."

"Yeah, he's uneven today. Weddings, as you know, can throw a man off a little. It can make him feel lopsided, like something's missing. You and I both know he's got something on his mind but we can only see half of what it is."

As Kate and her friends moved upstairs to start decorating the sanctuary, a young man limped into the fellowship hall they just left and began to scan the room. Talon decided that if he hid out somewhere in the church he was sure to see Molly tonight and maybe even get a chance to confront her alone. She was sure to come to the wedding for the new police chief, as every good, upstanding citizen in town would be here tonight.

Looking in every classroom and closet for a place to hide, Talon heard a man whistling as he approached the door. Just as the door began to swing open, Talon dashed into the men's room and stood just inside, peeking out at the man who had just come in.

The man sat down the large box of green vines he carried and headed towards the bathroom. When Talon saw him coming, he ducked inside one of the stalls to hide.

Bart came back from his expedition, well pleased with himself. No one was around so he decided to go to the men's room and clean up before looking for Kate. He walked inside and as he entered, he heard someone shuffling around in one of the stalls. Bart finished his business and looked at himself in the mirror as he washed his hands.

His face was dirty and sweat rolled down from around his hairline. On the counter, sat his bag with a towel and some personal items, so he could clean up and change before the wedding. He pulled out his old brown towel and began to wipe away the dirt and sweat, starting with his face and arms. Finally, he slapped the towel at some burrs and dirt he picked up on his pants when he walked through tall grass.

Bart looked the towel over. It still looked pretty good he thought, clean enough for him to take a shower with before tonight. He folded it back up and laid it on top of his bag, which lay next to the sink, and left the bathroom.

When Bart stepped back into the fellowship hall, he saw a tall man with fine dark hair standing and looking at the green vines he had cut. The man had a shocked look on his face.

"Can I help you?" Bart asked the man as he approached him.

Leroy looked up with horror and said, "What is this, some kind of curse on the wedding or somebody's idea of a sick joke?"

Bart narrowed his eyes, "This is my contribution to the flower arrangement. I just got back from picking them and I'm looking for Kate now." He picked a dead leaf off the vines and let it fall to the floor. Leroy stood still with his jaw dropped open due to Bart's flagrant disregard of the situation.

Bart was beginning to think Leroy was perhaps a little slow, so he said with patience, "Hi, we haven't been introduced. My name is Bart. I'm Kate's cousin."

But, when Bart reached out to shake his hand, Leroy jumped back as if it were a snake striking. "Are you crazy?" Leroy spat out.

"I was just about to ask you the same question." The two men stared daggers at each other for a moment before Leroy finally asked, "Don't you know what that is?"

Bart turned back to his vines in the box. "Yes, I know exactly what they are, they're vines for the flower arrangements. You'd know that if you were listening a moment ago."

Leroy had no more patience with this man who was clearly a little slow. "That's poison ivy!" He stopped himself short of calling Bart an idiot.

Bart jumped back from the box. "What? Poison ivy?"

❖ ❖ ❖ ❖ ❖

Talon laughed at the conversation between the two men. *'What a moron!'* he thought to himself, *'I can't believe someone could be so stupid!'* He washed his hands and then grabbed the brown towel someone had left lying there. He dried his hands and proceeded to wipe some of the oil buildup off his teenage face, scratching it slightly from a burr stuck on the towel. He pulled the burr off, folded the towel back up, and sat it back where he had found it. When he heard someone coming, he dashed back into his stall and closed the door again. He heard the same two men talking as they entered.

Leroy was instructing Bart about the woes of poison ivy as Bart retrieved his infected towel from the bathroom so it could join the evil vines that now lay in the dumpster out back. "I have your clothes," Leroy said, "let's go. I can show you where to get that special soap. You should wash everything on your body you think you touched, and I mean everything, everything! And then wash everything again, just in case. Trust me, there are certain places you especially don't want to get poison ivy!"

Talon stood pressed up against the wall until the men were gone. He hadn't thought of anything he could do to catch Molly off guard tonight and hanging out in the men's room clearly wasn't going to work. He would have to come up with a better idea or be stuck in this stall all night. So as soon as he heard the door close, he stepped out of the bathroom and left the church to plan his next move elsewhere. "Why did I come in here anyway?" He didn't know. "Wow, that was dumb!" He said to himself as he walked out, scratching an itch.

37
Girly Stuff

Then I, John, saw the holy city, New Jerusalem,
coming down out of heaven from God,
prepared as a bride adorned for her husband.
Revelation 21: 2 NKJV

Kate rushed into the shower at a little before two o'clock. She would be meeting Shel and Mandy in about twenty minutes to go and get their hair and makeup done in Bennington. The wedding would start at five-thirty and the reception following would go late into the night.

Kate quickly toweled herself off and pulled a comb through her hair as she looked in the mirror. Her cheeks and nose were still peeling slightly from the sunburn she had received as she and Chuck hiked through the river and over the mountain. One of the scratches she had received was still red as it ran across her forehead. She ran a finger over it, feeling scabs she wasn't sure were ready to be disturbed yet. Makeup would hopefully cover all of Kate's unwanted marks. Still, Kate felt a tear stick in her throat as she looked at herself undressed in the mirror.

Tripping repeatedly on slippery wet rocks had bruised her legs and with the passing of time, they had turned a yellowish green. She knew no one would see them except Sam, but he was the one she cared about most. Red lines ran parallel with each other across her arms where scratches from briars had healed over. Kate's ribs showed and her cheeks were hollow from loss of weight that had not yet been regained.

She moaned, "Lord, I don't want Sam to see me like this. I want my husband to see me as being beautiful." And in response, she heard the Lord say in a still small voice, 'He does see you as beautiful.' Kate pressed her hand on her heart and took a sudden breath as tears ran down her face. The words were simple but Kate knew they meant so much more.

Her bridegroom saw her as being perfect just like Christ saw His bride 'white as snow'. Kate reached out and ran her hand over the gown that represented purity. This gown and a little makeup would cover her scars well enough. But the Lord's 'white as snow' covering would not only cover the marks this world imposed on His bride, it would heal them.

"Thank You Lord," she whispered as she wiped her tears away and quickly got dressed.

"Where did the girls go?" Bart asked as he and Leroy walked over to Sally's Big Burger.

"They went into Bennington to do all the girly stuff."

"Girly stuff? What's girly stuff mean?"

"You know, hair, makeup... I don't know what girls do," Leroy finished impatiently with a smirk.

"That sounds dumb. I've never heard anyone say that before. No one says that."

"Of course they do, all the time!"

Bart opened the door and the two men went in and sat down at a table. Leroy picked up the small menu card that sat between the salt and pepper shakers, and studied both sides.

The manager quickly walked over to them and asked, "And what can I get you two gentlemen today?"

"You holding down the fort by yourself here today Fred?"

"Leroy! How ya doin' there buddy? I ain't seen you in a coon's age." The manager slapped him on the back.

"I'm doing good. The Lord is good you know."

"Amen to that. So what can I get ya two fellas?"

"Oh, just a couple of burger baskets and two sodas. So don't you have anyone helping you today?" Leroy asked again, never having seen Fred do his own waiting.

"Yeah, Rachel went into Bennington to do girly stuff with her friends. You know, for the weddin' and all."

Leroy gave Bart a pointed look, his hands out in a ta-da motion, "See I told you, girly stuff."

Molly would be serving cake tonight at the reception, so she took into account the colors of the wedding as she looked for the dress she would wear.

"Here, this is pretty!" Tess held up a lavender colored dress.

Molly shook her head, "No, the colors are pink, yellow, and blue - not lavender."

"Well, lavender is close to pink and blue," Tess argued. "Close enough anyways, it's pretty."

Rachel pulled the dress from Tess's grasp, "She wants pink or blue! Haven't you been listening?" Then she held the dress up in front of herself before replacing it back on the rack. "Oh, look at this one!" Rachel pulled an ice blue dress off the rack, overlaid with a sheer floral fabric. Pink and yellow roses stood out with blue forget-me-nots scattered around them generously.

"No, I don't like the style," Molly objected.

Tess snapped, "Look Molly, we have been here for hours and nothing is ever good enough for you. This is a perfectly pretty dress and it's the right colors. So you're going to try it on if I have to hog tie you and put it on you myself."

Molly had no doubt that Tess would do just as she had said. Maybe she wouldn't tie her with ropes but there would be no getting away from her just the same. But when she saw timid Rachel drawing up beside Tess, as if she was going to help her, Molly started to laugh.

Tess snatched the dress away from Rachel and stepped towards Molly who threw up her hands in surrender. "Ok, ok, I'll try it on!" Molly took the dress and held out the skirt as she grimaced, "Not my style."

Kate lay back in the beauty parlor chair as Sherry, the beautician, worked. Applying an astringent, she began to rub gently over the peeling sunburn and the scabs that ran the length of the scratch on Kate's forehead. "Oh this is working nicely," she continued, "I think you'll like the results of this Kate."

"Let me see!" Mandy stepped up beside Kate, "Oh Kate, it's perfect! There's just the tiniest little pink line where the scratch was!"

"And the makeup will cover that easily enough," Sherry added. Gently drying Kate's face, she began to apply the makeup that matched Kate's skin tone perfectly. "Mandy, could you give me an inch or two please?" Sherry asked as she motioned for Mandy to sit back down.

"Oh sorry," Mandy said as she turned and sat. Her black hair was pulled loosely up and braided around the top of her head like a crown. Woven into the braid were tiny pink and yellow rosettes and pale blue baby's breath. The flowers stood out against the dark backdrop that was her hair. Small spring like hairs softened the appearance of the flowers as they worked their way free of the hairpins.

Shel sat next to her with her nose in a magazine reading out loud every once in a while as it suited her. Her hair was pulled back into a sleek French twist that ran up the back of her head. She also had pink, yellow, and blue flowers tucked into her hair along the fold. Her blond hair shimmered with smooth lines as thin ringlets fell on both sides of her head, framing her face. She put down the magazine and said, "Are you about done, I want to see the full picture."

"It won't be the full picture until she puts her dress on," Mandy corrected. "But we can imagine her in it."

"There," Sherry said as she stepped back and pulled off the bib that protected Kate's clothes. "She looks like an angel."

Kate stood. Her dark brown hair was tied to one side and fell over her shoulder in thick ringlets. Her pink lips and cheeks gave her a youthful blush as her face pulled up in a, 'What do you think?' expression. Her large green eyes snapped to life, picking up the green that had lain unseen between the flowers in her hair. Kate's slender neck and pale skin gave her a fragile look, like a fine porcelain doll. Turning and looking into the mirror, Kate's lips parted with a contented smile.

When the dress went over Molly's head, a sense of dread washed over her as well. She wanted more than anything for Seth to ask her to dance tonight. So she wanted to look perfect for him. She knew that if she didn't like this dress, she might still have to buy and wear it for the sake of her friend's. They had gone from store to store, looking for the perfect dress for her, and because of it, they were irritable, hungry, and wore out.

The dress slipped over her head, falling over her curves like it was tailor-made. Molly fell silent.

"See, it's perfect!" Rachel said cheerfully, trying to convince Molly, but there was no need for convincing because she could already see that it was.

38
Mr. Weirdy!

Therefore a man shall leave his father and mother
and be joined to his wife,
and they shall become one flesh.
Genesis 2: 24 NKJV

As Cody fumbled with his tie in the men's dressing room at the church, he said, "Are you sure you want Martin to be your best man?"

"Sure, why not? Hey, are you saying you want the coveted position?" Sam pulled on his suit jacket.

"Well, I'm here aren't I? I'm the one making memories with you and giving you words of advice." Cody's voice tensed as he continued, "And I'm trying my darnedest to tie this worthless tie!" His fingers tumbled over the knot in frustration. "I think this thing is defective!" He pulled the knot loose and slid it from his neck. Holding it out to Sam, Cody smiled in jest. "It isn't too late to get your money back on this thing, is it?"

"Oh, come on," Sam took the tie and placed it around his own neck. "I thought you said you knew how to tie a tie."

"Well, it looks easy!" Cody said as Sam tied the tie with speed. "Wow, that's much better!"

Sam loosened the tie and slid it up over his head and back down over Cody's. Tightening it a little too snugly, he added, "There... perfect!"

"Yeah, if I wanted to suffocate." Cody twisted his face and stuck out his tongue as if he were being strangled. Then loosening the tie slightly added, "Now it's perfect!"

Sam turned toward the mirror to look at his reflection. "Oh, who is that handsome man?" His sun-bleached hair swooped up before lying perfectly combed to the side of his part. He pulled at his bangs trying to feather them over his singed brow, but they weren't quite long enough. He brushed them back into place with his fingers.

Cody said as he pushed him aside. "Handsome man, where? Oh, there he is. Wow, he IS handsome, isn't he?" He tried to brush back his own unruly hair, making it look no better than when he started. It just went back to where it was, waving at him in mockery.

"Oh, get out of here." Sam pushed the smaller man aside, straightening his tie and looking at himself once again. His tan face was clean-shaven. His suit lay crisp and pressed, draped over his broad shoulders, and the creases in his pants made his legs look longer than they already were. He was clean-shaven and smelled of aftershave, perfectly dressed from head-to-toe. His high-glossed shoes shined up at him. His jaw flexed as he smiled slyly at himself before turning to look at Cody. "You have to admit I look pretty good!"

Cody had his arms lying over the back of the small pew he sat on. "Sure, you look good, but you forget you only have one eyebrow, whereas I still have both of mine!" He bounced his eyebrows up and down and locked his fingers behind his head to lie back against the wall. Cody's boyish smile played on his face as his coat fell open, reflecting his nonchalant approach to life. His shirt was pulled tight across his chest and his gold belt buckle gleamed. His pants pulled up at the ankles as he stretched his legs out in front of him. Cody crossed his legs, revealing he wasn't wearing any socks.

"Where are your socks?" Sam asked in disbelief.

"Oh yeah, I don't wear anything but cotton on my feet and those nylon things were making my feet sweat."

"You have to wear socks!"

"Nah, socks are overrated." Cody sat up and pulled his pant legs down, not quite covering his ankles. Once again, he looked up at the clock and said, "I'd say if your 'Best Man' isn't here in five minutes, I'm the 'Best Man' for the job."

"If you're the best I can do then we're all in trouble!" Sam said with a coy smile, but he had to admit, even though he had only known Cody for less than a week, he had grown close to him. Secretly, he would rather have him standing in the honored position of 'Best Man' more than his non-Christian friend, Martin. But he had already asked Martin and it was too late to change things now, without hurting his pride.

Charlie looked out the hospital window as he watched those going to the celebration of Sam and Kate's wedding. He wasn't angry anymore nor did he feel like he had to protect Kate from Chief of Police Trusty. No, instead he felt a peace that she would now be happy. He knew there was a penalty to be paid here on earth for the sins he had committed, even if in eternity all had been forgiven. And so, he'd be going to prison for a while before he would be swept up into the arms of his Savior.

"God bless you Kate. Have a long and happy life," he whispered, standing at the window facing the direction of the church.

He closed the blinds and walked over to the bedside stand, picking up his Bible he propped himself up in bed. *'What will my Lord and bridegroom have to say to me tonight?'*

Sam's eyes were fixed on Kate's through her fine antique veil. Her eyes seemed to say 'come here'. It was all he could do to pay attention to the words being spoken by the pastor, words that he was expected to repeat. But somehow, he managed to say each word in order, without stammering, or being laughed at. Then Kate's own delicate pink lips began to move, pledging her undying love and promising to respect him, which was all he had ever wanted.

He leaned slightly forward, anticipating their first kiss, but it wasn't time yet. Sam made himself take a small step back, then shuffled his feet until he stood precisely where he had just been.

The second he heard the words 'you may kiss the bride', he lifted her veil and fell on her lips, drawing her in with his arms and holding her there, never wanting to come up for air. He had kissed women before but it had never meant anything to him like this one long awaited kiss. He felt Kate stiffen, slightly uncomfortable with the kiss. Remembering where he was and what was expected of him, Sam released her and stood up straight, his eyes never leaving hers.

It was laughter that brought Sam back to reality as he turned to see the men in his wedding party - Martin, Cody, and even Tad; holding up numbers as if they were the judges at the Olympics, rating his and Kate's first kiss.

Sam knew full well Cody was behind it all as he held up the lowest score of 4.9 and his face had a goofy 'got ya' look about it. So Sam made a mental note to get back at him later, but for now a playful glare and a point of his finger would have to do.

Laughter rang out once again as Cody flared his eyes and brought up one eyebrow as he ran a finger over the other. He was taking on the challenge and at the same time, reminding Sam that one of his brows was missing.

"Ok Sam, do you think you can hold that pose this time?"

Sam nodded, but just as the photographer was about to snap their picture he turned to look at Kate. This went on for some time, Sam tilting his head toward Kate, or pressing his left cheek into hers just as the camera was about to flash.

"What is the matter with you Sam?" Kate pushed him away. "We're never going to get done with this photo shoot if you don't behave yourself," she scolded, giggling at the unexplainably goofy expression on his face.

"I can't help myself. I just love you SO much!" He kissed her yet again.

Cody didn't seem to be able to wipe off the smile that was plastered across his face either. The two of them obviously had some kind of secret inside joke going.

"Ok guys, what's up?" Shel finally asked.

"Oh nothing, he's just a little off today. You might say, a little lopsided." Cody's eyebrows bobbed up and down.

Sam gave him a shove.

Shel poked him in the belly. "Cody Wiley, I know when you're hiding something from me!"

"Hey, I'm sworn to secrecy," he professed as he threw his hands up.

Kate turned to Sam with a surprised look on her face, "Sam are you hiding something from me?"

His smile froze, as he seemingly raised one eyebrow and leaned down to whisper something in her ear.

"What?" Kate snapped back to look at him. Taking his head in her hands, she rubbed her thumb over what remained of his left eyebrow. Pulling his head down, she kissed the stubble. "Oh you poor thing, are you ok?"

Sam smiled from his newly gained attention. "I'm fine. It took a little off the top too, so I went and got a nice hair cut." He ran his hand back over his hair.

"I wondered why you kept looking at me so strangely, it was weirding me out. I thought maybe I had married 'Jekyll and Hyde'! 'Sweet Sam' by day and 'Mr. Weirdy' after the wedding bells rang!"

39
Country Bumpkin

Trust in the Lord with all your heart,
And lean not on your own understanding;
In all your ways acknowledge Him,
And He shall direct your paths.
Proverbs 3: 5-6 NKJV

Seth sat nervously, picking at his second piece of cake as he nonchalantly watched Molly from across the dance floor. He could hardly breathe due to how beautiful she looked. She wore an ice blue dress sprayed with pink and yellow rosettes along with blue forget-me-nots. Her blond hair was pulled back into a French twist, smoothly turned in while shimmering like spun gold. A pretty hand-painted comb stood in the fold that extended up the back of her head. The blush in her cheeks and lips played with the pink in the flowers on the dress. And when her eyes flashed at Seth, his heart leapt in his throat.

He, on the other hand, had worn what he thought looked like the best of what he had. "How can I ask her to dance with me in my high-waters while she looks like an angel?" He pulled down on his pant legs once again. He wished he hadn't said anything to Molly's Dad yet about wanting to court her. Seth felt like he had to talk to her tonight, that now it was expected of him.

He tried to take another bite of his cake, but sat it down on the seat next to him when he heard a man speaking on the other side.

"Well, that's some pretty sweet stuff there isn't it? A man can only eat so much sweets before his stomach is just sick with it."

Seth turned to see Talon setting next to him and his face twisted with displeasure.

"Seth, I see you have your eye on Molly Mills. Now she's a sweet thing too." Leaning slightly over, Talon, mumbled something for Seth's ears alone.

Seth moved like lightning, standing and slugging Talon in the face with one swift move. Seizing him by the scruff of the neck and the seat of the pants, Seth quickly ushered Talon out of the church.

Talon's long legs and arms flailed out to his sides as he fought to get ahold of Seth, with no luck. He hadn't expected him to defend Molly's honor. He hadn't expected Seth, who was younger and shorter than himself, to have such strength. And, he hadn't thought for one minute he would find himself lying on the ground outside the church, watching as the door closed behind him. Nevertheless, there he lay. He jumped up and as he brushed himself off, he cursed with revenge in his eyes. But he couldn't afford a replay in front of his friends of what had just happened, so he walked away knowing full well he had better stay clear of Seth Barnett and Molly from now on.

"Is everything alright?" Leroy asked Seth as he came back in from throwing Talon out on his ear.

"Just give me a minute to cool down, would you?" Seth sat on the small pew by the door and ran his hands through his hair. "I can't believe I just did that."

"Well, he probably deserved it," Leroy paused then added, "I can see his kind coming a mile away."

Seth looked at him for a moment before putting his hand out, "Seth Barnett."

"Leroy McCoy." He shook the younger man's hand and sat down next to him. "So, what'd he say that got you so all fired up?"

"He said something about Molly that was crude and..." he stopped and clenched his teeth again.

"Molly, is she your gal?"

"Well she might be, if I could get up the nerve to ask her to be."

"Oh, I see. Well if you don't mind my asking, what are you afraid of?"

"Oh, I don't know. She looks so pretty tonight and well, just look at me! I look like the stereotype of a 'country bumpkin'. I'm growing so fast my clothes don't fit me from week to week!"

"Well, I hear women like tall men."

"You hear?" Seth looked at Leroy, "Don't you know?"

"Well, some buzz around me but I haven't found me one of those flirty ones I've liked yet."

"True." Seth sat back.

"Besides, I think I need me one with a little more fire to level me out a little."

"That 'opposites attract' thing, you mean?" Seth asked.

"Yeah. So this girl of yours, she's here tonight, right?"

"Yeah, she's here."

"Well then, just go and ask her to dance. Don't think about 'how can I ask her to be my gal'? Just think 'dance'. Then if your chance comes, you'll find your nerve and ask her. It's getting late anyways and how often do you get to dance with a pretty girl?"

Seth slapped his thighs as he stood up. "You're right, just dance! Thanks Leroy," he put his hand out again and Leroy took it as he stood. "It was nice to meet you."

"Nice to meet you too. God's speed!" and Leroy slapped Seth on the back as he walked away.

"Thanks!" Seth ran into the fellowship hall and before he lost momentum he scanned the room to find Molly. He sped across the floor and coming up behind her, he tapped her on the shoulder.

Molly had been waiting all night for Seth to ask her to dance. She flirted with him at the cake table and he had come back for seconds, exchanging small talk. She had stood off alone so it would be easier for him to ask her to dance. She had even danced with Markus Tillman who was several years younger. Purposely moving past Seth several times, laughing as if she was having the time of her life, acting as if she loved to dance more than anything in the world. But, it was getting late now and she was getting tired of the whole thing.

When Seth seemed to disappear, she found her friends. As she talked to them, Markus came up to her twice to ask her to dance. She had refused politely, but this time when he tapped her from behind she turned sharply and said loudly, "NO!" But instead of it being Markus, she looked up to find Seth standing there.

Seth's face went white as he spun around and moved quickly toward the door, leaving Molly standing in shock by what she had just done. She covered her mouth with her hands and gasped. Running as fast as she could towards the bathroom, she began to cry uncontrollably.

"Molly, are you ok?" Rachel asked from outside the bathroom stall.

"Would you ask my Dad to take me home, please?"

"Yeah, sure, but are you ok?" Tess asked.

"Please Tess, just go ask him, please!"

"OK, I will."

Gray asked his daughter as he drove her home, "So Puddin', did Seth talk to you tonight?"

"Just at the cake table. He hardly said a word to me all night, and when he finally..." Molly began to cry again.

"So, does this have something to do with him throwing Talon out of the reception?"

"What, what are you talking about Daddy?" She turned to look at him. "Was Talon there?"

"Not for long from what I hear!" Gray chuckled. "Those that saw it said it was the funniest thing they'd ever seen."

"Why did he throw him out?" Molly's tears had temporarily stopped.

"Now that I couldn't tell you, Puddin'."

Silence permeated the car as the purr of the engine pressed loudly in Molly's ears.

"Why are you so upset, what happened?" Gray asked.

Molly hesitated and then recalled the whole evening from her point of view, adding, "He'll never look at me ever again, and I love him Daddy!"

"Don't give up on him yet Molly. Seth's a good man and one thing I know for sure is men and women do not think alike."

"No Daddy, you didn't see him when I yelled 'No' in his face! He just turned and ran and he's probably still running. I would have ran if he had done that to me!" She began to sob once again.

"You yelled 'No' at him?""I thought he was Markus wanting to dance for the hundredth time tonight. I didn't want to dance with him anymore. I wanted to dance with Seth but..." She began to cry again.

"Well Molly, what would you say to you and I going into Ponder tomorrow for some ice cream?"

"Oh Daddy, I love you!" She scooted over and tucked herself up under his arm. "I'd love to go, but I don't think it's going to fix it this time."

"Oh, you'd be surprised what ice cream can fix."

When the two of them got home, Molly went to the bathroom to clean up for bed as Gray pulled his phone from his pocket and stepped out the back door.

"Have you had any of this wonderful cake yet?" Leroy asked as he sat down next to Shel.

Sitting by the door, Shel breathed in the cool evening air as she watched the couples on the dance floor. "Yeah, it was good too, but this is better." She smiled and pointed at Cody dancing with Granny. She seemed to be unusually tired and contented to just watch them enjoying themselves.

Granny was obviously thrilled to have someone dance with her who knew how to dance as well as she did. As Cody spun her around and around, she looked like she was reliving her youth as she giggled like a young school girl.

It was clear Cody had taken dance lessons some time during his life and failed to tell her, but she wasn't mad. It would just have to be incorporated into their lives now. Shel just hoped she would be able to keep up with him. She laid a hand low on her belly and smiled.

Leroy asked her with a thoughtful tone as he watched the dancers on the floor, "You don't have any more friends you'd like to see happily married with a great big guy like me, do you?"

Shel's eyes turned to look at Leroy as her mind whirled like a game show 'spin the wheel'. When the wheel stopped, her thoughts landed on her friend, Sarah. "Would you be willing to relocate to Ohio for a while?"

Already forgetting his question Leroy asked, "What, why?" looking puzzled.

"You know, for the love of your life."

"What?" He said, not understanding her.

"Well, I do have a friend for you Leroy. She's a little spitfire that has learned how to be a Godly woman and she's convinced the Lord is going to bring her a man in an extraordinary way. She wants a gentle, loving, kind of man, and I'd say that sounds a lot like you!"

"I haven't always been peaceful," Leroy said matter-of-factly, dropping his gaze.

"She hasn't always been a Godly woman either." She patted his hand and continued, "Why don't you just pray about it Leroy and see what the Lord has to say?" Shel dropped the subject and turned her attention back to the dance floor, watching as Sam kissed his beautiful bride.

The crowd had started to thin as the evening drew to an end. Sam and Kate danced their last dance before slipping out of the reception.

Shel looked back at Cody dancing with Granny, and felt as if life was very nearly perfect at this point in time, finding herself having to wipe away a tear. As her finger brushed under her eyes, Granny turned and smiled at her as if she knew what Shel was feeling. She smiled back, feeling now as if maybe this sweet old lady really did know. Granny had tears of joy streaming down her old cheeks, running to hide in the wrinkles of her dear old face. Cody spun the old woman around once again and winked at Shel. As she sat there, her heart leapt inside her with the love she felt for her husband.

From beside her, Shel heard Leroy say in a low murmur, "Yes, I think I would relocate, for love."

She turned sideways and wrapped her arms around his muscular bulk and said, "I knew you would, you're a softy, you big galoot!"

40

Mountains Move!

*...for assuredly, I say to you, if you have faith
as a mustard seed, you will say to this mountain,
'Move from here to there,' and it will move; and
nothing will be impossible for you.
Matthew 17:20 NKJV*

Sitting in a coffee shop in Bennington, Zeke said, "So, when the poor clod shows up at Sarah's door, she says, 'Look, I don't know you and I never agreed to a blind date with you. I'm sure you're a nice enough guy and all, but I'm not going out with you.'

"She knew her friend Clive had been up to something, so she told this guy, 'Clive set you up for a fall so you're just going to have to take it up with him'." Zeke slapped his forehead before adding, "My sister is never going to get married. She'll still be knitting socks when she's sitting in a nursing home waiting for Mr. Right to come along."

Leroy thought for a moment then said, "I don't know Zeke. I think the Lord can move mountains to bring the right guy along for her. Anyway, I think it's commendable that she knows what she wants and won't bend until she gets it. I'd like to be more like that."

"Speaking of Sarah," Leroy's smile twisted as he continued, "I dreamt the other night that we were kids again and you and I had climbed a tree to get away from her. She stood at the base of the tree looking for us, calling out our names as we covered our mouths to keep from laughing out loud. Were we really that mean to her?"

"Oh, I don't know, maybe. She's never mentioned it so it must not of scarred her too bad."

"So 'poor clod', that's something they call guys in Ohio?" Leroy asked.

"Yep, farm country. Oh and 'red neck', which I'm sure you've heard, but that's more a name others call them." Zeke smiled.

"Yeah, I've heard that." Leroy turned to look at him, "I'm going to be moving to Ohio next month."

"Oh really, what part?"

"A small town in the northwest corner, I think."

"That's where my folks are living now!"

Leroy smiled hopefully, "Well, maybe I'll run into them then."

"So school, work, what are you moving to Ohio for?"

"Both, I hope."

"You hope?"

"Well, I was answering the phone for the pastor back home after visiting Charlie the other day, when Pastor Hilby from Ohio called to ask about how Chuck was doing."

Zeke's head snapped up from taking another sip of his coffee.

"We didn't know each other, but he has a way of getting a guy to open up. Before I knew it, I was telling him about studying to be a pastor and working at a small church near my hometown. We talked about Chuck getting saved and when he found out I was the man who was there when Chuck murdered that man last year, he asked me to be praying about coming to

Ohio to work for him." Leroy continued as Zeke listened intently, "Well, I didn't think much about it at the time.   Then Mrs. Wiley was telling me about a friend she has in Ohio that I might like and asked me if I would be willing to move for love."

Zeke couldn't stay quiet any longer, "Shel?"

"Yeah!" A puzzled look passed over Leroy's face at Zeke knowing her name.

"Shel Wiley?" Zeke's eyes were big, but Leroy wasn't sure where he was going with this line of questioning.

"Yeah?" he said with uncertainty.

"And her friend's name is what?" Zeke leaned forward awaiting Leroy's answer.

"I don't know? It was something like Clara or maybe Sarah, yeah I think it was Sarah," he paused deep in thought, "Sarah Boon, I think."

"Sarah Bloom?" Zeke boomed out.

Leroy's eyes popped open, but he didn't speak.

"Leroy, Shel's friend Sarah is my sister, Sarah Bloom!"

Neither of them spoke for some time as they looked at each other with their mouths hanging open. When Zeke finally spoke, he stood and smiled, "Who would of thought, you and Sarah would get together? Well, I guess mountains do move!" He said as he slapped the mountain of a man on the back.

Brace knocked on the door, then stood waiting as the newspaper fell at his feet. He turned around to see the paperboy peddling away on his bicycle. He leaned over and picked it up off the porch just as the door opened.

"What do you want?" Talon growled, standing behind the screen door.

"I thought we were going to meet at the fishing hole this..." Brace stopped talking, taking in a breath of shock as he stepped back. "What happened to you? You look... what happened?"

Talon just glared at him and said nothing.

"I heard that Seth Barnet slugged you at the wedding reception last night, but...what is that on your face? What'd he do?"

"NO, idiot! Seth didn't do this. How would he do this?" He scratched lightly across his chin. "Ma says it's poison ivy." Talon was trying to look threatening but he came off just looking tragic. One of his eyes was black, while a rash grew on his face, stopping at the base of his neck and picking up again on his lower arms and hands. He pulled his face taut with anger, applying pressure to the blisters that had overtaken his lips, causing them to turn a bloodless yellow.

"How'd you get poison ivy like that, what'd you do, rub your face in the vines?"

"NO, I didn't rub my face in it! I don't know how I got it!" He narrowed his already slitted eyes, which only added tension to the hideous mask he wore. "I saw some idiot carrying a box of it around yesterday, but I didn't get near the moron," Talon said, never suspecting the infected brown towel he had used in the church bathroom.

Brace didn't know what else he could say to his angry friend so he let the silence run on before he asked, "So, are we still gonna go fishing?"

"It's going to be alright Seth, you'll see!" Granny said as she stepped over to the jukebox and put in her change, selecting three songs. "This last one's for you and Molly since you didn't get to dance last night." Seth watched her, wondering how she knew, but he said nothing as he saw Gray and Molly walking up the street towards the diner.

When they stepped inside, the bell above the door tinkled. He felt awkward and out of place. Tension and fear made him want to run. When Molly saw him setting there, her face dropped and she tried to steer her father back out the door. But instead of going out, Gray took Molly's arm and ushered her into the booth, directly across from Seth. He firmly nudged her into the seat and held her shoulder for a moment to show that she was to stay put. Then, he walked away to have a cup of coffee at the counter.

Seth's expression was blank with fear and his breathing was shallow and rapid. "Molly, your father said that what you said last night to me was a mistake?"

"Yes..." Molly started and Seth smiled slightly with relief. "I thought you were Markus and I was sick of dancing. I mean that I was tired of dancing with him. I really wanted to dance with you, but you wouldn't ask me." Molly paused and waited for his response. She didn't quite know what else she could or should say.

"You were so perfect, so beautiful last night, and I was so... well, 'country bumpkin' with my high waters."

"You were handsome!" Molly said with a blush.

"That wasn't what I felt like," Seth stated flatly.

"But you were! I don't care what you were wearing, it was a celebration and I wanted to dance with..." She paused before adding, "my friend."

"Molly, please." He laid his hand on hers. "I don't want to be just your friend."

Molly froze as she looked intently into his eyes.

"I want to be your beau." Seth sat frozen as he waited for her response. She said nothing so he went on, "I talked with your father and he gave me permission to court you, Molly."

Still, nothing came from Molly as her eyes got big and filled with tears.

"Molly, would you allow me to court you?" His eyes pleaded with her.

All of a sudden, she realized this was real and it required a response.

"Yes," she smiled as tears spilled down her face. "Yes, I will." Saying 'Yes' felt so much better to her than the word 'No' had felt last night.

Seth felt like today a mountain had moved for him as he asked, "Will you dance with me now?"

"Yes," she said again.

They stood as Seth stepped up to her and took her in his arms, holding her at a respectful distance, and they began to dance as she smiled shyly at him.

He smiled back and said, "Molly, there's one more thing I want to tell you, and this is very important to me, to us. Your father and mother will be talking to you about what is proper for you as a young lady to do, say, and how to act around me. We have an agreement that I will treat you honorably and..." He paused before saying, "I would like it very much if you would listen and do the things they ask you to do."

Molly watched his face seeing how important this was to him. Seth had made it clear he wanted their relationship to work, even at the cost of humbling himself, that alone made her respect Seth and trust his judgment. She wondered briefly what it was her parents would tell her but knew now more then ever, she needed some guidelines. "Yes, I'll listen," she finally said, "I promise!"

41
Father Figure

*"But anyone who hears My teaching and
doesn't obey it is foolish,
like a person who builds a house on sand.
When the rains and floods come and the winds beat
against that house,
it will collapse with a mighty crash."
Matthew 7: 26 NLT*

Old Lem stepped up to the door of Charlie's hospital room and stood quietly as the guard called the police chief to clear him to enter. The guard rummaged through the box the old man held in his hands before opening the door and letting him enter. Walking slowly over to the chair, he sat down, the small box in his hands. Charlie sat on the edge of his bed looking much healthier than he had several days earlier.

Lem sat the box on the floor and began with, "Charlie, I know you're off ta prison tomorrow but I have somethin' I need ta say right out. Now I know I ain't been much ta ya in the past, but I'm hopin' ta change that now. I been prayin' for ya son." Lem sat forward and took Charlie's hand, sandwiching it between his thin wrinkled ones, and said, "You're a good boy. I should have told ya that long ago and maybe ya wouldn't be in this mess today." The old man looked at him with troubled eyes.

A tear came to the edge of Charlie's eyes then retreated back as he blinked it away. He realized how long he had desired to hear a word of encouragement from another man who believed in him. He found it fulfilled a need, a deep-rooted thirst. It was a precious treasure he would hold near to his heart until his dying breath.

"What I'm saying is I know all the fathers you've ever had were no good, so I'd like it if ya would consider me as your father. Now, I ain't never had a son of my own and would be honored ta call ya my son."

Charlie fought back the tears as he said, "I think I'd like that sir."

Old Lem stood and pulled Charlie into his arms, "I'm so glad son!" As the men moved apart and sat back down, Lem added, "Ya know me and my Sally always wanted a son. While she can't talk for herself no more, I think it's safe ta say we were thinking of one a little younger ta start out with." He smiled for the first time since entering the room and Charlie laughed out loud.

"Now son, I know ya took a fancy ta those old slippers of mine and I want ya ta have them." He handed the box to him.

Charlie pulled out the slippers, laying them on the floor in front of his bare feet. Quickly brushing away a tear, he slid them on with a smile, "Thank you so much, sir!"

"That's quite alright, son."

Leroy began to speak as he came into the hospital room for his last visit. "I'm going to be moving to Ohio, Charlie." He sat down in the chair next to the bed where Charlie laid sprawled out with his arms folded beneath his head. "Ohio, why Ohio?"

"Well, I was answering the phone at the church the other day for Pastor Hilby when a pastor from Ohio called to see how you were doing. Well, it turns out that he needs help, like what I've been doing. So, he asked me if I would consider working for him in Ohio."

"So, that's it?"

"No, then at the wedding, Shelly Wiley told me about a friend back home she wanted me to meet. She thinks we might just hit it off. So since I had already been praying about moving to Ohio, I felt like God was opening a door for me.

"Then this morning, I found out this woman is Zeke's sister. It was really cool how it all..."

Charlie cut him off with, "So, you're going to run off to Ohio for some kind of a blind date?" he swallowed hard and brushed his hand over his brow. "Sorry," he chastised himself, "I'm just nervous about tomorrow morning. I'm happy for you Leroy, really."

Although Charlie said he was happy, his face was frozen with concern for what tomorrow would hold for him. Silence stood between the two men like the wrong sides of magnets, pushing them apart. Leroy looked at his friend with compassion and finally said, "About a month ago I had a vision and in this vision –

"I saw a man standing on the beach in the sand as the waves licked higher and higher around his legs, his feet slightly set apart as he tried to keep his balance. If no one approached him with the gospel of Christ, he felt as if he was doing well, because the sand beneath him didn't move as much. But, when the shakiness of what he believed was challenged, he panicked and in the process of beating back what he saw as a threat, he sank deeper, ever deeper into the wet sand.

"This man wanted closeness from others more than anything, but was afraid of giving up his position. He was angry, wounded, spiteful and proud, refusing to give up his hold on the things he knew he could control.

"What the Lord showed me about this man was he knew he was standing on sinking sand. He could feel it shifting under his feet and he thought if he could just get rid of all Christians, if he could somehow silence them, then he would be happy. He thought the waves would then stop coming in and the sand would stop swallowing him up. What he failed to see was Christ's scarred hands were the only life-line that would ever be thrown to him! And the longer he stood there, the lower he would sink, until it was too late for him. With his last breath, this man would curse the God he had fought against his whole life. A God he had claimed not to believe in." Leroy paused as he looked at Charlie, staring up at the ceiling above him.

"You saw all that in your head?" Charlie finally said quietly.

"Yes, it's called a vision."

"I had one!" Charlie said suddenly, swinging his legs over the side of the bed as he sat up.

"You had a vision?" Leroy asked as if he must of misunderstood.

"Yeah, I was in a courtroom and I saw the hand of God, 'The Judge', swinging His gavel, and as it came down on a spike, Christ's wrist was pierced. His blood spattered and covered me. It hit and sunk into the rough wood that was below it and I heard a loud THUNK and the word, 'FORGIVEN'!" Charlie said the word loud and deep with his fist hitting the table beside the bed, to show finality. "It only lasted a moment," he continued, "but I understood it just the same. It kind of scared me at first not knowing what it was but then I just figured God was talking to me, so then I was happy!"

"Wow! That pretty much says it all, doesn't it?" Leroy said. "That's the way God feels about us all. 'It is finished', is what Jesus said as He took His last breath on the cross."

"Wow!"

There was silence again as the two of them sat thinking. "I was praying for you," Leroy began again, "when I had that vision of the man in the sinking sand. It was just after I came to see you in the county lockup the last time and you didn't want to see me. I was pretty broken up by that and started seeking the Lord big time on your behalf."

Charlie turned toward him. "So, that man was me?"

"Yeah, it was you, but it also represents our sin nature. How blind we are, unable to see what we know must be true."

"That was exactly the way it felt," Charlie said thoughtfully. "That... that was me," he stammered as if in his own little world.

"The man in my vision was you, but he can also stand for anyone who is in rebellion to God. I'm telling you this because in life you're going to run into a lot of hurting people who are stuck in a prison of sin, like you were. Many have never known love. But He has turned you around and He can also turn others around, as well. This world is a mission field, for us all. Don't think you have somehow messed up God's plan and He can't use you now.

Very few of us will ever shake cities, states, countries, or even the world. So many of us, because of delusions of grandeur or not being able to see the urgency of the situation, or maybe just because of fear, do nothing as our neighbors are sentenced to die for their sins, when Jesus has already paid for their release. God has a plan for you and it starts right here, right now, right where you are. Wherever you go, for the short time that we have been given in this world."

Character Reference:

Chief of Police Burt – Retiring, making way for Sam

Samuel (Sam) Trusty – Police Detective, newly appointed Chief of Police.

Kate McClure (alias Kitty Knots) – Sam's love interest, works in family diner.

Granny McClure – wise elderly woman, Kate's grandmother, owns the family's diner / ice cream parlor.

Mandy Kimball – Kate's fun loving best friend.

Chuck Atteberry (alias Charlie Adams) – Prisoner convicted of murder.

Leroy McCoy – Chuck's former tough guy, now new Christian.

Martin Jones – Sam's replacement as Police Detective.

Cody and Shelly (Shel) Wiley – Husband and wife, Chuck believed that they had seen the murder (in Book 1). and tracked them with a hound named Duke.

-Duke – Shelly and Cody Wiley's recently acquired tracking hound.

Ezekiel Bloom (Zeke) – Christian and childhood friend of Leroy's.

Sarah Bloom – Zeke's unmarried sister

Paul Damascus - Deputy Sheriff in charge of transporting Chuck to prison; Paul's wife is **Susan**.

Lemuel Clayton (Old Lem) – talkative, wise old man.

Gray and Maureen Mills – Husband and wife, carpenter, owners of a Christmas tree farm.

-Molly Mills – their sixteen-year old daughter.

Gil and Mary Tillman – Husband and wife, Sam's neighbors and friends, parents to:

-Tad Tillman – their six-year old son.
-Markus Tillman - their son in his early teens.

Ken and Becky Barnett – Husband and wife, live in the mountains near a bigger town, parents to:
-Micah Barnett – their son in his early teens.
-Seth Barnett - their seventeen-year-old son.
-Skippy – the Barnett's energetic Jack Russell puppy.

Pam – Molly's false friend.
Talon - Pam's manipulative and possessive brother.
Rachel – one of Molly's true friends, a Christian, works at Sally's Big Burger.
Tess - one of Molly's true friends, a Christian, babysits the Tillman children.

Reader's Study Guide

1. What do you think Chuck saw and admired in Kate?

2. How did faith play a roll in Kate's life?

3. Was Kate right to think that Chuck could never change, never be saved?

4. When Kate could have ran off, do you think she did the right thing to stay and help Chuck?

5. Does God have a plan for broken people? Think of Bible characters that also were crushed in spirit and broken. And how did God use them once they were saved?

6. Discuss how it bothered Kate to hear people say bad things about Chuck, after she knew the root of evil that had poisoned him, compelling her to pray for him.

7. Do you think God was working in Chuck's life?

8. Before Kate's trial, did she apply her faith to help others, or was she prideful, puffed up, as though she was somehow better than the sinners around her?

9. Have you ever caught yourself feeling better than those around you who are not saved?

10. How did it make you feel when Old Lem asked Chuck if he would consider him as his father?

11. Do you think there are people in your life that you may feel differently about, if you took time to get to know them better?

About the Author

 When Peggy isn't caught up in the world of writing, she is working on half a dozen other projects at the same time. Included in these projects could be all manner of art, decorating ideas, murals, or even plays. Asking her husband about her many projects he said, "I love it! She's like 'Alice in Wonder Land'; she comes up with six impossible things before breakfast. At least they seem impossible to me, until she manages to do them all!"

Along with her husband of 40 years, Peggy has raised three children and has seven grandchildren. She is a graduate of both the 'Self Confrontation' and 'Inductive Bible Study' courses.

She has always been an observer of people and while dealing with personal trials, Peggy launched into writing in an attempt to try and sort things out for herself. Her stories jump off the page sparking a sense of adventure as well as believable relationships.

Peggy said, "In todays world we are constantly being bombarded, with dysfunctional relationships as though they are the norm, but in God, they don't have to be that way. Forgiveness, for one, is something the world knows nothing about. I wanted to show not only the trials of the characters, but also help the reader to apply this story into their own lives. Seeking the Lord we can begin to see things through His eyes."

Other Books include: Part 1 & 2 of 'HIS Eyes' series

Books 1, 2, and 3 of the 'Ash' trilogy

And 'Opposite Intent'